THE
JOURNALIST

DAN NEWMAN

DIVERSIONBOOKS

Also by Dan Newman

The Clearing

Diversion Books
A Division of Diversion Publishing Corp.
443 Park Avenue South, Suite 1008
New York, New York 10016
www.DiversionBooks.com

This is a work of fiction. Names, characters, places and incidents either are the
product of the author's imagination or are used fictitiously. Any resemblance to
actual persons, living or dead, events or locales is entirely coincidental.

For more information, email info@diversionbooks.com

First Diversion Books edition June 2017.
Print ISBN: 978-1-68230-810-3
eBook ISBN: 978-1-68230-809-7

For Laura and Ethan.

1

Today, fourteen more bodies were found. They were children, all of them, each carefully bound hand and foot, then lined up and shot in the back of the head. Their grave was a shallow latrine dug by the now retreating Hutu Interahamwe. That latrine—the sheer indignity of it—somehow made the discovery that much more grotesque.

I stand looking down on the crude blend of flesh, mud, and blood, and try hard to feel something. Anything will do. Pity is an emotion I lost long ago, so I check for anger, sadness—any of the usual suspects. But there is nothing.

Beside me, Vince heaves the camera to his shoulder and curses under his breath. I envy him. "Let's get this done, okay, Roly?" he says to me quietly, and I nod and turn to face him. He snaps on the light above his lens and gives me a three count followed by a sharp stab of his index finger. A sudden breeze snatches away the smell wafting from the pit behind me, and I breathe the clean air like a man surfacing from too long under water.

I fall smoothly into my role, as I always do, and gaze for a moment at the gaping hole behind me before turning back and fixing my carefully trained expression on the camera. "Behind me," I begin, with just the right amount of despair loaded into my voice, "lie the bodies of fourteen children, each executed with a single bullet to the head, then buried in a military latrine." I pause the way we do, all of us, carefully aligning ourselves with the sentiments of the viewer, even glancing momentarily, almost imperceptibly, at the ground, as if reaching for composure. "These boys and girls, none appearing to be above the age of ten, can hardly be considered fair game in this conflict, yet it has happened again and again with apparent impunity—a systematic elimination of what have been called 'tomorrow's soldiers.'"

I carefully weave in all three of the levels demanded by my craft—the horror before us, the immediate context, the overarching perspective—then leave the report with an open-ended question on the future of this land. Later, back at the hotel, we'll edit in some footage shot back at the crossroads: a ten-year-old girl, filthy and half naked, staring blankly with her arms outstretched toward the bloating heap that was once her mother. It is horrific, heartrending stuff. It is journalistic gold.

"Shit," Vince says, his eyes running over the raped land. "Now this is what I'd call a real bullet story."

I nod once in agreement. "Yeah, the genuine article." A bullet story is what we call coverage that can get you killed. Bullet stories, if ever recovered, usually end up with posthumous Pulitzers and memorial dinners attached to them. Being here when this evil deal was struck would have most definitely been a bullet story.

I look around again at the shapes embedded in the sludge below me and realize with no satisfaction that this grisly scoop will probably add to the Roland Keene mystique. Once again it is Vince who snaps me out of my thoughts. "Let's get it wrapped up and on the feed before the hordes arrive."

By "hordes" Vince is referring to the other members of our illustrious profession, the other forty-odd journalists here in Rwanda—forty-odd who hadn't yet got wind of this particular atrocity. It was one of the perks of being *hot*—stories often made their way to you first, bypassing all the other journalists, good and bad alike. This one had come in the form of an old man with his gnarled hand thrust out shamelessly for money.

A mere US$50 bought the location, along with his version of the event. He could have gotten more, but he knew the clock was against him, and that sometime soon someone else would come along selling the same story. Checkbook journalism is generally frowned upon, at least in public, by my esteemed colleagues. There was a time when I frowned upon it, too. But now I just don't care, because it's effective, for the most part. Vince certainly doesn't like it—I can always tell by the little knot of muscle flexing in the corner of his jaw.

At the hotel we edit the piece together, then bounce it off a satellite so it arrives in a tidy newsroom seven thousand miles away. Vince gently brushes off my invitation for dinner once we're done. I won't see him again until later, probably downstairs in the bar, where he'll be laying it on thick about how we scooped the big boys again. He'll raise his glass in my direction, I'll do the same in return, and that'll be it.

In the dining room I eat alone, until a young correspondent from England comes over and asks to join me. Despite the fact that I've had only five years on the road, my high profile has made me the consummate veteran professional in his eyes. "You're Roland Keene, right?" he asks, scooching his chair in tightly. "I'm a huge fan. Nigel Hoddle," he says, reaching a hand across the table. "BBC. I hear you lads were at the center of it all again today, then." It's not a question, and his tone is lined with something approaching flattery.

"Yeah, pretty grim stuff. Kids—"

"I heard. Never seen anything like that myself. Not so far, anyway."

"So you're new to…all this?"

"Yeah, mate. My first go outside the UK."

I chew on the rubber they're passing off as steak, hoping the fresh-faced boy in front of me loses interest. But he persists, apparently waiting for me to say something. Finally I do. "You guys having much luck?" is the gem I come up with.

"A bit, here and there. Nothing like the slaughter you covered today, though." There's a lingering question in there. An invitation to tell him something. He's waiting for me to set my cutlery down, to lean in close and pull him forward with a hooked finger and say something like: *Okay, kid. You're in the field now, so here's what you need to know…* But there's nothing there.

The silence stretches and sags uncomfortably, but Nigel presses bravely on. "Reckon we're heading east in the morning—to the Tanzanian border—apparently there's trouble brewing there with people trying to flee the country. There's a small press convoy headed out. How about you, then?"

"That sounds pretty solid," I say, knowing full well I won't be following the horde.

More chewing of rubber and the attendant awkward silence. Finally Nigel gives up, and I see in his exit that there's a small *fuck you* in there just for me. "Well, cheers, mate. Great chatting…"

None of the other veterans socialize with me, but I've always figured my disposition was probably as much a part of my mystique as my coverage quality. In my five years as a foreign correspondent I've learned a lot, and find that with every newsworthy atrocity I cover, I feel just a tiny bit more removed from my own dark doings. Today it's Rwanda, central Africa, but tomorrow it could be the Middle East, Europe, or Southeast Asia. It doesn't matter: white, black, yellow, or red—wanton violence is always in good supply.

Recent election results have stirred an ancient hatred, and all signs point to another bloody genocidal clash between the Hutu and the Tutsi. A good killing always catches the attention of the international media machine, and we dutifully clatter our way through customs with equipment cases and tripods, eagerly searching for the best of the worst. Our reputation—journalists as a whole—is that we are a tight-knit group, always looking out for each other. But the truth is something different; a thin veneer of collectiveness masks the reality of a story-thieving, source-corrupting, fact-perverting orgy where the knives come out early and find backs and throats aplenty.

Here in Rwanda, we all cram into the Intwan Hotel, a wreck of a place often haunted by journalists throughout the nation's history. The Intwan was once a grand affair, but was ransacked at the beginning of the genocide in '94. The majority of the structure has been left as it was, half burned and falling down, while a small section was rebuilt with something of an eye to economy. A very sharp eye.

My room is on the third floor, and as I make my way up the staircase of recycled fence wood, I can feel someone watching me. I don't think it's any special skill developed through my career in journalism, but instead a basic, rather poorly developed human trait. Surprisingly enough, I don't recall hearing anyone, as one might correctly expect thanks to the Intwan's questionable workmanship. Only the barrage of Africa's night chorus, the chirping, squeaking, clicking of the insects rises to my ears. I stop, halfway up the stairs, and turn.

She doesn't try to hide at all, in fact, I think she wants me to know she's there. She looks up at me for a moment with what I take for hatred, then turns and strides back into the bar with the Intwan creaking its own brand of disapproval. Donna Sabourin, the host for the television news magazine show *Foreign Correspondent*, has good reason to be angry with me.

She'd been a society reporter with the *Star-Telegraph* when I was working there, but it was no secret she was trying to land a spot on the international desk. She finally got her first real shot at the job and through an act of colossal insensitivity on my part—in the form of a few careless words—she never got it. How my comments got back to Donna I still don't know. But journalism is really just well-organized gossip, so I guess I'm not entirely surprised that she found out.

Yup, Donna is one of my great mistakes. If I were a biker, Donna's name would be tattooed on my arm in the middle of a big flowing ribbon through an even bigger blood-red heart.

I turn away from her and trudge on up to my room, then get that same feeling once again as I slide the key into the lock. I half turn and see her there again, arms crossed and lips tightly pursed. Again the creak of the building has failed to warn me.

"Hello, Donna," I say after a moment, unable to produce anything witty. In my mind I see her smiling, wrapped in my arms, the way it was when we were at our best. But the woman before me is bristling with hostility. The memory shrinks and disappears.

She closes the ten yards between us and simply stares at me.

I shift uncomfortably, and can feel my composure departing like a wet shirt peeled from my back. "What can I do for you?" Without my permission, a giddy smile creeps across my face—a dangerous habit I developed as a kid—and I realize with some regret that it will only infuriate her.

Her tongue darts out and sweeps once across her lips. "You think you're some big hotshot, don't you?" She is almost whispering. Nearly a hiss. "You think that the whole world owes you something."

This is a battle I am definitely not prepared for, so I reach for a look that says I am tired and really far too busy. "Listen, Donna..."

"No." She flicks a finger at me. "You listen. I'm tired of your smug attitude, marching around like you're better than the rest of us. Everyone's sick of you."

Something in Donna's face telegraphs her intent, and suddenly, without any tangible reason, I know what she is here to say. I find myself washed with alternating waves of panic and relief. The panic rises through me like hot vomit, then changes just as swiftly to a giddying sense of relief.

"I know," she says.

"You do?" I reply. Again, the schoolboy smile.

"You're finished, Roly. You're done." Her voice is solid with the confidence of the righteous, and looking at her becomes a suddenly impossible task.

I pick at the peeling paint of my doorway, and watch the fleck flutter to the ground. "What are you talking about?" It is pathetic and hollow, and seems to quash any latent respect that Donna might have held for me.

"You think you're big in the news now? Just wait till I'm through with you." She works her mouth as if to remove a bad taste, then continues. "And I'm not doing it just to get even,

Roly—and believe me, I'm due that—I'm doing it because you need to pay. That family needs to know the truth."

I push the door of my room open, step inside, and turn back to face her.

"Do you care to make a comment for the story, Mr. Keene?" she says, goading me. "Can I quote you, you son of a bitch?"

I stare at her one last time and hold the gaze, not through strength, but in an effort to collect myself. I read the entire story on her face, including the fact that the telling of it all will hurt her.

What she doesn't know is that there is no reason for her to feel any pain; I have already set my own plan in motion. I have always known this day would come, that I would ultimately be forced to confront my past.

Despite the surety of my plan, though, this confrontation with Donna strikes me, in an odd way, as a good thing. Her clear knowledge of everything is in fact an insurance policy: Her rage will make sure everything is public, even if I should falter or think of changing my mind. There is nothing left now but to go on.

I smile a cockeyed smile. "Thank you, Donna," I say, with so much sincerity that it registers for a brief moment on her face, displacing the anger with a fleeting confusion. I gather myself and gently close the door on her.

● ● ●

Vince is still down in the bar, and the flimsy door to his room is simple to pop open. Once inside, I load the camera with a fresh battery and stuff the keys to our rented Land Cruiser in my pocket. Then I set the letter down on his bed. I suspect that writing and leaving this letter is the only brave thing I have done so far. Perhaps ever. I leave it and move on to the practicalities at hand.

The Intwan is easy to leave without being seen—thanks to the charred back half of the structure—and I am soon on my way through the darkened streets of Kigali, past the still waters of Lake Luhazi on my way to Ngarama—a small village only a few kilometers past the scene of the slaughtered children. Not far after the lake, I am stopped by a police patrol and my hands grow clammy at the sight of the bright lights in front of me, and the silhouettes of men in combat gear with automatic weapons. I have no idea if it is the police, Hutu militants, or the Tutsi rebels, and my relief at seeing the silver coat of arms on the officer's beret must be apparent.

He flashes a perfect set of teeth as he looks at the press credentials I am thrusting out of the car, and speaks in halting English. "Whe' you go now?"

I start to answer but he speaks over me. "Very *denjaraas*. Lot pipples killed up dey. Lot pipples." His smile is insistent despite the warning he's giving me.

I nod gravely. "I'm a journalist."

"Lot jernlis, too," he says, then turns and shouts to the others by the car. They laugh and shout back things I will never understand. "Go if you wan'. Very *denjaraas*," he says again, stepping back from the car, still smiling.

I watch the patrol shrink in my rearview mirror, and feel a sense of abandonment as I round the bend and their lights blink out. In front of me, a pool of light surges with the motion of the vehicle, while at my sides the blackness of the forest hurries by. This far from town there is no ambient light, and the stars overhead are the brightest I have ever seen.

As I start into the hills, I know there will be no more police patrols and that the next group of armed people I come across will quite simply be in the business of killing. The group that had performed the execution of the children will almost definitely be in Ngarama—it is common knowledge that they have moved there, although no one has been foolhardy enough to go there and confront them. Until now.

Perhaps I actually have a chance of getting some useful material, especially since I'm coming in the night, and will therefore be unexpected. No one drives around at night in Rwanda these days. I hope to come across a small group, even an individual or two, who might be willing to answer a few questions on camera. Perhaps a little description of the dark deed itself. I play it through my mind that way a few times and almost start to believe it. The truth is, though, that I will probably be stopped, pulled from the Land Cruiser, killed, and left on the road to bloat with the morning sun. It is a common end for people foolish enough to travel this far into the country without the benefit of a military escort. But then again, that was half the point, wasn't it?

I lift my hand to my breast pocket and pat the letter folded there, the one Vince had given me when he arrived in Kigali yesterday morning, and realize that now is probably a good time to read it. I pull over in the darkness, open the letter, and read it by the yellow glow of the vehicle's map light. "So that's how they knew," I say quietly aloud, gently shaking my head at the revelation.

I pass the dirt road exit we had taken earlier to reach the execution site, and marvel at the fact that no one, save the police roadblock, has challenged me. It seems impossible that I could have come this far. It's right about then that I hear the first bullet.

Duh-plink. I never hear the shot itself, just the projectile whacking through the bodywork (*duh*) and then stopping against something hard—probably the engine block (*plink*). There are two more, both duhs—no plink—and then the car splutters briefly and coasts to a halt. I become aware of the fact that I am making a noise—an odd sound—a kind of high-pitched whine. I am scared by the bullets, but I manage to rein myself in and stop the sound. The Land Cruiser's lights are still burning, as are the dash instruments, but it is otherwise quiet. Nothing stirs outside the cab. Nothing inside, either.

This is it. This is where I will die for my sins. My mind tears off on an instant daisy chain: my sins, a dead girl. The dead girl, my career. My career, Rwanda. Rwanda, Donna Sabourin. Donna Sabourin, bullet story. In a flash, I recall why I am here, why I have placed myself in this predicament, and it gives me the presence of mind, if not the courage, to reach for the camera and slip out to the darkened roadside.

• • •

"Journalist!" I call out into the blackness, unsure of who I am addressing or where they are. I do a little circle with the camera, light off, sound wide open, trying to pick up whatever I can. There is nothing but complete blackness, save the pool of white from the headlights and the red dots that mark the tail of the Land Cruiser. "Media! Reporter!" I call out. "I want to interview you!" It sounds absurd even to me, and I snap on the light over the camera in some desperate effort to validate my claim. I turn the camera briefly on myself and repeat my entreaty, so that those in the blackness might understand that I am telling the truth.

It occurs to me that I am now a well-lit target, and I quickly swing the light toward the bush line, blinking madly and struggling to recapture my night vision. I wonder what people will say when—if—they see this footage. Do I seem scared? In control? I feel a sudden wave of self-loathing, as I realize that this little ending is a vanity of sorts—a last blast of ego. It seems I can't even be honest at the very end. What an asshole. And in the space of a fractured second I see my psychologist, Dr. Coyle, a haze of blue smoke about her and a broad grin on her face. She's not saying the words, but her grin is screaming it: *I told you so!* Then she chuckles briefly and is gone.

I pan the bush line on both sides of the road, and stop when I see what I take to be a man, a body anyway, just beyond the first line of low brush. The camera allows me to zoom in on it and expose it as a bloating animal carcass, not a man at all.

I blink away from the eyepiece at the sound of something metallic from the bush line behind me. I pan toward it, and the camera suddenly explodes into a shower of plastic and shattered lens glass. I drop the remains instinctively and hop backward, stifling the scream that's clawing its way up my throat. Remarkably, the light has stayed on, beaming innocuously skyward.

A harsh voice bellows from the darkness, all syllables to my ear, and I immediately shoot my hands into the black night above me. "Journalist!" I shout again. "Media!"

From the bush line steps a small man in rags, a member of the Hutu Interahamwe, going by the black swatch pinned to his shoulder. Again he bellows, and I jab my hands even higher, yelling a chorus of "Journalist! Journalist!"

He thrusts his weapon at me and fires, casually. No opportunity for discussion, for pleading, for barter. He just fires and knocks me backward into a wet heap on the road.

I can't move. I can only see what is directly in front of me, which is the Land Cruiser and a scattering of parts from the video camera. Several men climb into the vehicle with not so much as a glance my way, and begin pitching the contents onto the road.

And so this is how it all ends. It seems at least fitting. An eye for an eye, the Bible says, and as I think it, mine are snuffed out.

2

Seven years earlier.

I stare at the keyboard, and immediately Professor Bowman pops into my mind. He sits there in his tiny office on the fifth floor, surrounded by piles of paper and yellow Post-its scattered like dandelions across an unruly lawn. "There are two kinds of journalists, Roly," he used to say to me, leaning back and lacing his fingers behind his head. "There's Makers and Takers. The only thing you've gotta ask yourself is: which are you?" And then he would chuckle and tell me to get the hell out of his office.

But that wasn't unusual, nor was it rude. One on one, the Professor was like that—straight to the point. That's what I liked about him. If he wanted to talk, he talked. And if he was tired of it, he'd tell you to get the hell out. I suppose that's why I chose to study under him. That and his contagious passion for the news business.

His question rakes across my mind now: Which one would I be? A Maker or a Taker? I'd heard the expression before, several times before, along with everyone who ever took one of his classes. Professor Bowman would puff up like a peacock right before he launched into it, and students in their second and third year of journalism would groan and slouch a little deeper into the hard seats of the lecture hall. His lectures were distinctly different from his office hours, where Professor Bowman would lay it on thick to the point of theater.

The Takers, he would lament, were the kind of journalists who let things come to them. They thrived on press releases, loved the wire service, and basically inhabited the newsroom just to rearrange someone else's copy. Now, the Makers—that was where the real talent was. Those were the kind of journalists who went looking for the story. They frowned at releases and shook their heads in disgust at those who so much as skimmed what came in across the wire. Makers were professionals in an important field. Makers kept newspapers real, and saved them from being nothing more than billboards.

It was fascinating stuff—the first time. Around the third or fourth telling it got a little old, but you still had to respect the man's commitment. He was seventy but still had an absolute conviction in the power of a good story. "You might write one in your whole career—if you're lucky," he'd say. If you looked through his fifty-three years of work you'd find all kinds of remarkable stories—any one of which I would have been proud to say I'd written. The man was a genius of his time, and it's too bad that no one ever seemed to notice.

I look up from my keyboard. On the screen is my résumé, a static testament to my lack of achievement in life. Thoughts of Professor Bowman quickly depart, and I am alone again. I look at the résumé and hate it. I must have a thousand varieties, each one tailored to the specs of the job, then tweaked, tinkered, and shaped into something different again. Sixty-two applications, four interviews, zero jobs.

The people outside on Third Street all have places to go, scurrying with heads bent against winter's last kicks. In the street, cars crawl by, inhabited by people who presumably have jobs. And good jobs, too—judging by the parade of fancy BMWs and Mercedes.

I push through the doors, into the street, dragging what's left of my confidence a few feet behind me. I'll try again tomorrow.

"Roly! Hey, Roly." I turn and see that it's Warren, exiting his Beemer and struggling to do up his nine-hundred-dollar leather jacket. He's a good guy, but he gets on my nerves these days, what with his family money and his *I can do it without them* attitude. Somehow Warren doesn't get it. He almost always comes to the resource center in his shiny Beemer—and worse still, parks right out front. He gets a lot of looks from people itching to give him the finger, but he's oblivious to them.

He hunches against an icy city wind, a knifing cold that's channeled perfectly by miles and miles of glass and concrete. But despite it, his smile is still perfect. "What are you up to, Roly?"

"Just heading home. Sent off a bunch of résumés."

"Still nothing, huh?"

"More nothing than something."

Warren chuckles at my sarcasm and it makes me more pissed off. I think I'm developing happiness issues—more fodder for Dr. Coyle. "You wanna grab a coffee before you go?" he asks.

I am about to shake my head—the truth is a coffee would be nice but I'm pinching pennies right now—but then Warren seals the deal. "I'm buying," he says, raising both hands in the air.

I'm not normally a mooch, but I figure Warren owes me. I edit his cover letters—hell, I rewrite them most of the time, and help him with his job search whenever I get sick of my own. Which is a lot lately. It's not that I'm any better than Warren, but he seems to think my input helps, presumably because I'm a journalism graduate, and therefore a capable wordsmith. Warren, on the other hand, is a vet graduate from some exclusive academy on the other side of the country—Seattle, I think. Somewhere much warmer, anyway. He says he put himself through the school without Mom and Dad's money, but of course whenever he talks about that all I can hear in my head is, *What about the Beemer, Warren?* And I admit it, I'm jealous.

Warren seems to be picking up on my mood, so I make a conscious effort to lighten up. After all, he did spring for coffee.

"What about the interview with the *Sun*?" he asks from the other side of the little table in Starbucks.

"They said I'd more than likely get a call back for a second interview, but that was two weeks ago. Nothing since."

"Why don't you call them?"

"You think?" I've thought about this, but I'm paranoid about sounding desperate. Once you smack of desperation you're dead. It clings to you and hovers around you in interviews, seeps through the phone and stains your résumé. It's like getting sprayed by a skunk.

But Warren seems to think otherwise. "Sure. Why not?"

I explain my desperation theory and Warren nods in understanding. Great. I was hoping he'd debate me on it, but instead he's confirmed my fears. Now the follow-up call is out of the question, and I wonder if I already have the stench of desperation. Warren pipes up again before I can ask. "Have you thought about other places? Getting the hell out of the city?"

I have, and discarded it. "It's a money thing. Setting up in a new place costs big bucks." Of course, "big bucks" is a relative term, and I am talking to one of the heirs to the Barton fortune. So I back out quickly. "What about you? Any luck yet?"

He drains his coffee and spins the cup on the table. "Couple of nibbles, nothing much."

Warren, of course, is a lying sack of shit. He has at least two interviews set up. I know this because I pried it out of the aging administrator at the center. "It'll come," I remark with as much interest as I can muster, which isn't much.

Warren and I shoot the proverbial shit for another half hour, until the atmosphere is thick with the realization that no, I am not going to spring for the next coffee. Warren offers another, but I decline, mumbling something vaguely apologetic about cash flow and owing him one. Warren slips across the road with a wave, and I hustle down Third just in time to miss the streetcar.

3

By four I am home. My apartment is probably not the best place to be for someone in my kind of mood. I have a futon on the floor, a card table and two foldout chairs, a bar minifridge, a tube TV with bunny ears and, worst of all, a hotplate.

Tonight I retreat to my futon with a Coke and a ham sandwich. I thumb through a stack of magazines on the floor beside me, flicking resentfully past all the bylines of employed journalists the world over.

On the front of a copy of *Newsweek* I see the smiling face of Colin Dysart, owner and CEO of Newsco, the media giant that owns three of the major national newspapers, along with several others scattered around the globe. The caption, leading a story on Dysart's new sports magazine, is short and punchy, just the catchy kind of thing every journalism major learns how to do. *Dysart and Newsco: Major League News.*

Inside I find a story on Dysart's rise to media magnate from hardworking farmhand, complete with tragedy, comedy, and high commerce. It's a good piece, and I feel moderately pleased with myself that I can admit this without taking a cheap shot at the prick who wrote it. There are pictures with the article: his mansion in The Meadows, his wife Emily (his rudder, as he puts it), and his three kids—two sons and a daughter. All in all, a life that seems to be going well.

I toss the magazine on the floor where it lands beside a small pile of bills, some marked PAST DUE in bright red letters. *It's amusing,* I tell myself. *One day I'll laugh about it all.* In my pocket I find a five-dollar bill and a handful of change. Enough for a couple of beers. Also enough for about twelve boxes of Kraft Mac & Cheese, but I have little difficulty in convincing myself which is the priority. My nine bucks and I are going to the bar.

. . .

Dory's Printing and Office Supplies is a little business on the corner of Third and Main that's dying a slow and inevitable death at the hands of the big box stores. I work there for Rhona—hustling office supplies, printing and binding presentations, and running errands—and I should really be more grateful than I am for the few meager bucks it puts in my pocket. Without it I'd have nothing. I'm pretty sure Rhona employs me almost entirely out of pity—Christ knows she could handle the few customers she still has easily enough on her own.

But Rhona's all right, and I think she has a bit of a thing for me, which I don't mind. She's forty-seven, blonde, heavy in the chest and tight through the waist. I think her cleavage is the only reason she's still in business. She wears bright clothes and brighter lipstick, and calls everyone *honey* and *sugar*.

But the place is a hole in the wall and the job is the lowest rung on the "communications" ladder. I took it because I thought I could spin it into a perk in my résumé—that and the fact that it was all I could get. It sucks the life out of me. But it pays some of the bills.

Rhona reloads one of the copiers with her admittedly attractive hindquarters pointing in my direction—on purpose, I'm sure. "Hon, can you dash out back and bring in the case of toner from my truck? The keys are on the desk."

I say sure and squeeze past her, barely able to avoid contact.

"Oh, and sweetie, bring in my lunch, too, will you?"

And that's what my professional occupation is all about.

When I get back, Rhona yammers on about her date last night and I smile and nod in all the right places. Soon the doors are open and I'm given tasks by pimply-faced twenty-year-olds in suits, puffed up with self-importance. They smile at me condescendingly, then turn away with hands thrust impatiently in their pockets. I can hear their thoughts: *I wish that boy would get a move on. Doesn't that boy know we're career people here?* And so off I go to copy their little piles of paper, hating every moment of it, hating them and their puffed-up self-importance, and wishing I was one of them.

• • •

On Tuesday afternoon I get home and see the light blinking furiously on my answering machine. I slap the play button and wait as the little cassette rewinds, also furiously, and savor what I know must be an interview call. I know this because no one else calls me.

Hi, Mr. Keene, Irene Trent here from the Chronicle. *We had a chance to review your résumé and were hoping we could set up a time to meet briefly. If you're still available, please call me back on...* I scribble her number down and clench my fists—this'll be the one. I'll nail it, ditch the copy shop, maybe nail Rhona on the way out, too. I call Ms. Trent back and set the appointment for the following day. No time like the present.

In the bathroom, before bed, I wet shave in the mirror. Long, even strokes, just the way my father would have taught me. When I'm finished, I regard the face in the mirror, and check for any shadows of desperation. I tell myself I'm not there yet, not touched with the skunk stink of the hopelessly unemployed. Tomorrow I will sell myself to Irene Trent. I'll be the perfect interviewee. I know all the questions, all the answers. I've read just about every modern book about the hiring process, and I can almost predict the questions in advance. *How do you deal with conflict? What do you consider your strengths? What was the best job you ever had?* And my favorite, *What one word do you use to describe yourself?*

The face I see in the mirror now is sharp and prepared, honed to a fine edge by just enough rejection to make every chance count. I harden my eyes and set my jaw with conviction, and speak slowly to myself in the light of a naked sixty-watt bulb. *Tomorrow I am going to start my own success... I'm going to invite it in.*

4

My suit's not a bad one. It's only seen wear at my graduation and
at interviews, so it still has a lot of life in it. In the mirror, I give
myself a turn and I'm pleased with the results. My hair is getting
a little long, but it's still presentable. I look around my apartment
and promise to start living better once I nail this job. My eyes fall
on the hotplate and I know it will be the first thing to go.

At Union Station I move carefully. This is Trots's stamping
ground. Even though nine thirty is a little early for him, I still
need to be careful. He has a few kids that work for him, taking
bets and selling a little whatever-you-need on the side, and I don't
want to be spotted. I'll clear my slate with Trots, just not today. By
the ticketing booth, I see one of his lackeys, but the kid doesn't see
me—it must be the suit. I stand virtually next to him as I buy my
ticket, but he never shows any interest, and this is a kid who's taken
my NFL bets before. I walk away—already liking the changes the
news business has brought me.

In the train car I take a seat among people of every description
and start my run to the north end of the city. I am alone in my
suit; everyone else in a suit is already at work. Beside me is an
elderly woman with stockings wrinkling at her ankles. She smiles
at me, then gazes out of the window, watching as the bowels of
the city flick by. I search my pockets for the gum I always keep
there (always chew gum on your way into an interview—kills dry
mouth and freshens your breath) and find instead a soft, folded
piece of paper that I don't immediately recognize. I take it out and
unfold it.

The card in my hand is a gag graduation gift from the

Professor—a PRESS card like the ones reporters would wear in their hats in the '30s and '40s. But the quickly scribbled note on the back of it is something more—a kind of permission slip, a joke that I have somehow clung to despite its transient nature in the eyes of the writer. It was after the graduation ceremony, in the campus pub at the tables along the back wall. Professor Bowman and I sat and shared a pitcher or two and a plate of wings, as we often did during something we came to call Thesis Strategy Briefings. My relationship with Professor Bowman was tighter than most. He knew my history, knew what I did and didn't have, and in many ways I think he tried hard in those years to fill in the gaps. Maybe he was trying to play the part of those who couldn't. I knew he felt an unusual responsibility toward me—unusual in that it went beyond his duties as an academic bringing along the student—and that was never so clear as it was at the end.

The last TSB (although my thesis was long since complete and filed in the library) wasn't as jovial as they usually were, and the Professor employed his usual directness to nail the problem on the head. "Roly," he said, refilling my glass, "school's over now, you know."

"I know, I know," I replied with a certain resignation.

"No, I mean we're pushing you out. Out there," he said, gesturing to the world. His lecture theater persona was long gone now, as were his bombastic and practiced lines. Across the table from me was a man who struck me as, well, almost sad.

"I get it, I get it. Time to go out into the world and all that."

The Professor guffawed. He was the only person I've known who could actually do that—guffaw. "I don't think you do," he said. "You'd stay here forever if I let you." He shoved my glass toward me, slopping beer on the table. "This is supposed to be the most exciting time of your life, and you just don't get it." He shook his ancient mane at me and then tapped his forehead with two gnarled fingers. "Think about it: You've spent God knows how much money getting this top-class education, and now someone out there is going to *pay you* for it. That's a wonderful thing!" Then he pulled the PRESS card from his pocket and slid it across the table to me. "Here you go," he said. "Time to go be a newsman."

I smiled as I picked up the card, but somehow the moment seemed to falter, as if the little gag missed the mark and instead of being funny became something vaguely ominous.

The Professor sat back, took a long breath, and set his jaw. "Roly, can I be honest? I worry about you, son. You're a train on the same tracks I was on. Nervous starts in life can lead to a pattern of safe decisions. And safe decisions are often…limiting." Then he ran his hand across his hair in that way men do when they finally have to speak to something they've been avoiding. "When my wife died six years ago, I was pretty sure the world was over. I had no idea what to do. Everything had changed. But six years later, here I am. Still alive."

My blank face appeared not to be the reaction he was after.

"Look," he said. "The point I'm trying to make is that you need to go forward with…with more hope. More optimism. Just because you can't see the way right now doesn't mean it isn't there. You're a hell of a thing in the writer department, Roly, a hell of a thing," he said, topping up our glasses from the pitcher, "and not half bad as a researcher. But you've gotta lighten up in the living-life category. I mean, *expect more* from life, Roly. Don't fear it so much."

I tried to make light of what I knew was a deadly accurate fact. "Etiquette dictates that you're supposed to be giving me uplifting advice here, not blowing holes in my ego." It came out decidedly flat.

"My job is to prepare you for professional life, so by all accounts I've only done half the job. You've got the professional bit down pat. But that *life* bit… Here's what I'll do," he said. "I'll write you a permission slip."

And that's just what he did. He plucked the PRESS card from my hand, took out his pen, and scribbled something on the back of it.

"Here," he said, handing it back to me.

I read it and raised my eyebrows in mock surprise. "It says: *Carpe EVERYTHING.*"

"That's right. Everything."

"*Carpe diem* not enough for you?"

"Think bigger, Roly. Much bigger," he said to me with a charismatic smile and one raised eyebrow. "Follow that instruction and you've got nothing to worry about." And then he clinked his glass against mine and upended it.

"Now, take this as well," he said, scribbling away again, this time on a napkin.

And so I did. "What is it?" I asked. On it was written a name and a number. It said: *Dr. Cathy Coyle.* "And who is Dr. Coyle?"

Across from me, I remember the mood in the Professor's eyes shifting. "Cathy's a very dear friend of mine. She works with people to help them find a way forward."

"A shrink?"

"Cathy's a superstar. She's as laid-back as they come. She's a real person, not some stiff couch pilot. And she's a real friend." He paused for a moment, and I remember telling myself to honor that pause, because there was more coming.

And there was. "When my wife died," he went on, "Cathy put me back on track. She helped me see what I couldn't. Helped me see that I'd shut down and closed myself off. It's that simple. And for the record, Roly, no one necessarily has to die to make you lose your track. Some people just haven't found theirs yet. Take it from one who knows: your circumstances, where you start from in life, Roly—that can't be the definition of you. It's what you do next that counts. So do me a favor, hang on to her number, and when you get a quiet moment, call her. It's all covered, so don't worry about the cost. She'll be expecting your call."

I remember trying to be a little indignant at that but what really bothered me was how he saw me, that I was someone who needed help. But I guess he was right.

"Trust me and do yourself a favor. Call her. It'll just be an open chat."

I thought about it for a moment. "So it's just a chat with Cathy…with chatty Cathy."

The solemn air evaporated and the Professor laughed his old-man laugh. "Just promise me you'll call her, okay?"

I nodded, and he nodded back.

"It's settled, then," he said, raising a glass. "You've got nothing to worry about." But later on, as I turned and waved goodnight, I saw the truth in the Professor's momentarily unguarded eyes: I had plenty to worry about.

So now my mood has changed. The initial burst of confidence from images of the pub, the warmth of membership, the security of belonging, has faded. Now I feel decidedly alone. The old lady with the wrinkled stockings looks at me and I scowl at her. "What?" I hiss, and she shrinks into her coat and all but disappears into the seat. I feel worse now, and think about apologizing, but the train is slowing into my stop. It's easier to just slink off than explain myself, so that's what I do.

● ● ●

On the trip home, I sit slumped in the seat with my tie tugged open and my hair a mess from trying to pull it out with my hands. I try to analyze what happened, where it all fell apart. It's all a little blurry, but I'm pretty sure it went south in that very first exchange.

I remember that she smiled. She wrapped it around her face right before that question. But on reflection the smile seemed too wide, too Cheshire Cat. "And have you applied to all the major daily papers, Mr. Keene?"

"Well, um, yes…"

"So is our paper just a natural target for a journalism graduate to lob his résumé toward? Or was there something different about us that made you want to work here—here specifically?"

I remember thinking: *Is she pissed off at me?* Shit. But I pressed on. "Well, as a rookie—as someone fresh out of school—I'm looking for a place to learn the business. A place where professionals... I mean, a place like this is filled with some of the best in the business, and I can't think of a better place to grow."

"Hmm," she had said, jotting something on the pad resting on her crossed legs. "So really this is about what *we* can do for *you*, is that right?"

And like that Cheshire Cat, she began to disappear. Oh, she stayed there for the whole interview, sure, but it was just that disingenuous smile that lingered.

At my apartment, I check the answering machine, hoping for another message to focus on—I even allow for the wild thought that Miss Cheshire Cat might have called me back for a second interview—but there is none. I collapse into bed, feeling that I've finally reached the lowest point of my life, and will myself into a numbing sleep.

I awake to darkness, and for a millisecond, everything is okay as my memory and consciousness dance around in search of each other. But it all returns, first in my head, then in my gut. A low, hard, immovable object. The lingering element is simple dejection.

On the top of the magazine pile, Colin Dysart's smiling face taunts me. I pull the worn copy off the stack, thumb through to the article and gaze at the family picture. My eye settles on a paragraph below the shot, and I read a single line at random. *I started with nothing. What I have, I went out and got.*

And the simple act of reading that line is all I need.

I know this old sensation well. I know its promise—its price, too—but I let it flood in. Sparks of confidence are growing inside me, welling up to something larger. I find myself cross-legged on the futon, a notepad in my hand, scribbling furiously.

The writing seems to bleed from the end of the pen, which is scribbling so furiously the resultant scrawl is akin to hieroglyphics. But still I scribble on, each note making a clear point to myself, mapping carefully what I need to do, how I should do it, and what the result will bring. It's a simple plan—brilliant because of that simplicity and at the same time bursting with the courage and conviction of the Little Engine That Could.

At five thirty, the quality of the light through my window changes as the streetlights shut off and the day tentatively begins. I put down my five-hour labor and pad barefoot to the windowsill, eager to see the first day of my new life, of my new attitude, my new fortunes. There is no dazzling sunrise, thanks to the dilapidated buildings that tower above my little window, but if I lean out I can see the sky. It is dark and brooding. There will be a storm today, by the looks of it.

I smile as I watch the black clouds rake the building tops. It is a good sign, I tell myself, a genuine change in the weather.

5

The rain slaps at me as I hop off the streetcar and dash toward Dory's. As I swing the front door open, I can see that Rhona is peeved, and a glance at my watch confirms that I am indeed ten minutes late.

"Sorry, Rhona," I mutter as I slink in behind the till. "Storm killed the lights at my place. Alarm didn't go off." My ability to react convincingly to an evolving situation—some call it lying—is a capacity I am aware of, but somehow fibbing to Rhona, minor as it is, feels disproportionately wrong. And so I immediately chat it up with a customer, make him feel good about his Dory's experience, and get him to chuckle at some inane bit of wit; I know it has the desired effect on Rhona. She rolls her eyes, swats me with a set of sculpted fingernails and says something like, "Oh, you," and I know I am off the hook.

During a lull in the traffic, Rhona comes up behind me and places her hand on the small of my back. "So how'd the interview go?" I can tell by the way she asks that she's hoping I didn't get the job so I can still work for her. It's a compliment of sorts, really, and I don't take offense.

"It's down to me and another candidate," I lie again, this time to save a bit of face. "But I don't think I'll get it. They're looking for someone strong in science writing, and that ain't me." Rhona's hand creeps up my back from the position it has never left during our exchange and begins little circles around my shoulders. "Aw, shit, Roly, I'm sorry."

I smile at her. "No, you're not. You want to keep me here for life."

Rhona ups the ante a little and smacks me on the ass. "Can you blame me?" she says, winking at me in the exaggerated way that she does with the *best* clients. It's nothing new, but today it registers with me a little stronger. I feel it. In my crotch, I think. But it's not all Rhona; part of it is the new knowledge I have secreted inside me—the knowledge that I have a plan. A real plan.

I spend lunch in the library, researching in an environment that is pure comfort to me. I find most of what I need easily. The things that are harder to track down excite me, and please me more once I have them jotted down in my small notebook. As I glance over my scribbling, I know that with every fact carefully cribbed away in my book I am closer to the goal I have set myself.

By two, I know there is no way I can go back to Dory's. I would be useless, daydreaming about the execution of my plan, stapling and copying my way into Rhona's bad books with every goof—and I just know there would be many. That's how I manage to convince myself that calling Rhona and letting her know I won't be back after lunch is a good idea. Of course, I can't use this logic on Rhona, so I resort to the old standby: I'm sick. She takes it with minimal objection, which somehow worries me more than if she had put up a real fight. As I hang up the phone, another single note of regret hovers about me for just a moment; Rhona has been genuinely good to me since the day I started at Dory's, and like every other time, this minor deception feels like a much larger betrayal.

But that's something to worry about later. Maybe something for my next visit with Dr. Coyle, for those flat spots where I don't know what to say. I shrug it off with a deep breath and, for the moment, bury it. Right now I have to head to the university campus and make the first tentative moves of my bold plan.

• • •

I have her face burned into my memory, as well as her father's, her mother's and both of her brothers'. She has a lovely face, no question, but below that she expands too rapidly for my liking,

31

although in truth there isn't that much to complain about. The other concession I must make is that, having never seen her in the flesh, so to speak, I must give some allowance to the contortions of the photographer's lens. The only shot of her full body I have seen was in a newspaper, where she blurs somewhat into the background as she claps at her father cutting some ribbon or other. Even then, I can see a confident aura about her, as there is about all the family members, and I think that it must come from money.

At the registry office, I pull up a class schedule on the computer and spend the rest of the day crashing undergrad business lectures. They are first- and second-year affairs, so my intrusion goes unnoticed among the masses of keen backpack-toting undergrads. My exits, however, usually draw at least a pause from the lecturer, as learned eyes glance over bifocals to see who has the temerity to walk out halfway through a class. Only once am I challenged, and I simply ignore it and let the double doors swing closed behind me.

When I find her it is in the front row of an economics lecture, legs crossed and hair pulled into a single thick ponytail: Chloe Dysart. Given the size of the class—there must be 150 students in this enormous lecture hall—it's possible I'm the only one here who knows who she is, who she *really* is. Do the people on either side of her have any idea she's a Dysart? If they knew she was the daughter of one of the most successful media moguls in the world, that she was heir to untold millions, would they pay more attention? Would they look at her any differently—perhaps in the way I'm looking at her now?

She raises her hand and asks a tobacco-yellowed professor to please repeat the last point. Her voice is that of a woman, not the eighteen- or nineteen-year-old girl that she is, and it carries a casual authority. Immediately I conclude it is a confidence born of financial security.

I watch her for the full lecture, taking in her deliberate demeanor, her intensely furrowed brow and her strategically sloppy clothes that somehow stand out among the sea of sweatshirts and fleece. She has made deliberate efforts to blend, I see, but somehow the glint of money still shows through. She strikes me as a sharp individual, and her crisp, sudden moves betray the carefully selected college-uniform wardrobe. She is assimilating to the culture around her, but she doesn't belong.

"Notes, young man, are the key to retention."

Somehow I know the voice is directed at me, despite the fact that the steady monologue has not changed pitch since the lecture commenced. I look up from my scrutiny of Chloe and see a sea of faces swiveling toward me.

The lecturer is weed thin and beginning to succumb to the spine-bending pressure of old age. "Photographic memory?" he asks, and a ripple of laughter passes through the room. Not knowing what else to do, I raise my hands and eyebrows apologetically. He emits a low "hmm" and returns to his lecture. The heads swivel back and I try to drain the heat and color from my face.

Did Chloe turn and see me? She is now buried in her notebook, just as she was before I was singled out. I wonder if it matters anyway, and whether she would remember a face as common as mine.

At the conclusion of the lecture I make a hasty retreat, carefully eluding any lingering questions from the ancient professor. How exactly I will introduce myself to Chloe is still a bit foggy, but the sarcastic lecturer has bought me an opening. I can ask her for the notes. Nothing suspicious in that.

I approach her with what I hope passes as a casual demeanor, and note that she is alone—not just by virtue of the lack of bodies around her, but alone in a greater sense, in her temporary status within these halls. Something about her just doesn't fit in. But I accept that maybe it's just me; maybe it's just because I know that where she really belongs is with the super-rich, not down here with the trying-to-get-ahead crowd.

"Excuse me," I ask, only partly feigning my embarrassment, "I left my bag on the bus and couldn't take any notes. Any chance I could get a copy of yours?" I look into her hazel eyes and wonder what it's like to never have to worry about money. For the Chloe

Dysarts of the world rent is never due, grocery money never runs out, and bus fare is a concept that doesn't even exist. The financial struggles of the plebeian masses like me have probably never entered her mind. For her, wealth is eternal.

Chloe looks at me blankly, then purses her lips in what I can only describe as disdain. Perhaps my thoughts are too close to the surface. "I don't think so," she says, and turns on her heel, almost flicking me with her ponytail.

Beside me, a jock in a blue jacket with an oversized *T* on the front curls his lip and drops a beefy hand on my shoulder. "Crash and burn, bud. Crash and burn."

I give him his moment. Mine will come later.

• • •

Part of my plan is, admittedly, kind of ruthless. But it's good. After all, it's the result of serious thought. Nevertheless, the ruthlessness does bother me, and as I sit here in the chair across from Dr. Coyle for my weekly appointment, I wonder what she'd jot down on that yellow pad if I told her about the plan. Of course, that can never happen—regardless of doctor/patient confidentiality and all that shit. But even then I suspect she'd mostly just listen. Perhaps ask the odd, penetrating question, just as she has for the last four months.

I learned a lot about her in the first moment of our first session. She sat down on the simple chair across from me, lit up a cigarette, and said, smiling, "So, what's wrong with you? Evidently Leo thinks you're pretty fucked up." And I understood why Professor Bowman liked her so much. Birds of a feather.

"So what kind of day are we having today?" she asks, stubbing out her cigarette and mechanically lighting another.

"Okay, I guess."

"Making any progress in the world?"

Chloe Dysart's ponytail flicks through my mind momentarily. "Does *planning* to make progress count?"

The doctor takes a long drag on her cigarette. "I think it does. As long as there's ultimately an *action* phase to all this planning."

"Yeah, I think there is," I say, but even I hear the uncertainty in my voice.

"Well, good, then. So…" Another deep pull on her cigarette. "Tell me about it."

"Oh, well, ummm…"

"Roland," she says, raising her palms on stick-thin arms, "all this may not look like much to you, but it costs money, and someone's paying for the time, so let's not waste it, okay?" I look around her office. It certainly doesn't look like much. It's a tiny hole in the wall in the West End, up a flight of rickety stairs and perched above a laundromat. No swanky downtown digs for her. There is no couch, no carefully staged room with calming colors or expensive wall hangings. No receptionist. No tranquil music piped in through invisible speakers.

I swallow and respond. "Well, I *am* planning. Really. But there's risk, I suppose." Again, my voice carries a clear note of indecision. It's like a gambler's tell—something I have no control over.

"Risk isn't bad, Roland. Risk, weighed and contemplated, is not inherently a bad thing. You just have to be prepared to pay the downside price personally—should it all go to shit, so to speak."

I stare at the floor for a moment, then: "I guess it's that *personally* part. It's a little uncomfortable."

"Then I'd say you're not done weighing and contemplating. You need to run this through your coconut some more. It's what my old grampy would call *a thinker.*"

A thinker. My aunt in Ottawa, Pat, she always called me a thinker. Like the statue, all muscled and bent in deep concentration, fist pressed firmly into head. I always thought it was because she saw me as pensive and charismatically brooding. I believed it up until I was twelve, when my cousin bloodied my nose over a bottle of Coke, and, unsatisfied with his physical handiwork, proceeded to explain to me that nobody thought I was deep and thoughtful at all, just weird.

Twelve was tough for me. It was the first year that I really started to resent my parents. They left me two days after my fifth birthday, went out for a movie and the next thing you know I'm living with Aunt Pat and her meat-fisted son, Dwayne. It wasn't until I was seven going on eight that I found out about the accident, and again it was thanks to Dwayne and his particular brand of torture. He loved to be the one to let the cat out of the bag, especially if he could watch it flail its claws at your tender parts.

By the time I turned twelve, I had started looking for details. Aunt Pat, always smiling and nodding, obligingly handed over a small shoebox full of newspaper clippings and legal documents. There was big talk of a trial, the clippings indicated, followed by a preemptive settlement for the third victim. Apparently, my father was blamed for the accident—driver error, they called it—which killed my mother and him, and seriously injured a blonde teenage girl on a bicycle. Her picture made it into several of the clippings, but somehow my parents were never shown. I always wondered why that was, that the paper never printed my parents' pictures. They were a handsome enough couple, and there were plenty of photographs around if any reporter had cared to ask. And now, a journalist myself (albeit an unemployed one), I still have no idea why.

And, like a cartoon thought bubble, Professor Bowman pops into my head and begins nattering away with that lecture I know so well: "We set the agenda!" he cries, but the thought feels hollow just now, and so I stuff it back down. I rein myself in and get back to the conversation.

Cathy gently tugs me from my thoughts. "Talk to me about risk. About the risk you face. Personally."

"Well, that's just it. I'm okay with the risk—personally—but there's more at stake. Like other people."

At this the doctor just nods and smokes. It's one of her favorite plays; if she just sits and smokes and nods, she knows I'll eventually babble on and fill the space. But after four months, I'm on to her.

More sitting, smoking, and nodding.

I lunge in. "I mean, it's unavoidable, right? Risk is inherent in living. And so, risk to others, to people around you, is a natural part of, well, living, right? Being within a community, any community, is accepting of those risks—whatever they are." It's thin logic and I damn well know it. I need to shut my mouth; it's all getting too close to Chloe, to the parts of the plan that are flawed and ugly, but Dr. Coyle is like a magnet to the iron-filing thoughts in my head. Her brow furrows. "You mean risk to other people as a result of your actions?"

"…Well, yeah."

"And these *other people* are aware of the risks your actions expose them to?"

A pause. "Not necessarily."

"I see," she says, pausing in thought. "Well, I understand the dilemma, and it's actually indicative of a known condition—the clinical term for it is *being an asshole.*"

"I—"

"Roland, I get that you've not had it easy. But It's not a license for treating people like shit. This is the hard truth, and I've told you this before: the world does not owe you anything. There's no cosmic wheel that's out of balance because you got dealt the shittiest of shitty hands. And as long as you keep rationalizing and justifying being an asshole, you're going to have two problems: you're going to piss the world off, and you're going to be alone."

"I know."

"Yes, I think you do know. And I think that whatever you're planning has some measure of risk to innocent bystanders that you know is unreasonable. I think you're fully aware that you're going to piss the world off. And no matter how small a thing this particular instance may be—and I don't even want to know what it is, to be honest, but it doesn't sound like something good—it *is* a pattern, Roland. It's *your* pattern. So just think on that."

So, whether I am a thinker or perhaps just a weirdo is still unclear. Nevertheless, my plan has some real merit, and the risk to me, personally, is acceptable. And if nothing happens, then there was no risk after all. Thin logic again? Maybe, but nothing of value in this world comes without risk.

I leave Dr. Coyle's with a band of uncomfortable questions looping through my head. The streetcar jostles me all the way to the university, where I hop off to watch Chloe Dysart's evening class routine—from afar. But it feels creepier now, especially given that it's dark and I can stand in the shadows. *What the fuck am I doing?* Dr. Coyle's admonitions rattle around my head again but I'm already here, in the shadows, so I press on.

I follow at a distance, carefully, casually. My research will need to be meticulous here, and I watch intently for signs that she is aware of me, or that others are aware of my following her. I see none, and commit her schedule to memory—especially her route home.

But far in the back of my head, the question pops up again: *What the fuck are you doing?*—only this time it's Dr. Coyle doing the asking.

• • •

Trots is a dangerous man, and while I do fear him, I am also strangely drawn to him. He has a worldview that extends outward from himself, and if that worldview is ever contradicted, ever infringed upon to even the slightest degree, he becomes instantly enraged. Police, in particular, seem to upset Trots, and I know that his blatant contempt for them is also a source of personal pride. He is a charismatic man, six foot two, two-fifty, all of it muscle, and he walks with a long, loping gait that has his minions skipping to keep up.

I first met Trots through a guy named Dave Torentini, a part-timer at Dory's who was into betting on harness racing. He seemed to do well, and I eventually asked if I could tag along, maybe place the odd ten-spot on a football game. Dave said sure, but there were ground rules. "One—don't screw around with these guys. Pay up if you lose; they're pretty serious about their business.

And two—don't give them your real name. Just a precaution," he said, smiling. And so I tagged along, smiled secretly as Dave was greeted as Paulie, and then placed a couple of bets myself under the lamest of pseudonames: Joe. It was all I could come up with under pressure. But it stuck. To Trots and Company, I am Joey.

I claimed a few winners, just enough to get me hooked, and then came the losses. About a week after I started betting, Dave quit Dory's for a real job in advertising—fourteenth-floor offices at the corner of First and Main. And yes, I was jealous. Anyway, he pulled me aside before he left and repeated his warning not to cross our man Trots.

I recall that warning as I loiter in the lobby of the Royal Crown Hotel, watching the ebb and flow of humanity. I can see the train station across the street without being seen, and it isn't long before I realize that Trots is not at work today. The day is bright and spring seems to have taken a foothold. The tourists have once again invaded the heart of the city, walking around in cruise wear, staring up at the building tops and consulting their battery of free maps and coupons. They laugh and buy hot dogs from street vendors, spending money they've made at good jobs. Jobs they have probably landed with ease. I wonder about each of them, pigeonholing each one with a job—lawyer, doctor, accountant. Are there any journalists among them, I wonder? I stay an extra few minutes in my spot at the Royal Crown, just to be sure, but Trots is clearly not around. He does, however, have representation—in the form of a wiry little kid by the name of Bosco.

Bosco is maybe fifteen, pimply and dressed in a black-and-white tracksuit two sizes too big for him. He scans the crowd constantly, never reaching for the smoldering cigarette hanging eternally from the corner of his mouth. "Wussup?" he mumbles in my direction when he sees me coming toward him. "Doughna noya?" His feeble brain wrestles for a moment, then clicks in. His eyes light up and he points all four fingers at me the way military men do. "Shityah—yer dat Joey kid. Trots's looking fer yer ass, man."

It bothers me that a fifteen-year-old calls me *kid*, but I ignore it. I have more important things on my mind. "Trots here today?" I ask.

Bosco scratches at his zits and sniffles. "Naw, he ain't here, man. And I can't take no action from you. You froze out, man. Froze right duh fuck out." He swings his arms wide as he says it, then does the military four-finger point at me again. "Trots's looking fer yer ass, man," he repeats. He finally pulls the cigarette from his mouth and casually flicks it. "Now pay the fuck up," he says, and scans the crowd again.

I reach out and poke Bosco with a forefinger, which causes him to turn back with a look of revulsion on his face. "Duh fuck you doin', man?" he demands, rubbing the poke spot like a major wound. He is clearly annoyed and it makes me feel good.

"You tell Trots he'll get his money, but it'll be when I'm ready—in a few weeks."

Bosco is, as I knew he would be, flabbergasted. "When *you* ready? Duh fuck?" He shakes his head and blinks, clearly stunned. "Few weeks! Man! Trots ain't gonna go for no few weeks shit. Man, you askin' to get dead, man. Fuckin' dead." He screws his face up to the point where zits must pop and shakes his head. "Trots'll kill your ass, man. He's runnin' a bidniss, man. A frickin' bidniss." The zits hold. He shakes his head again. And then Bosco's interest is suddenly redirected to another client loitering nearby.

"Just tell him," I say in an authoritative tone, but Bosco has already made his way through the tourists and is striking up another deal. *No problem*, I tell myself. The message will be sent, and I will soon be on Trots's hit list—just the way I want it.

• • •

I originally thought that for my plan to work, I would have to get to know Colin Dysart's daughter, Chloe. The meeting with her after the economics class was an exercise to sound that possibility out, but I always suspected that she'd want nothing to do with the likes of me. It only makes sense. Still, she is a central feature of my plan, and I wanted to get a more intimate sense of the person I was drawing into it.

In the movies, the right move would be to simply woo the little rich girl, and marry into daddy's money and influence. But realistically, most people are not equipped to pull that off, and I know I'm certainly not. I think these thoughts with hands thrust in pockets as I stand at the edge of the road that divides the station from the Royal Crown Hotel, that edifice to opulence so completely juxtaposed to the grim reality of life in the train station.

I watch the ebb and flow of people from the hotel's entryway, mostly tourists, businessmen, and a variety of people whom I imagine are having affairs and secret rendezvous. Among them I see a face that I can't immediately place, although I am sure I know it. He is a thin, gangly man with posture so bad he seems to be a caricature come to life. I watch him as he shuffles through the door held open by the doorman and then disappears into the hotel. Nobody notices his departure, save me.

It is a few moments before it comes to me, and when it does I am not surprised that it took so long to recall him. I remember him with a small beat of self-satisfaction, realizing that very few people would have known who he was. Alex Joiner is the executive assistant to David Holt, the director for USCIS—Citizenship and Immigration Services...the proverbial big cheese. I recognize Joiner from a number of press briefings I attended during my postgrad research, and from a series of articles he coauthored on the issue of illegal immigration. For the most part he is a behind-the-scenes operator, but he's said to wield considerable influence in Washington, despite his low-key public persona.

I wonder if Holt is in the city, too, and I scan the crowd but find only tourists, businessmen, and cheaters. I know Holt isn't here—in any official capacity, at least—because if he were, we'd all know it. David Holt has that indefinable celebrity quality, and when he was confirmed by the Senate two years ago, an otherwise humdrum event became a call-in-all-the-anchors CNN lead. He's the closest thing in politics to a true superstar, and he's rumored to be a lock for higher office as soon as he decides to run. Hell, some tap him as a potential White House tenant at some time in the not-too-distant future.

I wonder casually what Holt makes in a year, and Joiner, too, for that matter. I resolve to look it up, but suspect that I never will.

Back in my apartment, I cook Kraft Mac & Cheese on my hot-plate and ignore its quiet mocking. I eye it—with as much malice as you can when wielding a plastic fork. "My day is coming," I say. "And so's yours."

6

I had no idea what I wanted to be when high school ended, so I just kind of shuffled into the college system like so many abattoir cattle. At the end of my second year I was coeditor for the university newspaper. By my fourth I had journalism firmly in my sights, enamored with the noble mission of the Fourth Estate, and returned for a master's degree after six months of résumés and cover letters failed to find their mark.

I believed that with a master's degree under my belt I would be a handsome prospect to the media industry, but soon discovered otherwise. Journalists are a strange lot, forever perched on a self-defined ideal of professionalism. We lack the board certification required of doctors, or the infamous bar of lawyers, but will argue our professionalism to the death. The ugly truth, however, is that to be a journalist, all you really need to do is write.

Nevertheless, I now have everything I need to lay claim to the title of Journalist, save a job. And so, with so much of me invested in defining myself as a journalist, I *must* have a job, whatever the cost. Not landing a job in journalism is to deny my personal definition of who I am, and that has taken far too long to discover in the first place. And so I cast my mind back, to the Professor, and to the unshakable ideas he instilled in me about what a noble profession it could be. It's a surety I have clung to over the last two years, and one I have no intention of releasing now.

I pull back the sheets and feel the morning wash over me: a strange blend of mild panic, excitement, nervousness, and perhaps a pinch or two of self-disgust. It is a sensation I scrub at in the shower, as I linger beneath the steaming jet and contemplate my life, my plan, and the mildew gathering strength in the far corner of the shower stall. By the time I have finished in the shower my resolve is set once again, carefully resurrected by the look in Professor Bowman's eye and by Colin Dysart's cash-laden smile beaming from the cover of *Newsweek*.

I make it to Dory's early today, to score some free coffee and to make sure I get back into Rhona's good books. I am agitated as I settle down in front of her TV, waiting for the coffee to brew. It's on account of the bank machine slip crumpled in my fist. I have a total of just over twelve dollars in my bank account. It sets me thinking, and I mentally tally my debts. Again.

Rent: $650. Credit card: $2,500 (but I'll just make the minimum payment and get screwed to the wall with interest). Student loan: $160 per month (with a grand total of $12,585). Then there's the small situation with Trots. Six grand plus the daily—Trots's term for interest on outstanding payments, which he calculates out at $40 a day, percentages be damned.

Still, if everything goes according to plan, I'll come away clear of debt and, with any luck, a new career in the making. I am beginning to surface from my self-doubt when the front door chimes and Rhona slinks in. "Hi, Roly," she says. "Coffee ready yet?"

"Just about," I say, automatically extricating myself from her desk chair. We move in practiced unison, setting up the equipment for another day of copy shop mayhem, then pause to splash some hot, black coffee into our mugs.

"So, what happened to you yesterday?" she asks, examining her cuticles at full arm's length.

For a moment I have no frame of reference, then it comes to me: my sudden illness. "Just hit me right after lunch. Headache and hershy-squirts."

Rhona raises her eyebrows in mock surprise. "Lovely."

I am now positive she doesn't believe me, and the regret I feel at my small betrayal seems again disproportionately large. I quickly change tack. "Hey, Rhona," I say as if everything is okay. "Have you heard if Holt is in town this week?"

Her eyes widen almost imperceptibly, but I catch it. "*David Holt?*"

"Yeah."

"No, no. Why? Is he supposed to be?"

I am about to blurt out that I saw Joiner yesterday afternoon, but catch myself in time. "I'm pretty sure I saw one of his staffers on my way in this morning."

"'Round here?" she asks, unconsciously adjusting her bra strap. My eyes flit to her large breasts, then back to her face. She sees me, I'm sure, and I think a tiny smile curls through her lip, but it's only there for a millisecond before she turns away to pick up her coffee mug.

I am a psychologist's wet dream when it comes to Rhona; in an unspoken truth, she is the closest thing I have ever had to a mother—or at least what I think a mother would be—and at the same time her overt sexuality is something I am constantly aware of. Freud would have a field day.

A man walks in and sizes her up with apparent approval. "'Morning," she purrs, still thinking, apparently, about Holt.

By eleven I get one of my many errands—to deliver a stack of freshly printed takeout menus to a restaurant down at First and Main—and set off just in time to catch the streetcar east along Park.

I hop off at First Street, hoist the box of printed paper to my shoulder, and head south. The pedestrian traffic is light: mostly corporate types with slicked-back hair, cell phones, and pinstriped suits. Among them are clutches of tourists, laughing and pointing, happily falling victim to the T-shirt, watch, and sunglasses teams hustling on the sidewalk.

At Main I turn right and start checking addresses for my delivery. I find it four buildings down, step inside, and see him for the second time in two days: Alex Joiner, Holt's executive assistant.

Now this strikes me as odd. Not just that I've seen him again, but also how he looks. In every press conference or news article I've seen him in, he's been wearing a dark suit and lurking unobtrusively in the background. Even yesterday at the Royal Crown, he'd been in a suit. But here he is, inside the foyer of the Waterhouse Building by the elevators, wearing jeans, running shoes, a dark blue sweater, ballcap, and shades. He looks nothing like the high-flying government player that I know he is.

He is standing by the glass wall across from the bank of elevators, glancing expectantly around every time a set of doors opens and spews out office drones. Seeing him makes me break the rhythm of my stride, just a slight pause, but enough to make him pivot his head toward me. I am already staring at him, and for a brief moment our eyes lock: mine wide open in full celebrity-stare, his hidden behind a pair of dark aviators—but I'm sure they lock. A fraction of a second later he flicks his head back to the elevator doors.

At the elevators, I punch the UP arrow, and scan the lights above the six sets of doors. Behind me and off to my right, I can feel Joiner's gaze. It is a palpable sensation, like the feeling you get with your back to an open fire, and in the end I can't resist a look as I step into the lift. He is still there, not facing me directly, but watching. Behind the sunglasses, I am sure I can feel his stare.

On the return trip Joiner is nowhere to be seen and I take the same route back to Dory's—a route that will keep me well clear of the Royal Crown, and the chance of accidentally running into Trots.

With my shift over, I head back to my apartment and eat a quick meal of Kraft Mac & Cheese and peas. I flip through the notes I made two nights ago, and check the plan once again for fatal flaws. There are a few spots where the wind creeps through, but no showstoppers. I realize there is little work I can do on it tonight, and to some degree I am relieved—partly because I know at some level that the plan is a stretch, and partly because I have another plan for tonight. Something much simpler—and noble by comparison. It's what the Professor would have called exercising the absolute necessity of the Fourth Estate. He'd stride through the hall, really selling it—I mean, laying it on so thick you could hear it sloshing around your ankles. *This weighty responsibility must not*

be shouldered lightly, my soon-to-be learned friends. It is the real seat
of power in a society. Not the politician with his hollow promises, nor
the businessman with his influential and highly mobile dollar. Not
even the soldier, bristling with arms and itching for a fight. No! The
real seat of power is here, among those who will decide—yes, decide—
what the masses will talk about tomorrow. Be not mistaken: we set the
agenda. We determine the issues.

Melodramatic? Perhaps. Accurate? Hell, there was always
truth in it for me.

I stuff my battered Pentax into my backpack and relish the
feeling that with that act I am actually doing journalism—something that seems to be increasingly rare for me these days. I set
off for the Royal Crown, not completely understanding what I
am going to do, but the reason, whatever it is, is connected to my
double sighting of Joiner. I tell myself that it smacks of a story, and
I even let myself believe I am following a "hunch." All I need now
is a trilby hat with that PRESS card the Professor gave me stuck in
the band and the corniness will be complete.

Perhaps Holt is here on a secret rendezvous. I have little weight
as a freelancer (two stories placed in larger metropolitan dailies and
a half dozen magazine articles), but I know that opportunities are
made by blending luck, knowledge, and persistence; I can hear the
Professor's voice preaching again in my head even now. Exactly
when the combination will occur is a crapshoot, but I'm not completely in the dark. I have the knowledge part, sort of—my double
sighting of Joiner—and I can certainly persist.

• • •

The lobby of the grand old hotel is impressive. The impression
is one of glass, brass, and fine deep carpets, wingback chairs and
marble coffee tables circled occasionally by doormen in short green
coats pushing decorative baggage carts. There is a hubbub of pros-
perity in the foyer, reflected in the tall mirrors and captured in the
giant oils bordered by velvet curtains.

In the bar I ask for a glass of water, muttering something about a headache, and find myself a spot in the corner that has a good view of the whole room—and not a bad line of sight into the lobby, either. I gulp back the water and, waiting until the bartender is busy at the far end of the bar, pull the tab on the Coke I have smuggled in. Budget surveillance.

It's a Wednesday and hotel traffic is light, and after an hour I am pulling quizzical stares from the bartender. Nothing has happened, and my hot lead is quickly fizzling out. Outside in the lobby I settle into a leather wingback, trying to look like a guest waiting on a friend—complete with regular glances at my wrist, occasional sighs, searching looks and, of course, subtle shakes of the head. Twenty minutes pass and nothing, save the odd forced smile from the artsy prick at the check-in desk.

By nine o'clock it's a bust, and I have to move on. Outside I decide to try my luck from across the street at the train station, and, after checking to make sure Trots is not pulling any night shifts, I pick a spot on the chest-high wall that surrounds Union Station. It gives me a perfect view of the Royal Crown's front doors. The spring is turning into a kind one, and the evening is unseasonably warm—enough, I see, for people to go out in shirtsleeves. I hoist myself onto the wall and see him immediately.

Alex Joiner comes through the revolving door and pauses at the sidewalk. He lights a cigarette—an act that seems somehow out of character given the sterile, public servant image I have of him—then paces slowly around the corner and up toward University Ave. Traffic is thin this time of night, save the odd car or cluster of late-night office types hustling by. I follow him at a distance, and slip into a dark alleyway when he stops at the corner of University and Fifth. He watches the traffic slide by, then strolls a few hundred meters up University, stepping back occasionally when big Greyhound buses or street sweepers rumble by. He paces up and down like a sentry, watching, waiting for something. I step a little further into the darkness just to be sure I'm not seen, and suddenly realize that I am shaking, not through cold, but through excitement. This is my first real stakeout, although just what I am staking out I don't exactly know. I wrestle my old Pentax from my backpack, and drop the shutter three times on one of the country's most influential players in Immigration, Alex Joiner.

Moments later a gray car rolls by. Joiner flicks his cigarette into the street and watches the car do a U-turn at the lights. The car cruises slowly past again, this time on my side of the divided road. At the next set of lights the driver U-turns once more—there's no traffic to challenge him—and pulls smoothly up to the curb where Joiner is waiting. Joiner leans into the window and I drop the shutter again.

There is only the driver in the car, but it's too dark to catch his face. Two more shots, just in case. I am now hoping Joiner will get into the car—an old reporter's trick; wait until the person gets in, dome light comes on, snap the photo and boom, you've got the driver. Easier said than done, but I set up the shot and wait.

Joiner looks up and around, then pops the door open. The dome light comes on and I snap away. The driver scans the street, swinging his head toward me. Snap, snap, snap. The car then pulls into the near-deserted avenue and rolls silently away.

I'm a competent photographer, and I'm sure I have some good shots—of exactly what, I don't know, but I have them. I'm shooting with actual film—an economic imperative just now because I've had to shop for camera gear within my budget at places like Liberty Pawn and Clarke's Cash Now. So just what I've got is hard to say, and developing the prints will be a job for another day, when I have some spare money (is there such a thing?). But for now I'm satisfied and I walk home triumphant. Of course, I don't completely delude myself: I know this whole evening has been more about *feeling* like I'm part of a profession. Doing something practical—regardless of the fact that I've likely got nothing more than some low-rent paparazzi shots—buoys me up and for now, that's good enough. What I have most likely means nothing, but by God it felt like journalism. Real journalism. Professor Bowman, if you could see me now.

• • •

I spend the next few days establishing that Chloe's route is pre-dictable, and that she follows it according to the day and her class schedule. It's easy to do; Chloe seems to be someone oblivious to the world around her—not in an absentminded sort of way, but oblivious because she doesn't *need* to be aware. Chloe is like a well-fed shark cruising through a school of minnows: everyone else is paying attention, but she doesn't need to.

My shifts at Dory's are all mornings this week, and afterward I head to the business campus to watch Chloe. I'm not stalking her—no, this is surveillance. A completely different thing.

Over the course of the week I discover, as I was hoping to, that she is a creature of habit. I have also discovered that, for whatever reason, Chloe chooses not to park her chrome Audi TT Roadster near the University. Perhaps it would clash with her slouchy college wardrobe, or it would identify her as a rich kid and draw undesir-able attention. Who knows. Maybe she's just trying to avoid door dings from Corollas.

Whatever the reason, Chloe follows the same route to an underground parking lot three blocks over and few more north of the campus. She also takes a shortcut through what I would call a slightly risky alleyway, although, in all fairness, it is a good shortcut. She even takes this route after night classes, and I suspect it's that sense of oblivion that lets her do it. If she thought for a moment that the damn minnows were dangerous, well, I suspect she'd think twice about that alley. I think this will be the place for it, though. It has all the dramatic elements I need.

The alley runs the width of a city block, and is wide enough for a single car to pass through comfortably. The buildings backing onto it are windowless for the most part, and in one of two recesses sits a group of large dumpsters—the kind people like to dump bodies in. The other recess, about thirty meters down and on the opposite side, is actually a back entrance to a building, but the door has no handle—just a keyhole—and the light overhead—the only light in the alley—is a spiritless low-watt thing set in a wire cage. It sits in exactly the right spot.

All in all it's not a really intimidating alley, but, like alleys in all the worst movies, it only has one way in, and one way out.

7

On my way to Dory's the next day, I pass the Employment Resource Center and a momentary flutter of panic races through me. I haven't written a cover letter or sent a résumé in over a week. The feeling is fleeting, however, chased away by the certainty of my plan—which is rapidly taking on a life of its own. I have already set part of the mechanism in motion, the part that involves Trots, and I am sure he has his minions on the lookout for me. Fair enough and rightly so.

I notice a black BMW parked out front of the center, and it makes me smile; I guess Warren is still struggling on his own without his family's millions. I step inside, search the ten cubicles, and find him in short order. Apparently only four people need to look for jobs today. Warren sees me and calls out. "Roly, buddy!" I think he's genuinely pleased to see me—or maybe just pleased to be pulled from the tedium of the job hunt.

"Did you land something?" he asks, already nodding his head.

"Naw, just been pulling a lot of hours at Dory's. How about you?"

Warren spreads his hands wide and smiles. "Still here, bud."

I check my watch and see that I still have a half hour until I need to be at Dory's. "You wanna go across the street and grab a coffee? I still owe you one." I only have a pocketful of change, but enough, I hope, to spring for a coffee for Warren. Today is a payday, so I'll have a few more dollars tonight.

At the coffee shop Warren tells me about two interviews he had last week, one at an upmarket clinic in the chic East End, and another at a dive an hour north. He got nothing from East End chic, but had an offer in hand for the dive within hours of leaving. He tells me the place needs to be torn down, and that he'd stock supermarket shelves before he'd work in a place like that.

"Still, you've got offers and that's something," I say to him, but clearly Warren can afford to wait for the *right* job. Must be nice. "Do you know Chloe Dysart?" I ask, surprising myself with the suddenness of the question that bears no reference to the current conversation.

Warren notes it too, twitches and raises his eyebrows for a brief second. "Well, yeah, I know her."

He is regarding me oddly, and I know an explanation is required. "I was wondering, because a friend of mine has classes with her Thursday nights."

Warren is still trying to figure me out. "...Right."

"And her dad is Colin Dysart," I say, trying to make it look like Warren is the odd one here, unable to follow my speedy train of thought.

His forehead is now in full spasm, so I lay my story out further. "Dysart owns Newsco..."

Warren makes the journalistic connection. "Oh, I gotcha. You wanna know if I can drop a good word about you to the Dysarts."

"You're making those connections at quite a pace, Mr. Barton."

He laughs and smacks his forehead in mock surprise. "Eat me, Roly."

"Sorry, man, but I had to ask. You know, turn over every stone and all that shit."

"Hey, no problem, and uh, do you know anyone in the vet business looking for a new man?" He chuckles and swigs his coffee. "I know Chloe, but not her old man. I will tell you this, though: she is one unrelenting bitch."

"Wouldn't date you, huh?"

Warren laughs again. It seems so easy to make him laugh, and I wonder if he's just a guy who laughs easily, or a skilled diplomat. "Well, true enough. But that's a whole other matter. But that just makes her a bitch with bad taste."

...

At Dory's, I am distracted and careless, spilling toner, wasting paper, and generally exasperating Rhona. She shakes her head at me more than once, and threatens to send me home if I can't pull it together. I apologize and try to focus on what I'm doing, but it's no use.

I never expected Warren to have a job-securing connection to the Dysart family, but I did suspect that he at least knew them. The ultra-rich keep the same circles, and it was likely that his family money and the Dysarts' had almost surely crossed paths at some time or another—debutante balls, lunch at the Yacht Club, that kind of thing. What I did hope to get was a little more information about Chloe herself.

I turn my attention to the next phase in my strategy—perhaps the most dangerous phase, one that involves putting myself at risk. It is time to set the entire apparatus in motion, time to launch kite and key to the skies and see if lightning will find it. What that effectively means is putting myself in front of Trots.

Because of me, Trots is out of pocket $6,000, plus his daily, which is mounting fast. I'm sure that if all goes to plan, I'll finally be in a position to start making good on the money I owe him, but in the strategy I had laid out I need his anger for me to be sharp. That's why I'd sent the rather abrupt message through Bosco, and why I'd made sure not to run into Trots since. When he does see me he'll need to be mad, and he'll need to see me in a place where he can do something about it.

After my shift at Dory's, and after a few choice words from Rhona on the questionable quality of my work of late, I take a streetcar back to my apartment and go through the paper draft of my plan one more time. I feel exhilarated at the prospect of its birth—like a kid when he finally gets that balsa-wood airplane finished and hustles his way to the park to let it fly. Part excitement, part dread: according to the instructions, the thing should fly. But there's always the chance that it'll roll over and nosedive straight to hell.

At six o'clock I head for the train station wearing a pair of old jeans, a worn-out T-shirt and a gaudy Giants sweatshirt I never wear, sent by my aunt as a present. My clothing choice is deliberate: all of it expendable. My exhilaration is turning to something else, something less light and buoyant—something heavy that seems to be growing in my gut and pulling the lining of my stomach downward. I've never put myself in the way of violence before, and as I look toward Union Station from the relative safety of the traffic lights, I realize that this part of my plan, if it goes wrong, could potentially change or even end my life. I'm scared…and there's no other way to put it.

The light changes and I cross the street with a throng of others: businesspeople, tourists, shoppers and more, all crossing Main Street and making their way toward the station. It's a Thursday night and both pedestrian and automobile traffic is fairly heavy. For this very reason it's an easy night to find Trots; he'll be taking action from his regulars tonight, and making a few specialty sales on the side as well. Up ahead I see his cornrowed hair a full head above the crowd, bent forward, talking with a customer. Beside him is Bosco, clad as always in his black Adidas tracksuit, a smoldering butt hanging from his mouth.

I veer away from them, careful not to be seen seeing them. I angle myself so as to approach obliquely, setting up my path so that at the last minute Bosco, but not Trots, should see me. I walk toward them with my head held high, trying to appear as nonchalant as possible. A few feet from the two, I see Bosco look directly at me for a moment—I see this in my peripheral vision—and then I am past. The urge to look back over my shoulder is powerful, but I walk on, and carry out my route as I had planned it.

I stride through the front doors of the station, through the great hall with its high ceilings and marble walls, past the ticketing booths and convenience stores, and on toward the men's room. As I turn the corner into the washrooms, the urge to flick a quick look back is so overwhelming I almost falter. A man emerges from the wide entranceway and jockeys with me to get past, and the distraction proves enough to get me in without glancing back.

The men's room at Union Station is a massive affair, designed to cope with the bladders and bowels of thousands of commuters every day. It's essentially a wide room divided by a freestanding wall down the center lined with steel basins and mirrors. To the left of the wall are the urinals, lining the entire length of the room, while to the right is a series of stalls. For the size of the place, it is remarkably clean and at the moment, only two other men are there: one is washing his hands and the other combing his hair in the mirror.

I walk to the urinals and strike the familiar pose, then move to the sinks once the two men have departed. I wash my hands thoroughly, killing time, waiting for Trots. An eternity seems to pass, and I begin to wonder if Bosco's limited intellect has failed him. If it has, I'll need to regroup, get out of the station and pass the two a second time—this time letting Trots see me himself.

It's incredible how quickly your legs can betray you.

On the floor of the washroom I am aware only of blood dripping from my nose. I know it's blood because I watch it spatter on the white tile of the floor. It's an odd sensation, because blood seems to have the ability to hang onto itself, and I can see my nose getting longer as the drips gather and fall, each time stretching the length of the red ribbon below me. I think for an instant of Pinocchio, and my red streak of nose grows longer.

I am confused. There's a force on my shoulder, and then I'm rolling onto my side. It's not a violent feeling, just a determined force pressing into me, pushing me sideways and over. As I come to rest I can see it's a large boot, a boot attached to an even larger black man. It's Trots, and he's smiling.

I look around, still bewildered, but starting to vaguely remember the fact that I'm the architect of this situation. There's no one else in the washroom, save the figure by the doorway with his back to us. I can tell by the outfit that it's Bosco.

"Joey, man," Trots says in his deep West Indian-accented voice. "Where you be, man? Me look fah you plenty time, but me nah fine you." He stoops down to my level and peers at my forehead. "You arright, man? Dat some cut you got dere, man." He laughs and stands up. I hear Bosco saying something to someone by the door, most likely turning people away.

My senses return now, and with them a sharp pain in my hairline. I reach up and touch it, which hurts, and my fingers come away bloody. I look up at Trots and remember that my plan called for me to *look* scared at this point. It strikes me as ridiculous now, because I'm no longer playing a role here, and my fear is anything but an act. I cower away from him, and I see immediately that he's pleased.

"Wha' wrong, man? You scare I gon bos you face some?"

I raise my arms just in time to meet his boot, this time sent at me with a quick jab. I take it down the forearm and feel the skin beneath the sleeve gather and pull away. "Wait...please, Trots."

My fear, all of it real, is something he's enjoying. It's a factor I'm counting on.

"Where my damn money?" he says, the word *money* coming out like the French painter. He drops his foot onto me again, driving the wind from my chest.

I scuttle backward as best I can, struggling to take a breath. With no air in my lungs I can't speak, can't tell him what I need to tell him. Panic washes through me like a cold current, and I realize my plan and I could both die here. I fight to breathe, heaving, wheezing, making small grunts and squeaks. Trots follows me, but holds off the beating. I reason that he needs me alive to collect his money. He puts his hands in one of the pockets of his green military-style pants, and pulls out a straight razor, which he slowly opens in front of me.

"Man, I gon cut yah trowt clean troo. 'Less you can forward I some dollars." His eyes are almost sympathetic, and I struggle harder to find my voice. I nod frantically, eyes fixed on the straight razor in his hand, dreading the damage he could do with a simple flick of his wrist. Finally I have sufficient air to form a word. "Yes," I say. "Cash."

His West Indian drawl is slow and melodic. "You have my cyash, man?"

"No, not right now."

The razor arcs upward.

"No!" I say as loud as I can. "I have something better, plus your money, I swear!" I sound convincing—desperation will do that—terrified as I am of the disfigurement the razor can so swiftly deliver. "I know where you can put your hands on an easy twenty grand. Real simple, I swear." I gasp for breath, one hand raised hesitantly against the razor's imminent flash. "And I'll get you every penny I owe you. I swear Trots. I've missed a few payments, yeah, but you know I'd never screw with you, right?"

The number stops him cold and the razor glides slowly back down to his side. I watch it intensely; it has become the central facet of my life, and when blood momentarily runs into my eye I flail at myself, wiping frantically. I cannot lose sight of the blade for even an instant, because I know that's when he'll use it.

"What you talk 'bout, man?" he says quietly. He is right where I want him, and now, with blood in my eyes and death only a single slash away, I must make my play.

I am scared of what Trots can do to me right now. He holds the blade casually by his side, swinging it in his hand as he talks, as he moves. He holds it as casually as I might hold a pen, and that frightens me still more. It is like watching a child with a loaded revolver.

I rub my eyes with jerky, panicked movements. For that instant I'm blinded and my fear squeezes at me with renewed vigor, tensing my muscles to tearing point, crushing my bladder. I see Trots's face through a red filter, which clears gradually in a flurry of blinks, fingers, knuckles, and thumbs.

"What you talk 'bout, man?" Trots says again, flicking the blade momentarily toward me. "What twenty-towsand?"

"There's a girl," I begin, praying he will believe me. "There's a student at the university. She's selling and making a ton of cash. She's a rich kid, and she's hooked into all the rich dopeheads on campus."

Trots's face is wrinkled in question. I can't afford an error here, so I press on before he can form the question on his face. "She's a bored rich kid. Works a regular routine, including a cash run every three weeks. I swear it's true, Trots. I swear."

"How you know dis?" he asks, pointing the razor at me. "How you know all 'bout dis cyash run?"

"I've been watching her, for months now. I was gonna take it myself, so I could pay you back, and…" I swallow hard—my voice is squeaking and threatening to quit. "And keep the rest for myself." I glance about the bathroom rapidly and take in the scene: sinks above me, shards of a shattered mirror around me. I realize suddenly that it's my face that shattered the mirror.

The big West Indian stoops close to me and for the first time I can smell him: cheap cologne, tobacco, and sweat. "Tell me 'bout dis woman," he says.

And I do.

• • •

As I wake the pain wakes with me, clawing at my sides and lancing me with every move I make. In the mirror I check the damage from the night before: The skin on my forehead has a weight all of its own, seeming to tug downward with every step, blurring my vision with the brightness of the pain. The bleeding has stopped overnight, and the T-shirt I had pressed to my forehead fights me as I try to remove it. It's hard and angular with dried blood, and when it finally peels away fresh pearls of pinky-red blood well up through the scabbing.

My right side is the color of rainclouds, shades of blue and black, and where it has yet to scab over, the mangled skin on my right forearm weeps tiny bubbles of clear plasma. Still, these physical injuries will pass; what really scares me is this new sense of doubt. Somewhere in the night, between refusing a stranger's help and stumbling gracelessly home, somewhere on the darkened, cooling streets of the city, faith in my plan evaporated. I have accomplished what I set out to do at the train station, and I have come away with the result I wanted in hand. So why am I so shaken? Why do I suddenly feel a sense of hopelessness? It's the girl, I think. Chloe.

I have now drawn her into the plan completely. Up until last night, until my face shattered the mirror on the men's room wall, the plan was just so much shadowboxing. It was a series of mute maneuvers, a cocky solo diatribe in a closed room. But all that has changed. The plan has become real, and will unfold with its own momentum. Innocent people are now part of it, and that reality is cold and without comfort of any kind. Dr. Coyle said it out loud—that word that I never let settle: Unreasonable. *I think that whatever you're planning has some measure of risk to innocent bystanders that you know is unreasonable.*

I think about last night, and wonder how I found myself at Union Station, wonder how I convinced myself that all this nonsense was something I could really play out. I think about it enough to scare myself, on two fronts: first, I see now that Trots could have killed me. Second, I am scared because my own counsel has been so off-the-charts awful. I stare at the bare wall, at the dripping faucet over the kitchen sink, at the hotplate.

Carpe EVERYTHING, Roly.

Professor Bowman's face flashes before me for a second, and I wonder if he ever hit a tough spot in life. Did he know what it was like to wake up one morning and realize that you had completely betrayed yourself? That your sense of direction, your sense of fair-mindedness, your belief in yourself as a shaper of your own future had just gotten up and walked away?

"What am I doing?" I whisper. I can feel my eyes flicking about the room now, looking for I don't know what, but stoking some fiery panic with each glance. I have thrown the switch in this lunatic plan, like throttling up in a plane I have never learned to fly. I hold my head in my hands and feel the panic rising. It comes from my chest, I think, expanding outward and engulfing me like a dust storm, filling every part of me, owning me.

Down, down I go.

• • •

Hours later, I wake. I am curled on my futon, hands wrapped around my knees, and it's some time before I move. There's light coming in through the window, and the clock by my head says it's nearly noon. I have a shift at Dory's today—or at least I did, at eight thirty this morning.

I move to the bathroom and shower, cupping my hand around the cut in my forehead, wincing as the water and soap conspire against me. I dress, put an old baseball cap on, and make my way into the street, walking slowly and keeping my gaze on the side-walk in front of me. On the streetcar I can feel stares but I'm too bruised to care. I get off a block from Dory's and walk the rest of the way, and wonder if I should go in at all.

Inside, I see Rhona at the counter. She looks up as I come in through the doors, and dismisses me with a heavily drawn breath. Only when I am closer does she acknowledge me, all cold and prickly until she sees the bruises and the hitch in my gait.

"Roland? What the Christ?" She abandons the line of cus-tomers and comes over to me with open arms and unlimited compassion. She walks me into her office, sits me down, and puts a hot cup of coffee in my hands. "Let me just get rid of these, wait here…"

I watch her dispatch the customers, glancing back at me occa-sionally and locking the door behind the last one. She hurries back into the office and squats before me, cupping my face in her soft hands. "What in God's name happened?"

I stare back at her, unable to tell her all that I am thinking, all that I am feeling.

"Did you get attacked?" Her hands flutter to my forehead and quickly shed the cap and bandage. "Oh, Roland. How on earth…"

"I got mugged is all," I say, my voice hitching of its own accord.

She disappears for a moment and returns with a first aid kit and dabs at my forehead. "Have you told the police?"

I shake my head, thinking that the police are the last people I could turn to.

"What about a doctor? This is a serious cut, Roly. Where else are you hurt?"

I point, and she looks, biting her lower lip and gently touching me. She looks at me, into my eyes. I look back, and I know she knows there's more here than a ten-dollar mugging, but she won't ask. She draws me to her and hugs me, the first time ever, and it is an embrace I completely accept. It's only a moment before I cry.

8

It's been two full days since Rhona dressed my wounds and cradled me, and I've not left my apartment once. I needed time to retreat, to regroup. I told Rhona I needed some time, and she said she understood, and even offered to pay me out for a couple of eight-hour shifts. I've stayed in my room with the curtains drawn, the door locked, and mostly with the lights off. I know it seems dramatic, but I need the protection, the respite the darkness offers. But I'm moving now. Breaths that are slow and steady—or at least steadier.

I dial the numbers on the phone and hear the familiar, gruff voice on the other end. "Bowman," he says, tired and slightly bored.

I take a breath and speak, reaching for casual and finding a bad facsimile. "Professor Bowman, it's me, Roly."

There's a pause, a millisecond of silence, but one into which I read volumes: he has forgotten all about me. Worse still, he's embarrassed by my call, trapped and unable to dodge me.

"Surely not the great Roland Keene?" His voice is warm and welcoming; I can hear the smile on his face.

I'm relieved in proportions that make no sense, and catch myself flat-footed. "Yeah, it's, uh, it's me."

"How the hell are you, Roly? Where are you?"

"I'm doing okay—living right downtown." I scan the single room, the futon on the floor, the telephone. The hotplate.

"Are you working? Got a job?" Professor Bowman's questions carry hope. I can tell he's not prying; he's hoping, willing me on. His enthusiasm for my life is like nectar, and I feel myself growing calmer as he talks, and it doesn't matter much what he says.

We chat for a few minutes, popping and answering questions for each other, until the line goes quiet. Somehow he knows I have something to say, even if I'm not sure what it is. His tone is different as he speaks now. Calmer. Perhaps even fatherly. "So, what's up, Roly? What's going on?"

My response is automatic. "I just wanted to let you know that I did call Dr. Coyle."

"That's good, Roly. That's really good."

"Yeah. I've been meeting with her every week or so."

"She's great, isn't she?"

I think back to that word: *unreasonable.* "Yeah. She's great. Really."

"That's good, Roly."

"So, thank you. I just wanted to say that. Thanks. Really."

He pauses, and I can almost see him bobbing his old graying mane up and down. "You'll be okay, Roly. You'll be fine."

And with that we both run dry. Mercifully, I hear a knock on his door in the background, a "Who is it?," and a "Sorry, Roly, but I gotta go."

I hang up the phone and sit back. Things are beginning to gel again. And tomorrow is Thursday—the day I told Trots that Chloe does her money run.

9

This morning spring seems to have made a real claim on the city. The streets are dry, the sun is bright in an entirely cloudless sky, and the black icebergs that cling resolutely to the curbsides are all gone. I move down Park, feeling alive again after my three days of confinement. I can tell the summer is nearly here, mostly by the fashion barometer. Women's skirts are creeping north, and the colors are getting bolder. It's a different city this morning, and I smell hope. I know that tonight I'll expose myself to another risk, but this time things will be more controlled—and controlled by me.

I realize there's risk to Chloe, who is nothing but a patsy in my scheme, and is about as much a drug dealer as I am a fighter pilot. But what risk there is is minimal, and will ultimately be negated because I'll be right there to make sure things work out. I'm moving easier now, and I can feel myself coming back, my confidence welling, filling my soul like cool water poured into parched soil. I hop on a streetcar and work myself toward the university, then hop off and make for the alley: the scene of tonight's performance.

The alley, the one that Chloe Dysart uses as a shortcut to the parking garage where she lodges her silver Audi TT, is perfect. I watch from the street as a man in gray overalls pitches cardboard boxes into one of the dumpsters—the one I will hide behind later tonight, in fact—and then disappears through a flat steel door in the brickwork. The alley looks innocent enough in the daylight, and to be honest, not much worse in the dark. It is the nature of the alley that makes it my choice for tonight. Like all good alleys, it forces its occupants to follow a definitive course to the end.

As I survey the lane, I imagine tonight's scene in my mind's eye: I see Chloe come into the alley from Harbord Street, where I'm standing now, humming or maybe listening to headphones, with not even a glance over her shoulder (her social status makes her immune to events as common as muggings, or so she must believe). I see another figure enter the alley, also from Harbord Street. He follows her silently. I can't see his face, but I know it's Trots.

That's when Chloe hears him, spins quickly and takes a step backward. There are words, Trots grabs for her backpack, and although that's when I *want* to enter the fray, I wait. I know Trots will strike her, just as I know Chloe won't give up the bag entirely without a struggle. He threatens her with his straight razor and Chloe cringes. A second later it happens: a backhand that spins Chloe and drops her to one knee. Now the timing is right.

Stepping out from behind the dumpsters halfway up the alley, my features well hidden beneath a hoodie, a ballcap and the upturned collar of an old leather jacket, I shout bravely at him, my voice husked down a few octaves for effect. "Hey, back away from her!" I yell, hefting my aluminum Louisville Slugger above my head. The only light in the alley is behind me, a stark glare they must look into that reveals me only as a featureless silhouette. A silhouette with a very large bat.

Trots springs backward, startled, and darts for the exit. Once I'm sure he's really making a bolt for it, I take up the chase, but give up at the corner. I turn and jog back to Chloe, who is crying quietly, and I offer to take her home. She resists, but it's a shaken and limp resistance. She says that she has a car, but I am firm, and insist on making sure she gets home safely. I tell her she's in no shape to drive, and that the car will be fine until morning. I hail a cab, she gives the address for the Dysart mansion, and we set off through the night. In the back of the cab I examine her cheek, which is split slightly from one of Trots's rings. I press a clean handkerchief to it. We talk, mostly about what happened, and I'm careful to let her know my name, and the fact that I work at Dory's. I mention it casually enough at least three times, making sure she'll remember Dory's, if not my name. When we arrive at the mansion there's a swirl of activity as her family circles the wagons. I leave quietly at the front door—never entering the Dysart home—as she is drawn in by her mother, and, I see in the background, by her solemn-faced father.

Once her family has tended to their daughter the questions will come, including questions about the person who intervened on her behalf. Later, perhaps the next day, there will be a phone call, or a letter, or perhaps a black-capped chauffeur with an invitation to dinner. Either way, Mr. Colin Dysart will be sure to reach out, and inevitably the phrase *If there's anything I can do to repay you* will be uttered. Of course, I'm not banking solely on Mr. Dysart's good nature to reach out to me, but on his business sense. On my return taxi ride home, I am careful to mention to the cab driver who the young lady was, and what had happened. I see his eyebrows rise at the name Dysart. I also mention that he could probably make a few dollars off it, by calling the papers and giving them the story. I give him my name and tell him what desk to call at the paper, whom to ask for. When the news hits the streets Dysart will come calling, eager to publicly thank the stranger who stepped in on behalf of his little girl; it's the stuff his PR people have wet dreams about.

And I won't ask for money. I'll ask obliquely for a break, delivering a passionate story about the journalist I want to be, about the career I am trying so hard to launch. It will be a simple gesture for Dysart the media magnate, and even simpler for Dysart the man. And that, as they say, will be that. I'll finally have my start.

• • •

The dusk comes later and later these days, but the temperature still drops rapidly once the towers cast their long shadows across the streets. The alley, my alley, grows dark at a rate that seems faster than that of the city itself, and after a while the one remaining light, the one cradled by a rusty cage, flickers to life and sets the scene completely. I walk casually through and make sure my spot behind the dumpsters is clear, then settle in for the wait.

Chloe's class is over at seven o'clock, and she passes through the alley at around a quarter after. I told Trots to watch from a coffee shop across the street, where he would be able to see her as she made her turn into the alley. He will probably be there from around six or six thirty, which is why I put myself behind the dumpster almost an hour earlier. I watch as the darkness grows thicker, and test my cover with two other people that make their way through the dimly lit alley. They pass within feet of me, but never know I'm there. I sit among cardboard and plastic bags, concealed by the dumpster with the bat on my lap, watching and waiting for the next phase of my bold enterprise to begin.

Through the slit between the wall and the dumpster's steel side I finally see her. She walks into the alley briskly; I can't see if it's her for the first forty feet or so, because she's in shadow, but I can tell by her walk. Once she steps into the light it's confirmed. She has her backpack slung over one shoulder, and I breathe a sigh of relief—it was a potential hitch if she decided not to carry a bag tonight. Moments later another figure enters the dark alley, and immediately I know something is wrong.

Again, the first forty feet are in darkness, and the figure moving through seems smaller than Trot's six-foot frame. As he enters the penumbra of the alley I see that it is not Trots at all, but a smaller, younger man, dressed in an Adidas tracksuit. He is skittish and jerky, throwing glances back to the street and moving forward with one hand against the wall. His other hand is deep in the pocket of his tracksuit top. My heart skips a beat as I realize it's Bosco.

Be calm, be cool, I tell myself. *This is okay. It doesn't really matter who it is, as long as the result is the same.* But a ripple of panic gets through and enrages me for a second. I should have seen that. I should have known Trots would send one of his lackeys; he's probably across the street awaiting the outcome. Never mind. It can still all work.

I watch as Bosco slithers along the wall, quickly making up the ground behind Chloe. A moment later she senses him and whips around, her hair fanning out like a Spanish dancer's dress for an instant. Bosco speaks and I hear him clearly; he's edgy, and his voice is higher than normal. "Gimmeduh fugg'n money!" he shouts at her. Chloe backs up a few steps. "Gimmeduh fugg'n money NOW!" he shouts again, this time flicking a glance to the street. Before he can turn back Chloe has begun running. In a second, Bosco is on her, reaching out and taking a handful of her hair, bringing her down hard on her buttocks. She shrieks once and I pull myself to a squatting position, ready with my bat. I wait—I knew this would be the tough part, waiting for the blow to come, that high-credibility moment that only violence can deliver—and finally I see it: a glint of something as it skitters across her face. She shrieks again and I come around the side of the dumpster, still a good fifty feet from Chloe and Bosco. I raise the bat, fill my lungs, and freeze at what I see.

Ahead of me Chloe begins to scream in earnest. I hear Bosco shout once, "Shudafugup!" And then I see the thing in his hand. He is pointing it at her and she is cowering, screaming, flailing her arms about her head. "Shudafugup! Shudafugup!" Bosco is yelling, his voice cracking under the pressure. He's hopping from foot to foot, glancing all around but somehow not seeing me. There is a flash between them, then a pop, and Chloe Dysart rolls back and stops moving. The change is more rapid and definitive than I have ever imagined—from moving and screaming to silent and still in a fraction of a second. There is no wind-down, no preparation. It is a case of on and then off.

Bosco is still yelling "Shudafugup!," still hopping about. He reaches in and grabs at Chloe's backpack, but her body is lying on it and Bosco can't seem to pull it free. He looks up, directly at me, and I can see the terror in his eyes. He raises his arm and punches at the air toward me with the gun. I hear both pops, and something stings my forearm. The bat goes rattling away across the alley, and the momentum in my arm tugs me around to my right. Bosco frees the bag and runs for the street. I stand rooted to the spot, my mind a crescendo of bright sparks, half words, and a strange whimpering that I soon realize is coming from my own throat.

Finally, I move forward to where Chloe is lying. There is no blood on the ground, no dramatic last words. There is only a carcass. I look at her and see the girl, Chloe, but it's not fully her. Her eyes seem to stifle the light, absorb it somehow and stop it from reflecting. They have no vibrancy, no sparkle, like the flat white of a ping-pong ball. Something vital is missing.

The panic that grips me is so complete that it prevents me from doing anything. My breath hitches and my vision goes spotty. I pull air into my lungs in snatches, each one giving birth to a strange barking sound as I struggle. I look down at my right hand and see it's black and glistening wet. My sweatshirt too, is wet, and sticks tightly to my forearm. I know it's blood, but there's no pain and I'm confused. In front of me is Chloe. She is completely still.

"I'm sorry," I whisper pathetically, but I know the girl before me is too dead to hear it.

• • •

I analyze the emotions within me. I am sorry, guilt ridden, angry, scared, ashamed, confused, horrified, and, most frightening of all, amazed. I am amazed for a number of reasons, the most incredulous of all being the fact that I'm not falling apart. I feel terrible about Chloe's death, about the years of suffering I have delivered to her family, but I'm somehow still keeping it together.

Another source of amazement is what's happening to me. My arm is encased in a clean white cast, and the operation, I am told by the orthopedic surgeon, went well. In my hospital room there are bouquets of flowers, fruit baskets, and a number of get-well cards, all from people I've never met. On the bedside table there's a copy of the *Daily Sun*, and on the cover is a large photograph of Chloe Dysart, smiling. Another photograph below that one, smaller, shows Colin Dysart and his wife, holding hands and scuttling down the front steps of what appears to be their house. The headline reads, DYSART HEIRESS MURDERED.

Lower still on the front page, and smaller again, is a photograph that I don't recall being taken. It's a picture of me sitting on a chair with my arms behind my head. I too am smiling. Below my photograph is a simple cutline. It reads, *Roland Keene: Good Samaritan shot aiding Chloe Dysart.* I read the entire article and it tells the same story that appears to be unfolding around me.

A doctor arrives and smiles at me, then explains my condition in medical jargon that makes no sense to me. Apparently my face reveals the confusion, and he smiles again and repeats it in English. My ulna, he explains, was shattered by the bullet, which exited my arm after nicking the major artery that feeds my hand. Apart from that, the bullet did no real damage. The real panic was the amount of blood I had lost, and the ensuing blackout—which explained the fact that I remember nothing after kneeling beside Chloe.

He asks me how I feel, and when I answer that I feel fine, he asks if I feel up to a visitor—a police officer. Suddenly I'm scared, and again my face betrays me. I didn't mean for any of this to happen, but it's my fault—and there's no escaping that.

"There's nothing to worry about," the doctor assures me, "the police just want to ask a few questions." I nod and the doctor ushers them in, two of them, smiling sympathetically. They introduce themselves and ask me to run through what I saw, and I do so, altering the part about me hiding behind a dumpster, of course. Instead I say I was walking through—on my way home from a late delivery. The police ask where I got the bat, and for a moment I am befuddled. The bat. I had forgotten about it completely. I say it was there, leaning against one of the dumpsters, and they seem satisfied. They thank me, wish me a speedy recovery, and leave.

They visit me just once more, the following day, have me make my statement on paper, then leave. And that's it. That was all the dealings I would have with the police over the matter. I remain in the hospital for two days in total, and return to my apartment to find a stocked fridge and Rhona's small TV in the corner. Remote and all. I call and she gushes over the phone, asking if there's anything else I need. I thank her and hang up.

I take a cold Coke from the fridge, snap on the TV, and recline on my futon. I find the news channels and watch the story unfold again and again. The death of the Dysart heiress is the lead, but I'm always there, a footnote, but there nonetheless. At one point I find myself smiling, but then the image of Chloe fills the screen and I feel tendrils of shame.

It was never meant to happen like this. She was never meant to get hurt—well, only a little—more scared than anything. She was just supposed to get hit once—to give the whole thing some legitimacy. I watch the footage of the family scuttling down steps to a waiting black Mercedes with drawn, tired faces. The doors close one by one, and as the last one closes, I know my mood is changing.

I can feel myself closing up: drawing curtains, switching off lights, growing smaller.

Only the glow of Rhona's TV lights the room, flicking images at me with no sound, casting shadows until nothing but that single cone of light before me exists. In it I see the Dysart family in black. I see mourners at churches, limos, dark sunglasses, and enormous flower arrangements. And the journos are there with roof-mounted satellite gear, cameras, cables, lights and microphones, and in the middle of it all, a solitary coffin. It's the color of pewter, ringed by eight men who heave it down the steps to a waiting hearse. The coverage lasts only seconds on each station, but I can find it again and again. Different angles, different stock shots, different nodding heads. But in the end it's the same dead girl. My dead girl.

The family I see in the small, flickering cone of light from the TV is collapsing. I can see it happening before me. They are adrift of one another, none of this "bonding together in times of adversity" bullshit. They are now individuals, their links severed by individual pain, unable to see any kind of collective family unit. They are a group of staggering survivors, each blasted from the comfort of their privileged lives by the simple and selfish assertion of my needs. I have put them where they are and I don't know how to be sorry for something of this magnitude.

What have I done? keeps running through my head, but the truth is I know exactly what I've done, and had I thought it all through completely, I would have known—I would have predicted this outcome. And while this thought sickens me, one thought sickens me more: maybe I did know.

I roll onto my side, eyes still watching the glow on Rhona's TV. The news hour is over, and in its place there are people cracking jokes to laugh tracks, catching each other in odd situations, chasing bad guys in fast cars and battling it out in courtrooms. The world, it seems, doesn't care much that Chloe Dysart is gone. And what's worse, it doesn't care much that I'm still here. And so, with the apathetic approval of the world, I switch off the TV.

• • •

After two days in my dark room, I manage to plug the phone back into the jack, and almost immediately it starts to ring. It's the news agencies—one after the other, begging for an interview, looking for a quote. With an irony that doesn't escape me, I turn them all down, politely but firmly. They all seem empathetic, and soon I realize that my two-day hiatus has heightened my status as the hero. I never meant for this to happen, but when I finally turn the TV back on I see images of my own apartment building. I see the super being interviewed, and another photograph of myself—a shot taken but never used as part of the Faculty of Journalism brochure. It's a picture of me leaning against the stone building marker outside the Journalism building. I'm smiling, with my arms crossed and a backpack full of textbooks hanging from my shoulder. The picture's four years old at least, and somehow the Roly of then and the Roly of now seem miles apart in every way. In the photo my hair was much longer, I was a lot thinner, and I wore a goatee that never seemed to have filled out properly. But those were just physical differences. The real differentiator was the obvious carefree disposition of the Roly in the picture; it might as well have been an entirely different person. The photograph was never used in the brochure, but the photographer gave me a copy and it somehow made its way onto Rhona's corkboard at the copy shop.

Seconds later Rhona's face is on the screen, but she's gone before I can find the remote on the floor and restore the sound. "…and it's a tragedy that's touched so many," says the narrator, and my photograph once more flickers on the screen. I turn off the TV and snap on the desk lamp I keep on the floor beside the futon. The room is a disaster: bedding strewn all around, bowls of half-eaten cereal and Kraft Mac & Cheese, Coke cans, a pizza box, and magazines. I shuffle through it all and step into the shower, run the water as hot as I can stand it and sit. What I have done seems like news about someone else. The death of a media magnate's daughter is too far removed an event to be part of my dreary existence, and as I run the scene in the alley through my head over and over, I slowly realize that, at least in part, I was a victim too. It is a weak and thready argument and I know it, but I tell it to myself over and over again, until steam is rolling out of my bathroom and into the apartment. Finally I allow myself the narrowest of spaces to slide through: what I did was wrong, but I never intended for Chloe to die. And with those words, I start to breathe.

By the next day I am thinking straight again.

• • •

I know this part well. I have inside information and know how to build the effect.

To complete the final stage of my plan, I must play this new role carefully. I reject the reporters with subtle comments, quiet words. Things like *I'm not ready*, *I can't talk about it*, and the real gem, *I'm so sorry I couldn't help that poor family.* Chloe is dead, and I can't change that. And no amount of self-loathing can. And so I resolve to go on, to complete the play.

Chloe is gone, and to fold everything now would be to make it all in vain, her death included. No, quitting now makes everything a waste. I think I even say to myself that if I stop now then Chloe died for nothing. It's a lie I will tell myself for many years, and on occasion I will almost believe it.

The phone rings and takes me from these heavy thoughts. I pick it up and know what to expect. I take a deep breath and put my persona in place. I am hurt. I am saddened. I am racked with survivor guilt. But this time the call that comes is not from a reporter but from a man with a quiet, soft voice.

"Mr. Keene?" he inquires.

"Yes, this is Roland Keene."

"Mr. Keene, my name is David Mahoney; I'm Mr. Dysart's assistant."

It is the call I have been waiting for.

10

The man on the phone speaks with what I take to be breeding. His words are deliberate and well chosen, but his voice is rough with grief. He pauses often as he speaks, and I know without question that the gaps are handholds for composure.

"Mr. Dysart—indeed the whole Dysart family—would like to meet you—if that would be all right with you."

"They want to meet *me?*" I ask humbly, my tone saying, *why would they want to meet such an insignificant person as me?*

Mr. Mahoney is so eloquent it makes me actually smile on the phone, until he mentions Chloe, and I banish the smile and replace it with a clenched jaw. "Certainly, Mr. Keene," he says, addressing me as if I were someone far above his station. "The family feels indebted to you. They would like an opportunity to meet the man who stood up for their daughter when they could not. It would really mean a great deal to them, Mr. Keene."

A short silence hovers between us, until Mahoney leaps in as if to up the ante on a decision that might go either way. "We would, of course, send a car for you."

"Are you sure they don't just want their privacy right now?"

"Indeed they do, Mr. Keene, but they explicitly asked if you could spare an hour."

"Well," I reply, sounding flattered and nervous at once—with none of it faked, "okay. I guess that'd be fine."

· · ·

At eleven the following day the car arrives for me. The sun is burning with the kind of glare that forces your eyes closed, and the white of the limousine nearly blinds me. A guy my age pops out of the car as I approach, and asks simply, "Mr. Keene?" I nod and he smiles, then holds the door open. Inside there's more room than in my apartment, and I shrink self-consciously into the corner, the leather seats grunting and muttering at me with every move.

The glass divide slides down with a low-pitched, automatic whine, and the driver regards me through the rearview mirror. "If you'd like a drink, please feel free to help yourself, Mr. Keene." I decline, even though my mouth has suddenly dried and my heart is racing.

The driver swings off of First and in moments we are surrounded by treed-in mansions lined with BMWs and Mercedes. The quality of the air here is different, the light better, softer, although the biggest difference is the fact that I can see not a soul.

Wealth, at least the kind of extreme wealth up here on The Meadows, means you never have to be seen. Cars slip into driveways that wind behind thick, well-established trees, or disappear behind gates that close so slowly they seem arrogant. On the streets themselves there are no pedestrians, only a lone jogger clad in running gear that probably cost more than I pay for a month's rent.

The driver slows and turns left, and stops as an enormous wrought iron gate swings back and opens. We glide through it, and I watch as the gates pause before closing. Anyone could run in now and be inside the estate—but the gates clearly believe no one would dare try. There are no streetcars here. No bus services that I can see. There is nothing to bring in the common folk, and any that dared enter would stick out like the proverbial lost fart in a perfume factory. No, this enclave just north of the city core is an invisible community.

The limo crunches to a stop on crushed gravel, and the door is opened for me.

"Mr. Keene," says a man with his hand extended to me. His voice tells me this is Mahoney, but he looks nothing like I imagined. He is a short, rotund man, probably once well muscled, but now just plump. He smiles briefly to me, and I can't help but smile back. "Mr. Keene, thank you so much for coming."

Before me is the Dysart home. It's a new building, but one that has been carefully crafted to appear old. The structure is faced with stone, and ivy is carefully trained up and around the many window frames, each anchored with a solid plinth of polished granite. The windows are all darkened with heavy curtains, all drawn tightly save one directly above me. It pulls closed as my gaze reaches up to it.

Mr. Mahoney smiles in that drawn-lip way that says smiling just now isn't quite right, but here's a close facsimile, and nods in the direction of the front door. I follow like a puppy, then thrust my hands into my pockets in a desperate grab for composure.

I follow him through the double doors with their heavy stained-glass inlay: no thunder crash, no band of accusing fingers, just a slight pressure on my eardrums as the door sweeps closed behind me and seals me in.

I am shown to a small library, where the furniture is the real deal when it comes to old. Shelves line three of the walls, ceiling to floor, and are filled with books. Old books, too, judging by the wide dark spines and faded lettering. Two graceful leather wing-back chairs guard the window, where more stained glass catches the light and breaks it into shafts of gold, pale yellow, and green that tumble through the drifting dust onto the thick piling of the luxurious rugs. They are old and show some wear, but no doubt they are priceless imports from some exotic place a million miles from here. Across from the chairs and backed by one of the book-lined walls, a low desk polished to a high gloss sits piled with more tomes, some held open with heavy glass paperweights or carefully marked with ornate bookmarks. Its owner has left his scent all over this room.

It's a moment before I realize Mahoney has left without a word, and that he has somehow managed to close the door without my hearing it. After several minutes, I opt for a closer look at the books, rather than attempting something so irreverent as sitting on one of the wingbacks.

The books, I realize with wonder, look to be first editions of classic works; Tolstoy's *Anna Karenina*, a host of Hemingway novels, Solzhenitsyn's *Cancer Ward*, and many others I've simply never heard of. I pull a worn copy of *Things Fall Apart* and sweep back the cover. I'm correct. It too is a first edition. Behind me the door opens—this time audibly—and I turn, too quickly, caught neck-deep in my own treachery.

"Roland Keene," says the man before me. It is a statement, not a question.

I nod yes, and he reaches for the book in my hands and takes it—not possessively, but collegially—like a man sharing a secret. We stare at each other for a finely stretched moment; he is drinking me in, I think. Looking for some quality that put me into his daughter's life. Suddenly he is aware that the moment has been stretched to its limit, and he breaks away, dropping his eyes to the spine of the book in his hands. "Achebe," he says. "One of the most underrated great ones." His look asks me if I agree, and I nod again.

"I hope I haven't made you too uncomfortable—inviting you here like this," he says, replacing the book and gently pulling it back to line up with its neighbors.

I realize I have to say something now, no more nods. "No, it's fine, really. I just thought that when you called, when Mr. Mahoney called, that you all might just want your privacy." Dysart nods approvingly.

He waves us into the chairs. Leaning forward, he peers into me, and for the first time I can see the hurt around his eyes. His face is a familiar one—to virtually anyone in the news business—but this close perspective reveals lines and bags that have never made it to the cover of *Business Week*. He shuffles further forward on the seat, hands clasped together. "Can I ask you about it? About that night?" He is aching for answers, and I have them. I have them all.

"Sure," I reply. "What do you want to know?"

He stands and moves briskly to the desk. "When she was…
when she was shot. Did she…"

I know where he is going, and I can at least spare him the
indignity of the question. "From what I remember, when the shot
went off, she went limp right away—I don't think she even knew
what happened. And up until that point she was putting up a fight.
I don't even think she was scared—just, well, pissed off."

He half laughs and runs a hand through his hair. He spends
another half hour with me, pitching questions—not probing me,
but searching for something in her death that just isn't there. It was
an accident, something that just shouldn't have happened—and
even I believe that much.

Finally, after settling back into the chair across from me, it
comes. It is a half measure, an afterthought, but an opening I am
ready for. "So what about you, how are you doing?"

"The arm's pretty good—I'll be back out pounding the pavement pretty soon." He looks at me quizzically, so I clarify for good
measure. "Job hunting—that's what I was doing when I came
across your daughter."

"What are you looking for?" he asks, his eyes and mind somewhere well past me.

11

I answer the knock at my door with a no small degree of trepidation; in the time I've lived here, only one other person has ever knocked on my door—and that was the super looking for a late payment.

"Mr. Keene?" The guy I see through the guarded sliver of an opening is dressed in bike gear, a satchel slung over his shoulder and half-moon sweat stains in his armpits.

I let my defenses slide and open the door some more. "Yeah, I'm Roland Keene."

"Sign here," he says. No small talk.

I sign and he hands me an envelope, then turns away without so much as a *see ya*.

I close the door and see that the envelope carries the Newsco logo, and a small butterfly bats its wings once in my stomach. It's been weeks since I sent them my résumé, so if not that...

I quit trying to reason my way through and shred the envelope open.

Inside is a single sheet of paper, folded once and emblazoned at the top in a copper-colored ink with FROM THE OFFICE OF COLIN DYSART. The note is written in longhand—all swirls and loops—and signed simply: *Colin.*

It is brief:

> *Roland,*
> *I've made a couple of calls and set up an interview for you down at the Star-Telegraph. Give Ed Carroway a call—he's expecting to hear from you. Best of luck.*
> *Colin.*

I read the message twice more, soaking it in. I hear the words in my head spoken clearly in Colin Dysart's voice. His tone is authoritative, crisply delivered and leaving no room for discussion. I somehow know that I am not meant to contact him again. Ever. I fold the note slowly and slip it back into the mangled envelope, then lean against the doorframe and try to understand the magnitude of those words. The note feels almost hot in my hands, and I know with utter certainty that if it had elbows it would gently dig one into me.

It knows, just as I do, that I've done it.

Somewhere in the background, deep in the quiet spots of my mind, a dead girl is trying to get my attention. I ignore her. I have to make the best of it and push on. After all, I never shot her, and I did take a bullet trying to save her. A few more well-aimed chestnuts and she's gone. For now.

I sit on my futon and look at my world. The hotplate, shrouded by a dishcloth, is remarkably quiet. My magazines litter the floor, and Colin Dysart regards me from the heap, eyes wrinkled in a smile. There are clothes strewn everywhere, a pizza box, Coke cans, and shoes, and, on the single table, a notebook with all my sins. I thumb through its mad-dash handwriting, and on the last page of my notes are only two words, the destination that everything must come to. It is something that I have not yet achieved, even with Colin Dysart on my answering machine, but it is something that I am now rolling inexorably toward. Those two words: my byline.

• • •

The start of Dr. Coyle's sessions are always weird. Maybe *uncomfortable* is a better word. Her opening salvo today is: "So. This whole thing's a real shot in the arm for your popularity, huh?" I think it's her idea of a joke, and she smiles through a cloud of smoke. "Funny," I say.

"Oh, come on. Gallows humor is a time-honored strategy for dealing with grim situations."

"I guess."

She shakes her head lightly—not so much at me, but at the world. "How many times have you had to tell the story so far?"

"A bunch."

"Feel like telling it one more time?"

And so I do—but of course it's the version where I came across Chloe Dysart by fluke as I made my way home that night. I finish at the hospital, where I woke with a neat white cast on my arm and a chat with the local constabulary.

"Wow," she says, stubbing out another cigarette. "Heck of a story."

"Yeah, it was pretty unexpected."

"I bet. But, as great a story as it is, what I'm really interested in is the next part."

"What next part?"

She lights another and nods as she draws the smoke in deeply. "Right after you got home. That first night after the hospital. What happened then?"

I have to think about this. "Nothing special…"

"So you saw a girl get murdered in front of you, then you got shot yourself and were almost killed. Just wondering how you're doing with all that."

I'm unsure here. "Am I supposed to react a certain way?"

"No, no. Now, if this were a Saturday afternoon made-for-TV-drama, then yes—you'd process this on day two, go through your grieving, rage a little, briefly cry *why me* with your fists in the air and then get right into survivor's guilt. But here in real life people hold on to that shit for years."

The sarcasm is dripping and I'm not really sure what I'm supposed to say. So I just stare at her.

"Roly—and this comes directly from the Shit We Already Know file—your brain marches to its own drum from time to time. Now, granted, any kind of clinical diagnosis is still a ways off, but we both agree that you perhaps trend toward the occasional extreme. That 'clarity of thought' you've talked about, and the other end of the spectrum—where you end up feeling hopeless—all that gets kicked off by a catalyst of some sort. By an event—a trigger. And my fancy education tells me that almost getting killed, and seeing it happen to someone else, that might qualify as a trigger." The cigarette glows once more. "So I'll ask you again: what was that first night home like?"

I stare at her for a long time, and while I understand what she's saying and fully agree, it's with a small beat of astonishment that I finally tell her the truth: "Honestly, nothing special."

She pauses for a long time, the cigarette in her fingers burning away and sending up little swirls of blue smoke. "Okay then," she says finally, the way people do when they don't believe you. "But just be aware that these events may yet come home to roost."

• • •

The following morning I start early at Dory's. I arrive well before Rhona, clean the glass on the copiers, fill the paper drawers, check the toner levels, make coffee, and generally straighten the place up. I print off two fresh copies of my résumé on crisp white paper, along with five sample articles I've written and published in various less-than-mainstream publications. I place them in a large envelope with cardboard inserts to stop them being bent, and slip it all into my bag.

When Rhona comes in I smell her, heavy on the perfume and hairspray. She glides over to me and smiles. "How you doin', Roly?" Her hand flits across my shoulder and comes to rest on my upper arm. I wonder if she knows the effect it has on me. Her cleavage is ample as usual, and it is physical work to not let my eyes dart downward.

"Good, all things considered. Thanks again for the TV and all the stuff in the fridge."

She waves her hand dismissively. "Oh, that's nothing."

"I would have brought it back today, but my hand…" I say, raising my cast.

"Never mind about that." She picks a speck of lint off my sweater and then brushes my shoulders in an oddly maternal yet sensuous way. "So what happened out there? You're a regular celebrity!"

I pause for a second, reaching for my prefab story, but Rhona takes it as some difficulty on my part, as if I'm not ready to talk. "Look at me, prying already." She moves off in a near-graceful waddle, her feet tortured in three-inch pumps.

It's a Friday and traffic is light at Dory's, and my mood is good. The air in my lungs seems to exist only in the very top of my chest, and it makes me feel quick and new. I will prep for my interview over the weekend, but with any luck, Colin Dysart's call to the *Star-Telegraph* will make my new position a slam-dunk.

The door chimes and a group of young, upwardly mobile professionals comes in, momentarily distracting me from giddy thoughts of my future. I greet them warmly; after all, I'll soon move among them.

• • •

"Tell you what: you and me, up at the cottage. You'll love it. What do you say?" Warren's voice is warm and I'm glad he called. He feels like a safe distraction from everything swirling around me these days.

"You mean your place upstate?" I ask.

"Mm-hmm."

"Will there be cold beer?"

"Does Dolly Parton sleep on her back?"

It's my turn to laugh. "Really? It's pretty swanky for a guy like me. It's all movie stars and millionaires, right?"

"Nah, don't worry, you'll fit in. There's lots of guys like you up there. Pool boys, maintenance people, that sort of thing…"

"Okay, I guess I asked for that."

"Yes, I believe you did," says Warren, and I can hear his smile right through the phone.

"All right, then, I'm in."

"Lemme see when the old man's not using it; I'll set it up."

The drive to cottage country in Warren's Beemer comes the very next weekend. It's easy and relaxed, with the conversation meandering through sports, movies, and the various personalities that will be showing up at the little get-together later. Two hours north of the city we leave the main highway and wind our way through a birch forest, cutting gently down toward the lake. The road is barely more than a track, two bare ruts really, and as we sweep through a final bend the forest gives way and opens to a wide grassy hill tumbling down to the water. The Barton cottage sits midway down the hill, facing an open arc of water with a boat-house and an elegant dock at the center of a wide private bay.

Of course, to call it a cottage is something of an understatement: the structure is wide and low and follows the slope of the land. It's all glass at the front—to take in the wide expanse of the bay—and elegant stone with dark wood accents at the back and throughout the supporting pillars. There is a series of decks and landings at the front of the structure, servicing rooms that fall at different levels as the house blends into the curve of the hillside. As the day turns into evening a series of soft lights twinkle on, skillfully hidden beneath stone landings and wooden walkways, casting a soft glow that seems to raise the structure lightly from the manicured lawns.

From where I sit now, nestled in a deeply padded lounge chair on the dock, a cold beer in my hand and a comfortable buzz running through me, the building looks more like an exclusive resort than a private home. I glance at my watch and see it's a little after three in the morning. The folks at the little get-together—all sixty or seventy of them—have somehow evaporated into the night. All that's left is the moody drone of *The Dark Side of the Moon* coming from the main house.

I look up the lawn and see a few last souls, stragglers left up there at the house, passing it around and searching the walk-in pantry for Cheetos. But down here at the dock, beside the twenty-foot Chris-Craft hoisted out of the water, high and dry in its nightly berth, I am alone but for the gentle sound of the lake lapping at the dock beneath me.

My eyes track a path along the gorgeous lines of the Barton cottage and on up into the stars. They are so bright up here, so silvery against the perfect black of the sky. I think hard but can't remember seeing any stars in the city; it's all too bright, too busy.

"There you are, Roly." It's Warren, and he's carrying a pair of beers in each hand. "I was wondering where you'd got to." He settles into the next lounger and sets two of the beers beside me. "Reinforcements," he says, hoisting a bottle in salute.

"Well, I'll tell you something, Warren, you know how to throw a party up here."

"Yeah, it's a good spot, isn't it?" He tips the beer to his lips and then, "I told you that cast would work for you; Margo was circling you like a frikkin' shark."

I think back but I can't remember Margo, or any of Warren's friends' names for that matter. Jeez, I suspect I'm a little more trashed than I thought. "Nah, I was just enjoying the party. Wha'bout you?" Yup. That was a slur all right. I try to think how much I've drunk, how many beers, but I can't recall.

"Nope. Same as you. A few beers, a few laughs. That's about it." Warren finishes his beer and grabs another. We fill an easy fifteen minutes with chatter about the resource center, the characters that populate it—like the sad posters (*Your Career Is Waiting!*) that seek to project hope but say something entirely different with their curling corners. Eventually we fall silent and sip at our beers, watching the night sky wheel past us.

Up at the house the music has stopped, and it's hard to tell if anyone is left up there. We sit quietly for what feels like a long time, staring off at the house, at the night sky. In another situation the moment might have been uncomfortable, requiring conversation, filler. But not now. Not with the post-party yawns and the *bloop* of cold beer running the length of a tilted bottle and back again.

"Man. Lotsa stars up here," I say. It's official, I've drunk way too much.

Warren says nothing, but looks up into the night sky along with me, drinking his beer and letting time wash over us. Finally he lolls his head toward me. "Hey, man. When all that shit went down with Chloe, you know, the shooting and all that. I want you to know I called, you know, after. But your line was always busy."

For a little while there she was somewhere else, busy with other pressing matters of the dead. But now, with Warren's simple comment, she is once again beside me, close enough to touch. "No sweat, buddy," is all I can say.

But Warren is not to be dissuaded; he has a few beers in him, too. "How are you with it all, man? I mean, it had to be pretty scary."

Warren's tone is caring, and while I know the subject is a dangerous one it cuts through me with remarkable ease. He might be the closest thing I have to a friend right now, and the thought quickly wilts my resolve to avoid the inevitable conversation. Still, I give it my best shot. "It was. It was scary, but it's in the past now, you know?"

"Aw, shit, Roly—I didn't mean to…"

I feel immediately guilty. Warren is one of the purest people I have ever met. He's never crossed me, never criticized me, and he has no reason to pal around with a penniless guy like me—other than the fact that we seem to laugh at all the same things. I feel the need to backpedal. "No, no, it's not like that. It's okay, I mean, I'm okay talking about it."

"You sure?"

"Yeah, sure I'm sure. And in answer to your question, yeah, it was scary. But mostly afterwards—when it kind of dawned on me that I was well on my way to being a dead man. If they hadn't found me there… I was bleeding buckets, man. It could have easily been two of us there."

"Fuck." There is wonder in his voice, but I know it's not the voyeuristic kind. Empathy is washing off Warren in sheets.

Maybe it's the beer, maybe the weight of Chloe pressing down on me anew, but somewhere inside me I yearn to tell, to unload this secret and confide in someone who will say *Yeah, I understand. It's not your fault. You had no choice*—even if none of it's true. I look at Warren and wonder if he could give me that. There's relief in telling someone, I know. What's the old adage? *A problem shared is a problem halved.* And then there's *the truth shall set you free.* I look at Warren again. Would he understand?

And then he begins to speak. "Man, what a fucking nightmare. For you, the Dysarts, everybody. You think they'll ever catch the guy? I mean, did you get a look at him or anything?"

My head bows slightly even though I don't intend it to, and I look down through the neck of the bottle, spinning the amber contents around and around. I don't want to drink any more of it. I don't want to think about the answer to Warren's question. Instead I just shake my head gently.

He goes on. "I tell you, if her dad ever gets hold of that fucker..."

A cold sweat rises in prickles at the back of my neck. *The truth shall set you free* suddenly morphs into *the truth shall put your ass in jail.* Telling Warren—shit, telling anyone—is a thought that suddenly terrifies me. And even more frightening is that I considered the option at all, no matter how fanciful the thought.

No one can possibly understand what happened. *How* it happened. And certainly not how I've managed to move on, and actually benefit from this wholesale tragedy. Chloe is dead and decomposing—despite her little incursions into my life—and I'm sitting on a two-thousand-dollar lounge chair sipping imported beer on a dock bigger than my apartment. There's not an explanation in the world that could cover the gulf between us.

I must stop it here. I can't risk another moment like that, another little stretch of weakness where I start wondering about understanding and forgiveness—from anyone.

I don't know a better guy than Warren, but I have to remind

myself that he knows more than just the facts of the shooting. He has other strands of the story, other threads he can tug at and worry.

No, I have to stop hard, turn and run. Warren is too close, too tied to the Dysarts, to Chloe. I suddenly understand that I have to disengage, distance myself, and let Warren sink quietly into my past. I guess in a way, I'm killing him, too.

I sit up from the lounge chair and swing my legs to the floor. "I'm shitfaced, man. I gotta go to bed." I nod once, set down the bottle, and leave Warren alone at the dock.

12

My first impression of Ed Carroway is, forgive the pun, that he's a seedy little man. In another life he would have been a bean counter in the Wild West, with a green visor and black bands around the arms of a shirt that was once white, and a dead cigarette hanging from his permanent scowl. But today he's a long, meatless man in a very tired cardigan. His face is tired, too, but his eyes are sharp and miss nothing. His first glance at me, brief and almost dismissive, cuts deep. I see that he is immediately suspicious.

He talks quickly about nothing, everything, expertly rifling the stack of yellow-jacketed files on his desk, moving from one to the next with a practiced tempo: a note here, a circle there, the occasional head shake of exasperation. His chatter is about the business, the pace of it, the unrelenting lava flow of events that surround us and demand reporting. Finally, he turns his focus to the business between us, but his transition is so seamless that it's a moment before I realize the subject matter is now me. "So, I've read the pieces. Some promise there. What kind of journalism are you hoping for? Investigative, hard news?"

His questions are obvious and on some level embarrassing. He means to test me from the very get-go, checking to see if my journalistic credo is borrowed from some Hollywood version of what it means to be a newsman. But I'm ready for him. "Look, I'm as green as they come," I say, realizing with some small splinter of surprise that while my route to this meeting was contrived, my response is not. I believe what I'm saying. "I'd just like to learn the trade—a cub reporter. The most I can offer is maybe some modest writing ability. That and the fact that I really want to do this." My lowball has silenced the yellow jackets; his pencil is still.

Carroway's eyes dart at me for only the second time in this meeting. Something in his manner changes, and he leans back into the leather of the seat, suddenly a little more human. I see a tired man now: a man driven to do what he does, and with no say in the matter. Perhaps there's something of me in there.

His glasses ride up to his forehead as he pinches at the bridge of his nose. "I'm sorry about the whole mess with Dysart's daughter. That must have been difficult." I nod, still uncertain of how to deal with the strange apologies I have been receiving daily. "Let me be frank," he continues. "Dysart put a call in here, so you're hired—that's the bottom line. There's a lot of people clamoring at our doors, so make the best of your good fortune—this is the *what have you done for me lately* industry, got it?"

I nod again, thrilled at the admission that there's a job for me, but struggling to look suitably distressed at the circumstances surrounding my appointment.

He presses on and I listen gravely. "You'll be in the general pool, which means stories will be doled out at the beginning of your shift, and that's what you cover. Do it quickly, do it right the first time, and do whatever it takes to make friends with the editors. That's the sum total of my advice to you. Take it to heart—especially with the editors. Bring them coffee, shine their shoes, babysit their kids, hump their wives—whatever it takes. Am I making myself clear? Think of it as the sole purpose in your life at the moment."

I nod again, this time a laugh tickling the back of my throat.

"Any questions?" he says, and as I open my mouth to ask, he says, "And no, you won't get your own byline. But that'll come with time—if you turn out to be any good."

● ● ●

Day one—hell, month one is mostly about fetching coffee and

doing other people's research. But I don't mind. It's a kind of penance, a time-honored internship for those who are willing to kill for a career in journalism. I commit to memory important information for a rookie like me: who likes lattes or long blacks, the difference between a Reuben from Findlay's and one from The Lunch Pale, and when to hold the mayo or ask for pickles on the side. I do it cheerfully, knowing full well that I have nothing real to offer this group of professionals that I so badly want to be part of.

At first they just nod at me for the most part—"Put it there," they say, pointing with an elbow at some spot on their desk where the coffee should be left. There's barely a thank you, just a grunt and then back to the screen. I learn to move quickly among the low cubicle walls, among the clutter, the paper piles, the TV monitors and hat stands laden with sports jackets and ties for those occasions when reporters need to look something akin to businesslike. I stop only briefly, weaving through the wide expanse of the open-concept newsroom that stretches the length and breadth of the entire floor, setting down cardboard cups and plastic sandwich boxes with a *here-you-go* and a *this's-for-you*. I learn names, schedules, and habits, make mental notes of kids in picture frames or dogs on screen savers. I study the seemingly haphazard layout of the vast newsroom, a place that appears to have taken shape organically, creating a maze of desks and cubicles that seems to detest straight lines and clear walkways.

But in time, after enough coffees and sandwiches have been delivered, someone asks my name. They ask what school I went to, and, eventually, if I can proofread a story here, verify a fact or two there.

I stay connected to Dory's, but my shifts get fewer and fewer; it's a cord I'm not willing to cut quite yet. But at the *Star-Telegraph* I rack up the hours. I fact-check like my life depends on it, knowing full well it's a dying service among the journos. In the golden age of broadsheet newspapers, subeditors would comb through stories submitted by reporters and check, correct, and confirm all manner of claims. But today the reporter is largely on his own, writing frantically against a pressing deadline to feed the insatiable machine. I know the reporters eating their Reubens and sipping their grandes have little time for the fact check, vital as it is, and I know I can offer real value here.

I call offices and confirm titles, verify attributions with named sources, reach out to the police services and get ranks, names, and dates confirmed. I trawl the web for background, authenticate place names and street addresses, pore over public records, comb through government websites, validating, corroborating, and attributing as I go. I do thorough reads, find typos and spelling errors, but I'm careful to touch nothing related to style: I want to add to their work, not criticize it.

The experienced reporters on the floor learn to use me, hell, abuse me, but I don't mind. The tradeoff is a slow death of my coffee duties: *Hey, Stan, go get your own goddamn coffee, I need Roly on this.* Eventually someone tosses me a recorder and asks me to do them a favor and cover an insignificant announcement going down at City Hall. They know, as do I, that the formation of some inane subcommittee will never make the day's paper. But it has to be covered, written, submitted to the editorial meeting, and, predictably, killed. But I relish the moment. And while I sit in the media room at City Hall covering a story no one will ever read, I am absolutely thrilled. This is the thing I have been chasing. This is journalism.

Once my first couple of paychecks clear, I hustle down to Union Station to put a small wad of cash into Trots's meaty fist. This is a nervous moment; he knows me as Joey, some insignificant kid in a hoodie, but my face has been plastered about in the media ever since Chloe. I tell myself that the photo they used—the Faculty of Journalism brochure picture—was from years ago, and I looked different then. Clean-cut. Preppy. And the name with that photo is Roland Keene. Not Joey. I tell myself that Trots doesn't strike me as a current events kinda guy, but it doesn't matter. It's a chance I have to take. I know he'll be looking for me soon if I don't start paying—something I can finally do now with my new and steady income.

Trots is not there but Bosco is: taking cash, paying wins, and selling a little of this and that. As he looks at me I feel a sense of relief—there is no telling reaction, no sudden realization; he has no idea it was me he shot that night in the alley.

I ask him where Trots is and my lucky streak just keeps on streaking. "Trots got his ass pinched, man. Fuckin' pinched. He's doin' a stretch inside for boosting a ride." I wait for Bosco to tell me that I need to start paying, that Trots left instructions on how much and how often. But it never comes. Bosco just stares at me and shakes his head gently in a knowing, almost forlorn way. For a moment I consider giving him the money, but instead I push it deeper into my pocket. Do criminals have succession planning? Are their accounts handed on when one or the other gets sent away? I guess not, and before I consider it any more, I simply drift off into the crowd, my debt suspended—who knows, maybe erased. Surely it can't be this simple? Probably not, but lately my life has been making all the right moves, and maybe this is just one more. I'll take the win and leave it at that, because I know it won't stand up to a thorough examination.

• • •

Later that day I have my first real meeting with Donna Sabourin. I've met her once before, shortly after I started at the paper—that is to say, I was introduced to her and was likely immediately forgotten. And I've seen her around since then, of course, and even said a fleeting hello to her while passing in the corridor in a pathetic (and hugely unsuccessful) attempt to get on her radar.

When I see her today she is down in the archives, two stories underground where copies of the paper are stored for posterity. She is struggling to heave a dusty legal box from the top of a wobbly steel shelf and I arrive, much like Spiderman, just in time, and help her with the box. Somehow we get chatting about whatever it is she's researching. Something on cosmetic procedures. She says she knows it's fluffy and light, just filler, and that the international scene is where she really wants to be. I don't really care; I'm just happy that she's talking to me.

For a moment I try to understand why talking to her is so important to me. I also notice that I'm suddenly making conscious decisions around functions that my body usually takes care of without thought: why is it that I'm standing a little taller right now? In fact, why am I even thinking about how I should stand? Should my hand be placed casually on the steel shelving rack beside me? Or shoved aloofly in my pocket? Is my hair sitting awkwardly? And am I smiling and laughing in the right places? It's a rabbit hole I can slip easily into, so I fight my way out and refocus on Donna.

She's looking at me oddly.

Shit.

"Are you okay, Roland?" Her brow is furrowed in concern. Not just the pretense of it, but the real thing.

"No, yes. I'm fine. Good." Jesus. I'm close to panic. I don't know what to say; I haven't been listening for the past few seconds. I lunge in blindly. "You got me thinking—about what you just said…"

"Oh?"

The frying pan I just left was much more comfortable than the fire I am now standing in. "Yeah, what you said just before. Before the am-I-okay thing…" I don't know if she's figured me out yet, but she throws me a fire extinguisher without so much as a blink. Generosity comes so easily to her.

"You mean about getting taken seriously—covering real stories?" she asks.

Relief. "Yeah, yeah. I mean, being relevant, as a reporter—that *has* to require credibility, right?"

Now, I know instinctively that someone with Donna's looks is well out of my league. Mice don't chase cats, asses don't race stallions, and Roland Keenes don't date Donna Sabourins. Still, perhaps it's the realization that I don't have a prayer that lets me speak to her without any of the pressure that goes along with the half chance. It's oddly liberating, that simple knowledge that I can't lose because I'm not in the race at all. For a moment I feel bad for all those well-groomed, carefully coiffed guys who have all the right things to say at a chance encounter in a bar. They have so much to lose and so many competitors to lose to.

We spend a few more minutes chatting, and I notice suddenly that the conversation has left the research subject that got us talking in the first place. I then do one of the smartest things I've ever done: I simply leave. I say, "Okay, I gotta go, see you later," and I leave. That's it. And it feels like a victory. I know I'll see her later in the halls or across the cubicles, but for now I'm content to let that light and airy feeling hover, and to revel in the fact that I have managed not to screw it all up—whatever *it* is. I head back upstairs, roll up my sleeves, and refocus on the trade, and on the development of the man I am determined to become.

My early experiences in journalism quickly change me. I am soon keenly aware of the sharp financial imperative pressing into the back of every journalist on every floor. I also begin to understand *hardening*, a distinct layer that forms about you, like the calluses on so many bare little feet in Rwanda, and through the course of the first fifteen months, I finally come to understand the core tenet of journalism—and it is this: journalism is a business.

I spend time doing errands and research for others—others whose names will appear atop stories they write and publish. One of those, perhaps the most talented of them, is Dave Barret. Dave has been at the *Star-Telegraph* for six years. He has a good name, a solid portfolio of work, and is widely seen as a rising star—the kind whose face will peer at commuters from a ten-meter billboard as they pour into the city every morning.

But I quickly realize I will never be one of his fans; he talks down to me, and takes every opportunity to make me look like nothing more than an errand boy. And in fairness I really did try—for a while, anyway—to please him and accommodate his menial requests. There were lattes, lunches, and last-minute web searches, and I really did make an effort, as I did with everybody. But where Dave was concerned I just couldn't seem to get it right. Eventually I stopped trying, and just accepted that I'd reached that point where, well, I just plain didn't like him. And the feeling, I suspect, is mutual. I like to think it's because his finely honed journalistic intuition tells him that I'm his biggest threat.

Dave becomes, in some ways, the springboard that puts my world at the *Star-Telegraph* in motion. A little over fifteen months into my shiny new career, on a Monday, he hands me—tosses me—a piece of paper with two names on it, and tells me to pull whatever we have on the two of them. I recognize one right away, but the other means nothing to me. The first name is Alex Joiner. Easy—executive assistant to David Holt, the celebrity director at USCIS. The other is Mike Peelman.

Barret is something of a closet conspiracy theorist, although he's smart enough to publish nothing too sensational without solid supporting facts. And to date, his stories have been written on concrete foundations. The two names don't fit together for me until a day later, when I finish wading through reams of information on the web. There is a glut of information on Joiner—his career is well documented—but there's next to nothing on Peelman. The reference I do find on him is unearthed as an afterthought, a quick search through the *Federal Reporter*—a legal publication that catalogues federal district and appellate court rulings—a kind of catch-all for decisions that percolate through the courts. Mike Peelman's name comes up twice: once in a fraud conviction and then again for theft. He did a total of six years for the two offenses. The documents provide little detail otherwise and I am left with a vague sense of curiosity.

The following day, I drop a stack of documents four inches deep on Barret's desk. It's a carefully selected collection of the most bland and obvious Joiner factoids: a list of coauthored federal publications, contact information at the offices of David Holt, travel schedules, letters of reply on behalf of Holt, mentions of Joiner's name in several Holt speeches and a host of other insignificant citations. The stack contains nothing of Mike Peelman.

It takes me a further two days to establish what it is about Peelman and Joiner that piques my interest. When I find it, which I do in a FedEx envelope sent to me by way of a *Star-Telegraph*-friendly contact at the District of Columbia Metro Police Department, I immediately understand the significance of my discovery.

Everything in my world is about to change. Again.

13

How Barret suspected the two names somehow fit together in the beginning is still a mystery to me, and frankly, I really don't care. The real juice here is the fact that the two names *do* fit together, but only for me, and no one else.

In my tiny apartment I lay out my next moves and document them in the same tattered book. I see this thing in three parts, and I know that a gamble is in the cards, too. I scratch "Part 1" at the top of a fresh leaf, flip a few pages and then do the same for Parts 2 and 3. The fourth heading is simply "The Gamble." I close the book and lay back on my futon, hands cupped behind my head, and follow the plotline before me.

It's been months since I last wrote in this book, and I venture a brief reflection by flipping the pages backward. I scan through the earlier notes, Chloe's notes, and immediately feel a creeping, gnawing guilt I have wrestled with on many nights like this one.

My mind floats to Dr. Coyle, whom I've not seen in probably six or even eight months, and I wonder if I should change that. I know I should. But things have been good. No *extremes*. I'm okay. Things are okay. But her last comments are never far away: *these events may yet come home to roost.*

• • •

Between coffee errands and research tasks I catch Donna's eye from time to time. We develop a quirky relationship, although to call it platonic would be an understatement of titanic proportions. It's fun, though, and built on nothing more than comical glances. There is the James Bond: one eyebrow dipped and one raised as high as possible. It's cast across the room at almost any occasion—when people say something controversial, when people say something redundant, when people say anything at all and we manage to lock eyes. And there's the Get Me Out of Here: a pained look that conveys the angst of the modern cubicle dweller.

But today it's the Slow Blink, a move best delivered in concert with the Nearly Imperceptible Head Shake, which acknowledges the more spectacular gaffes of the mere mortals that work around us. At the far end of the floor someone has just dumped hot coffee into their lap, which gives birth to an attendant scream and a flurry of cusses. Of course, the rest of the newsroom stands immediately, prairie-dogging over cubicle walls to see just what happened. I lock eyes with Donna and let fly with the Slow Blink/Head Shake combo, and she stifles a laugh with her hand and disappears behind a cubicle wall. I know she'll pop back up so I keep going, and when she inevitably does look over a few seconds later I'm still there, slowly blinking and head shaking away. She dissolves into giggles and I admit it makes me feel every kind of wonderful.

For me, it's an exotic form of foreplay that will surely never to reach fruition. For her, an amusing office distraction—a silly and immediately forgettable exchange that will never even achieve the status of flirting.

Reenergized, I push the tasks assigned to me aside, and begin to hammer out the structure for the three-parter that will usher me into mainstream journalism. Each piece is about 750 words—short and punchy, but driven by as much fact as I can pull together. Each story leans against the next for support, like books on a shelf, building momentum and leaving just enough unanswered to draw in the questions—and the critics. I know that selling this to Ed Carroway will be the toughest part, as he will want the story's conclusion—the payoff—up front. Editors always do. They don't want the well-crafted path that weaves through a story—not at first pitch, anyway—they want to know where it's going, and hear about the details that got you there afterward.

But for this story to fly, and for a cub reporter like me to fly it, I will have to sell it to him the way it was designed to unfold. Blurting out the payoff would likely get me little more than an embarrassed smile from Carroway—and a bulletproof glass ceiling inserted directly above me.

No. Carroway has to open this story like a carefully wrapped gift. The story's payoff is so big, so significant that even if I did get past the pitch it would be stripped from me and assigned to a veteran known and trusted by the readership. It's a career killer and a career maker all in one. My mind runs back to the notebook, briefly brushes up against Chloe, Professor Bowman, and then Dr. Coyle, then on through the pages to my overly dramatic heading, "The Gamble."

I will bet it all here.

• • •

It's nine forty at night and the *Star-Telegraph* is quiet, relatively speaking. Most of tomorrow's stories have been committed to paper, submitted to editors, rewritten, and are now sitting on plates in the press center just north of the city. Deadlines have been met, and journalists are sipping specific drinks in specific bars— the journalistic equivalent of cocking a leg. I'm through with my assignments. I have spent the last three hours working on my own story, and I can already taste the cold beer at the bar where my cubicle mates—and Donna—are gathering.

Outside, summer's first early surge is in full swing, and the restaurants are spilling their business into the streets with table-cloths and candles. The city is stirring from the deep chills of February; the sidewalks have been swept, the awnings are rehung with new color, and streetlights have been dressed with banners. It has all the makings of a beautiful evening, but out of the corner of my eye I catch a quick, darting movement. And without fully turning my head, I know it's Trots.

As I sprint through the crowd of prospective diners, all I can think of is that after fifteen months Trots is now out of jail, and he'll kill me if he catches up. I don't mean that he'll kick the proverbial shit out of me; I mean he'll put a knife in my gut and smile as I juggle the mess of blue-black hosing that used to be inside me.

I clip an older woman and spin her around, but I can't stop. Trots has nearly a foot on me in height and he's built like an Olympian. But fear is on my side. My high school bio teacher pops into my head, shadowboxing in his cardigan: *It's the fight-or-flight gland, folks!* The sidewalk is a blur below me, and as I whip my head back for a glance at Trots, I know I've made a mistake. The hydrant I hit is hard and immovable, but I feel nothing. All I register is the sensation that my feet are no longer in motion, no longer propelling me forward and away from Trots. My hands go out ahead of me, and I feel the skin smear as I fall face first into the street. Within seconds hands are upon me, hauling me upward by the back of my clothes and popping the seams in my shirt as it bites into my neck.

His voice is winded but victorious nonetheless, and I can feel the satisfaction in it as he pulls me up easily by the back of my sweatshirt with two balled fists. "Got you, you fucker."

I am jerked round and dragged onto unwilling legs. I throw my bloodied hands across my face, but I know the act is futile; Trots will gut me, and as I reach for my stomach he will arc the blade upward and carve a neat smile below my chin.

But what I see momentarily confuses me: I can see Trots, but he's not the one holding me. There's a small crowd, and I'm being held by two large, well-dressed men, both of whom are huffing and catching their breath. At the back of the crowd I see Trots. He's watching me, his eyes narrowed and his index finger flicking back and forth across his neck. I can hear him in my head, hissing at me: *I gwan cut you latah, man. I gwan cut you latah.* Then he's gone, and a sharp shove turns my head to the men holding me. "You knocked down an old woman, you prick."

"Kick his ass, Derrick."

"What's the matter with you, man?"

I look around again, bewildered, muttering apologies, but my focus is on finding Trots's face in the milling crowd. I put up no resistance and Derrick and his pals shove me to the floor with an entourage of threats and boot soles. The crowd thins as a policeman wades in and I'm once again hoisted to my feet. In five minutes it's all over, and I'm sent nervously on my way. Derrick and his friends are gone. The police have moved on. I quickly stop a cab and flee with my tail well tucked.

Upstairs in my apartment, I look at the hotplate and can't seem to understand why I still live here, why I still live this way, the way I did before the job at the *Star-Telegraph*. It occurs to me that I have to move—not just because I'm living like a squatter, but because if Trots can find out where I work then he can sure as hell find out where I live. But I know that this logic chain is not all that's worrying me: there's been a question lingering for a while, unformed but quietly making itself known: does Trots now know *who* I am? Has he put it all together: the photos in the paper, the interviews? A surge of panic ripples through me. No, I rationalize; he can't. The photo is old, I had a beard, and Trots isn't a follow-the-news kind of guy.

But I need to move. And I need to do it soon.

. . .

I'm at my desk by seven thirty the next morning, the brief chase of the night before a memory I can shake—temporarily—from the safety of my cubicle. I know leaving the building later on will be an exercise in paranoia, but for now I can immerse myself in a sense of safety—however fleeting. Focusing on work will bring calm, so I throw myself headlong into the job given to me by the assignment desk the day before. One of the senior writers, Paula

Cross, is working on a story about municipal overspending, and my task for the day involves getting copies of invoices and expense sheets submitted by certain city councilors. We're looking for fat, for good times at the taxpayers' expense—for anything that helps support a story pointing directly at greed.

I spend the first part of the morning making formal requests under the Freedom of Information Act, a handy piece of legislation that compels government agencies to provide copies of public documents. I make requests against expense reports from every city councilor named in the story, and pick up the phone twice to speak to federal employees known to be *Star-Telegraph* friendly, asking for help on shaping the request, and making it move through the system at its best speed. I play my rookie status to the hilt, coming across as nervous, in awe of their role but enthusiastic to learn how "all this works." They are flattered and eager to help.

After that it's the real grunt work of journalism: calls to the lowest-ranking people associated with the councilors' offices, people who just work there, and who will have little allegiance—if any—to the fat cats running the show. They are also the people least likely to toe the standard corporate line of passing all media requests up to some communications team close to the councilor himself. I ask them pointed questions about spending, try to get them to speak, to open up, bluntly using the *Star-Telegraph*'s name and its strangely inferred sense of authority in the hopes they'll get flustered and say something, anything that might open a way forward.

I get one warm hit: a clerk who says the councilor he works for plays golf every Wednesday with his buddies and it irks him that the invoice always goes to the city. It's something. So I note it, document the call and the contact, thank him, and hang up. Paula will like that one. I feel good; it's ten in the morning and I've already done more than some of the folks here will do all day.

That's enough for now, I think; time to focus on my real future. But before I can get into that the phone rings. It's Donna. She asks what happened last night, why I never showed up. I apologize and make excuses, all the while feeling thrilled that she called. But I convince myself it's just that friendly affection that Donna dispenses so freely to everyone. It means nothing, I tell myself. She's just that kind of person.

I spend the rest of the morning appearing to work on assigned stories, while actually laying out a mockup of the first chapter of my three-part story. I lay it out as it would appear in any generic mainstream paper: columnar, with carefully matched font and size. I am cautious to omit any masthead or reference to a publication. When the layout is complete, I print it, tear the edges around the story, then immediately scan the print—slightly angled—and repeat the process until I am left with a hard copy that's slightly fuzzed, and looks like a legitimate photocopy of a story torn from the pages of a real newspaper.

I read through the piece and try to see it from the perspective of a new reader—someone who knows none of the details, has none of the facts. I think it plays well, and immediately begins to stare accusingly in the direction of very lofty players. The piece stacks the facts rapidly, logically. It ties previously published stories together, plots a suggestive timeline, and builds a steady momentum that halts in midstride with the line "Read Part 2 tomorrow." I nod silently. It's as good as I can make it. I set the piece in a folder and place it in a drawer, then go about bringing the two following pieces together. They, too, stoke the fires of suspicion—still maintaining a sense of fairness and balance—but nevertheless push the reader to the desired conclusion.

The last of the three stories is the clincher. It holds the key, the hard proof that anchors the story and brings absolute credence to the facts that came before it. As I stare at the finished photocopy of Part 3, scanned, copied, and suitably fuzzied, I focus on the simple, explosive item that rests there. It sits in its own box at the top of the page across two columns, and it is brilliant. I realize for the first time that I am looking at something the best minds in journalism would just about kill for.

14

In the two days since completing my stories, I have been focused exclusively on two things: avoiding Trots and meeting with Carroway.

I'm taking a little heat for research I haven't done and for dropping the odd ball here and there—but it's a price I'm willing to pay for the opportunity I'm making for myself. The little barbs and snipes from those looking for me to do their grunt work are insignificant now; if things go my way, these people will be a memory. If they don't, well, I suspect they'll be a memory just the same.

Again, I dedicate some considerable time to the prepping of documents—this time, a fax cover sheet.

The fuzzying of documents seems to be something of an art I'm developing, and it serves me well as I create the page. It's a fax cover sheet designed to look like it comes from a news agency, but I've purposely placed a fold through the header, then photocopied it numerous times until it's practically unreadable. Still, it manages to convey the impression of size, maturity, and importance—as if the corporation from which it hails is old, established, and not particularly tech savvy.

Next, I scrawl a suitably cryptic note across the body of the page, in the large, looping cursive of some older, confident hand. It reads, "Ed, you should read these—quite incredible…" I then sign it with a patently unintelligible signature, and repeatedly photocopy the sheet until it, too, is of poor quality. Nevertheless, the note remains understandable.

I sit back and flip through the entire production: a fax cover sheet that looks like a transmission from a low-end machine, and three following sheets (my stories), that look like clips from a legitimate publication. I leaf through them, mesmerized by my own sneakiness. For the moment I am alone in the universe, until I am suddenly aware of Barret and his pinstripe suit.

"What the fuck is that, Keene?" His tone is condescending, but at the same time lined with something else. I drop my hand to my side, instinctively pulling the papers out of sight. I am unsure of what—if anything—he has read. How long was he standing there?

"Just some notes," I reply. "Nothing important."

But Barret, true to his reputation, hangs on to the bone. "Let me see that." His hand is outstretched, his finger pointing to the sheets at my side.

I realize I have no response, no cover.

He pushes on. "Let's see what you've been working so hard on, pal. Cuz it sure as hell isn't the research I told you to do."

Again, total brain stall. A flat buzz. And then, out of nowhere, it pops into my head—and I think it actually makes a popping sound as it is born. And then it bursts out of my mouth, with a surprising degree of what I can only classify as, well, aplomb. "No," I say, to the *Star-Telegraph*'s Golden Boy. And then I add a finishing touch. "Fuck off."

Two things happen in quick succession. One: Barret takes a step back—not a figurative one, but an actual step backward, his face tightening like wrung towel. Two: the entire floor goes silent and every head swivels in our direction.

"Excuse me?" His face is now wearing an incredulous smile that has absolutely nothing to do with humor. And I think he is blushing, too. Or perhaps it's more like an allergic reaction, a hot flush of blood to the face as his entire being rejects what he has just heard. He's a sharp thinker and there should be a stinging response, but so far, just that strange smile and nothing else.

The silence stretches to breaking point. Everyone on the floor has a look of wide-eyed desperation, begging for release. The smile and red flush have been joined by a quivering chin, and I can take it no more. I stand up and turn away. As I leave the floor I realize I have just made a mortal enemy, and secured my berth in what surely must be one of the best "did you hear" stories that this paper will ever have.

15

At the *Star-Telegraph,* the morning after my run-in with Barret, I think people are looking at me differently. Perhaps it's just that they are actually looking at me now, actually seeing me, like a ghost that just went *poof* and became flesh and blood. Or maybe it's me. Maybe it's the way I'm looking at them. There's the beginning of a knot in my shoulder this morning, and maybe I'm projecting something. All I know is that so far no one has come and asked me to fetch any damn coffee.

It's a powerful feeling, this potty-mouth afterglow, and even though I know it (and me) might not last the day, I revel in the sensation. God, I wonder if Donna has heard about it? It's one of those things that you need those who are important to you to hear from someone else. Part of its power is lost if you have to do the telling; no, with any luck someone has already sidled up to Donna and said, "Oh my God—did you hear what Roly did?"

At my desk I knead the little knot in my shoulder, but I can feel it tightening up and hunkering down. I pull the file from my backpack and check to see if Carroway's personal assistant, Janet, has taken up her post out front of his office. She's always an early starter and today's no different. She's there, sharpening her claws and doing not much else. On the other side of the empty newsroom, I stack my four pages in the fax and dial Carroway's number. I hear the machine chirp next to Janet, then wander back to my desk.

A few minutes later I check to see that she has collected the fax, and of course, she hasn't. I watch over the course of the next forty minutes as the floor comes to life, Still the fax waits in the tray, a mere arm's length from Janet. She's surfing the web now, some kind of site on porcelain dolls, and a glance at the clock above her tells me Carroway will be here in a matter of minutes. I'm starting to sweat now.

There's really no reason that her lack of attention to the fax should bother me—Carroway will get the fax soon enough—but it does nonetheless, ratcheting my anxiety notch after notch. At eight thirty, Carroway appears at his desk, as if by magic. I've been watching for him but never saw him enter. By lifting myself in my seat, I can see over the short wall of my cubicle and through the glass wall of his office, and soon he's sifting through the morning's missives—my fax among them.

As with any watched pot, the process takes forever. Carroway is on and off the phone, flipping through papers, making notes and posting sticky notes with wild abandon. Only the computer seems to have escaped his attention. Then, like a fish with a set hook, he finds it. Carroway's entire body shifts, not becoming erect or animated in any way, but rather more relaxed. He's hunkering down for a good story. I have to sit back down as people are starting to notice my prairie dog impersonation. When I pop back up, he is speaking to Janet, whose posterior is pointed directly at me as she hovers half in and half out of his doorway. Janet is motioning "No," and I can just hear her say, "Just that. It came in this morning." He motions her in and hands her a page. Janet squints hard at it and shakes her head. She says something to Carroway and then shrugs, hands back the sheet, and retreats to her station.

In his office, Carroway pulls at his bushy eyebrow in contemplation and I know the moment has arrived. Without another thought, I am up and walking to his office, freed by the knowledge that one way or another, my career as a news clerk has just ended. I make straight for his door; it's important that I catch him now—while he's still captured by the implications of the story, by the heady ideas that it presents, and before he picks up the phone and involves another colleague. The chances of Carroway making the decisions that I am about to push for are slim to start with, but diminish exponentially the minute another person is involved. But my timing is on. He's still yanking on his eyebrow, the phone sits quietly in its cradle, and I am primed, set: a raised hammer about to strike.

Then, like a glass sliding door, Janet glides in front of me.

16

Janet is small. At five-foot-nothing and a handful of pounds, she's little more than gossamer. I should be able to sweep her away as easily as a spider's web. But I can't. This woman is skilled in the art of the shutdown. She nimbly positions herself between me and the doorway—between me and a career, a real career, in journalism. I lean to the right, but she's there, one agile movement ahead of me.

"You don't just wander in. Oh, no. You don't just wander in," she chirps. Then she follows up with a sharp jab. "I'm speaking to you, Mr. Keene. I'm *right here.*" Reluctantly, I glance at her and she tweets away like one of those territorial birds on the Discovery Channel that will gladly take on a lion that strays too close to the nest.

I blunder into the usual recourse of the rebuked, "It'll just take a sec, honest—I'll be in and out before..." but she's a pro and is having none of it. My jaw is starting to clench and the air in my lungs is rising to the upper part of my chest. Over her shoulder, my world is starting to show tiny fractures. Carroway is now leaning forward, peering over the top of his glasses and pecking away at the phone. I glance back at Janet. The bitch now has her hands on her hips, and the blood that is working its way up under my collar and ruddying my cheeks is apparently pleasing her. There is the beginning of a smug smile there somewhere.

Again, over her shoulder, the fractures are widening. Carroway has replaced the receiver and is tapping his upper lip with the arm of his glasses. Janet pokes me with a bony, extended index finger right in the sternum. "You'll have to back up, young man. Mr. Carroway's far, *far* too busy..." The second *far* does it, and the apparatus inside me that keeps up the civil front collapses. "Don't poke me!" As the words cross my lips, I feel instantly ridiculous. *Don't poke me?* Have any of the great journalistic minds of our time ever uttered those words?

The rattle of glass in a door frame snaps my attention back to the moment, and I see the fractures have given way to a full-scale, carcass-swallowing crevasse.

Barret is in Carroway's office.

· · ·

Inside me a small and hasty battle rages as my sense of proper behavior is attacked head-on by panic—induced by Barret's sudden presence in Carroway's office. My sense of proper behavior loses the fight almost instantly. My jaw tightens, my eyes narrow, and Janet sees it. For a second she loses her powers. I look away and she is dismissed. With my blood up and the air in my chest compressed to tight ball, it's a full three or four seconds before I realize both men are staring at me, apparently waiting for me to deliver whatever it is I'm so clearly carrying. I look back and see the door has been closed—I must have done it—and behind it there is a small woman with crossed arms and a bruised expression. In front of me, two different expressions: Carroway's, incredulous and teetering on the edge of annoyed, and Barret's, positively disgusted. The three-way Mexican standoff stretches to infinity.

"It's mine." I don't plan these words, they just pop out. Carroway's brain has momentarily seized, and Barret is fighting some foul taste in his mouth. "The story. It's mine."

Barret performs an impressive emotional full-gainer and replaces disgust with disappointment. "This is what I'm talking about, Ed." He shakes his head almost imperceptibly, runs a hand through his well-sculpted hair, and lands it across his mouth in mild horror. A new level of revulsion for this chameleon surges up through me like a burst of flame in a hot air balloon.

It must be some kind of Barret-induced reflex, a primal motor response because it's not the kind of thing that I would do. Not the kind of thing I would say. But there it is. "Fuck you, Barret."

The old editor is awakened and he throws up a pair of withered arms as he sees Barret straighten up. "That's enough. What the hell's going on here? What's the matter with you two?" The scene is instantly transformed into some kind of bizarre father-and-sons clash, with Barret and me casting cutting glances at each other and the floor. If I didn't have a serious agenda I'd probably shrivel from embarrassment.

As much as I can't stand him, I am forced to acknowledge that Barret's mind is quick, and he is the first to weigh in coherently. "Look, Ed. As I've said before, this guy is a management challenge." Barret begins to physically puff up. "He's come in here under some bullshit charity pretense and he's adding nothing to the place. He's confrontational, uncooperative, not to mention foul-mouthed. Quite frankly, this kind of thing detracts from the level of professionalism we should be shooting for here."

Carroway is processing. "What do you mean it's yours?" he says to me, dismissing Barret's carefully crafted diatribe. As he says it I notice a little of the air squeak out of Barret's inflated self.

"I wrote it. All three parts."

Carroway's mind isn't making the connection between me and the story in his hand. He struggles to ask me a question, but nothing comes, so I blunder in. "I put this story together over the last few weeks and as you can see, it's pretty heavy. I knew that getting you to read it on face value...well, I didn't think you'd take it seriously."

Carroway's face knots in confusion, so I press on. "Look, if I walked in and just told you I wanted to do a story that could conceivably pull down one of the city's most important politicians, you'd roll your eyes and send me on my way. I needed to do this to get you to see what it *could* be, what it *is*, and get you past the fact that I'm just some rookie. It's about perspective; you saw the story as credible because of the perspective I made you read it from."

"What's with this guy?" says Barret, struggling to bring himself back into the conversation, but Carroway shuts him down—albeit gently. "Hold on, Dave." He turns back to me, his expression stretched somewhere between confusion and pain. "You wrote this? And what about this," he says, jabbing at the picture on the third page, "you took it?"

"Yes, I…"

"Ed," says Barret, stepping physically into the conversation, "if I may." He has completely regained his composure. He's going for the calm, if slightly condescending, demeanor of the wise village elder—and he's actually doing a pretty damn good job of it. "I think we're all getting a little ahead of ourselves here. Let me explain something, Roland."

Somehow Ed has bought into the ploy and is giving Barret some latitude. Barret goes on. "As the senior staffer here, any information about affairs at this level comes to me—it's a question of experience. There are delicate political nuances at play here that take years to understand, and…"

"Alex Joiner is selling citizenships, and I have the story nailed, including a photograph of him and Mike Peelman having a clandestine chat."

Barret's composure crumbles. "Listen, you little shit, I'm the point man at this paper and you know damn well I've been sniffing around this. Anything—I mean ANYTHING on this goes to me directly. Who the hell do you think you are?" He looks to Carroway for support and gets it.

Carroway works to smooth the air with both bony hands. "Look, I'm not sure how this story came to be or about this smoke-and-mirrors business of faxing it in, but Dave is right. He's the senior writer here and there's a logic in how we do things, how we bring news to the public—if indeed something like this were proven to be legitimate. Let's all calm down and see what we have here, get it to Dave and see what we can salvage. And Roland," he says, gesturing at the faxed pages on his desk, "this whole thing… jeez." He shakes his head.

Across from him, the puffing begins again. As I watch Barret inflate, I realize that the time has finally come. I take a slow breath, steady myself as best I can, and speak. "This story will be the biggest story of the year. I get the byline. Nothing will go to Barret. And I also want the beat of my choice." There is a rigid silence, and I can't tell if it's the one that precedes laughter or applause.

After a moment, Carroway speaks. "Roland, that is one very large set of balls you're lugging around there, son, and on some level I have to say good for you for swinging for the fences. But on the other hand, you're fucking insane. If there's any truth at all to this, Barret will run with it. We'll talk about you assisting."

"No. The story is solid. Every fact will check out. But it collapses without the photograph."

"Yes, it does," agrees Carroway. "The picture is the key— assuming the rest stands up to a fact-check. But like I said, Barret will be the…"

My jaw sticks out just a shade further. "The photograph is mine."

Unable to control himself, Barret chimes in, oozing satisfaction. "Well, we're all in agreement the shot's a great one, Roly, but even the interns know that everything you do as a journalist for this paper belongs to this paper."

A quick, calming breath and I am steady again. "I agree. You should also know that the picture was taken prior to my employment here, and the rights belong to me in totality. The story has no anchor without the photograph. And the photograph is only available if it appears in conjunction with my name, on my story, on my terms." I glance at Carroway and see that his eyebrows have made a brief but sharp migration to the north, and somewhere on his face, well hidden but in there somewhere, is the beginning of a wry smile.

17

"Fuck you." Barret is an intelligent journalist with a pretty damn good command of the language, but for now, he's completely lost it. "I mean fuck you, you little fuck." He's in my face, breathing into me, using all of the two inches he has on me to try to look down from some place way above—physically and professionally. I've said nothing in return and the cleaning woman in the corner of the otherwise deserted cafeteria is backpedaling for the door. He fires a glance at her and she's gone, her mop abandoned to clatter on the floor.

"Do you have any idea who I am? I'm the fucking paper, you little maggot. I'm the fucking anchor here! Jesus!" He backs away, as if my proximity has somehow become instantly revolting, performs a half turn, then spins back and unloads some more. "Where the hell do you get off stealing my story? I fucking asked you to do some research, and you write this high school bullshit and try to end-run to Carroway? What the fuck is that? Jesus fucking Christ!"

I stare at him and say nothing. I am remaining silent as part of the deal I made with myself, holding everything until Carroway makes his ruling. The issue is a mere day old, and I knew Barret would corner me somewhere. It took him all day to time it just right: two near misses in the men's room and a false start by the photocopier. But now, a full seven hours later, he has me solidly cornered. I cling to my silence and I think it's goading him on. It's a side effect I don't mind at all.

"You've just pissed away the best fucking opportunity you'll ever have. Do you think anyone is going to take you seriously after this crap? Do you think Ed's going to back you on this? You're a goddamn green fucking rookie and you haven't got a clue about this business."

Although sticking to my silence is working, I realize, suddenly, that I have no plan to get away from Barret. I feel no threat of physical violence from him, but I suspect he won't let me simply walk away. I drop my head and step to his left, but he follows my lead. I try right but he's there, spewing more of the same. The door opens again and this time Barret unloads on the cleaning woman—a clenched-teeth, arrogant bellow delivered with not so much as a glance in her direction. Unfortunately for Barret, it's not the cleaning lady.

Ed Carroway walks into the room, disregarding Barret's mumbled apologies, and inserts himself between us. Somehow, Carroway manages to suck up all the hot air in the room, absorbing it like some cardigan-clad box of Arm & Hammer. He places his hands slowly in his pant pockets, eyes fixed on a spot on the floor between us all, and lets out a long puff of air. I watch him and realize for the first time that little about Carroway is the result of happenstance. The way he walks, moves, the way he dresses, the tilt of his head, every furrow in his well-furrowed brow—all of it suddenly seems to me to be the result of a lifelong studied practice. Not some dollar-store impression of an old-school editor, but the real deal. Everything about this man is the paper business.

He takes a moment to bring a hand from his pocket and scratch the stubble on his chin, then pinches a spot of lint from a cardigan that should have been retired years ago. Barret and I have both lost the plot of our confrontation, still polarized but somehow stopped cold by Carroway's downright eerie composure.

The judge has returned a verdict.

• • •

Confidence, I have found, is a temporary, fleeting emotion. I say *emotion* deliberately, because that's what I really think it is: it's a sensory experience, a kind of arousal that picks you up and stretches your frame a good six inches, just enough to give you the height advantage over those around you. But the sensation is fickle, like happiness; it only settles on you in passing, then moves on. You can never be sure what moves it on, but today it's a pair of words that steals every other vertebrae in my back and shrinks me down to the boy that I really am. *Look, Roland.*

Perhaps it's not even the words, but more the delivery. *Look, Roland* comes out with that unmistakable softness, that pursed-lipped *dammit-son-life-just-ain't-fair* empathy that's socially required but oh-so-very hollow. I lift my head up and watch Carroway, feeling slightly detached in the knowledge that I have absolutely no backup plan. It's an all or nothing proposition, and right now nothing looks to be the big winner. Carroway goes on.

"Look, Roland," says Carroway. "You're new to all this…" He tilts his head forward and looks at me through bushy eyebrows, his lips pursed as if what he has to say is hurting him more, as the saying goes, than it will hurt me.

18

"Dave here is the real deal," says Carroway. The sentence somehow tugs my head down so that I am staring at a spot on the floor between us. "He's put in his dues, he's thorough, and he's a damn fine writer." Without looking, I can sense Barret's feathers fluffing, his chest puffing out. I can also sense my teeth approaching their shatter point as I clench for all I'm worth.

"I think you've shown some interesting, um, initiative here." Barret snorts and it brings my head up to look at him, a reaction I curse myself for inwardly. My loathing for this man plumbs heretofore unknown depths. I take some consolation in the fact that Carroway catches the snort too, and pauses just long enough to make a point to Barret. Nevertheless, he continues on, like an executioner bringing the blade to just the right edge.

"Stories—any stories, but especially big stories like this—need more than just fact. They need credibility from the institution. They need to be anchored in the local culture by a recognized, trusted source—someone they perceive as part of their intellectual community, or they just won't buy it—and I mean 'buy it' in every sense." His expression is pained, as if he's passing a small stone. Unpleasant, but manageable.

Barret's expression is at once gloating and strangely paternal; he's enjoying the one-sided slant of Carroway's discourse, but at the same time he's growing this enormous chin that seems to be jutting out in self-righteousness. It changes as soon as Carroway says, "But..."

A flash of concern darts across Barret's eyes, only for a second, but I catch it with a sideways glance.

"On the other hand, new blood is something of a necessity in the business. People are strange creatures. They want the credibility and trust of the established anchor, but at the same time there's no denying the need for new, young talent. Christ, I don't know. Maybe it's the combination of the two, the juxtaposition and the underlying inherent conflict..." His last remark is not lost on me, and I suppose it's not lost on Barret either, judging by the widening of his eyes. The tide seems to be ebbing.

"I've thought about this all day and I think we should go back to my office and sit down..."

Barret's arms cross defensively. "It's just the three of us in here, Ed. Let's hear it." Carroway looks at him and gets a shrug for his efforts.

"All right," says Carroway, appearing to gently submit to Barret's sudden coolness. "This story has some legs. It's legitimate, it's timely, and with the elections looming, well, Christ, it's just plain important. You'll collaborate and you'll both get the credit, byline and all. Barret's name will run first through seniority, and—"

I can't help myself. "No," I say in a voice that sounds removed from me.

Carroway either doesn't hear me clearly or does a damn good job faking it. "Pardon?"

"I said no."

"I thought you might. If the byline order is a big deal I'm sure Barret will—"

Again. "No."

"No to the order?"

"No to Barret in the byline. No to collaborating. No to all of it. It's mine. It'll run bylined by the writer. Me." I am in a state of sheer panic inside, while outside I am nothing less than Mr. Botox. I lift my gaze to meet Carroway's solely; Barret means nothing at this point. He's just a sack of organs sucking in lungfuls of perfectly good oxygen and taking up space.

And that's when I see it. It's almost imperceptible, a miniscule arching of a single muscle buried well under the folds of fifty-three years of facial skin. It tugs at the corner of his lip, and I catch it.

This whole fucking thing has worked.

• • •

I report to Carroway's office just after five o'clock, where he offers me a seat and has Janet bring us both coffee—something she does warmly, as if being asked to bring me coffee is some secret handshake, some Masonic rite of passage to the inner sanctum. I feel almost giddy with victory, my chest still filled to capacity with a new, lighter kind of air.

"I thought he might storm off like that," says Carroway. "He's a hell of an asset to this paper, and a hell of a talent."

I nod and mumble that I know, unclear of exactly how to respond.

"Have you ever had any enemies?"

Again, no real answer forms to his question.

"Because you've got one now," he continues. "Barret is set to be just about the best in the business at this point, and you've made a five-star enemy out of him. Have you seen his office? That fella's got an entire wall of awards, he's on a first-name basis with nearly every person of prominence in the city and he has a reputation of being a real sonofabitch at the best of times. And now you've handed him perhaps his first professional embarrassment. How's that grab you?" Carroway lets the moment linger, knowing full well I'll fill the void, which I do. "I guess he'll be pretty upset."

"Oh, don't worry about Barret's feelings. If he's nothing else, he's a professional. I suspect by the time he's done, it'll all look like a bone he threw to some shiny-faced greenhorn. He'll likely have it looking like he was fulfilling his obligation to the journalistic community, bringing the new talent along, as it were."

He squares a set of papers in a stack in front of him, chopping at his desk twice briskly with the stack's edge: a clear end to this part of the conversation. "Okay. Here's how it'll work. You will be placed on special assignment. You'll publish the two-parter—"

"It's a three-parter."

"Not anymore. We're running it as a two-parter and in case you haven't figured it out by now, you ran out of no's in the lunch room. This is how it is. This is how it will be. Understand? I need this teased and closed in two days. By day three the *Post* and everyone else will be all over it, so we're going shorter. You get the full byline, and the latitude that comes with picking your next assignment. Play your cards right and this is your ticket, although somehow I think you already knew that."

I nod once with a shallow dip of the head. I feel the adrenaline coming fast and it makes my hands tremble in my lap. I have no idea if Carroway can see my excitement, as I am bottling it up as best I can. It occurs to me that the whole thing—the creation of the story, the delivery of it, the confrontation with Barret—Jesus, even this conversation with Carroway—it all adds up to one thing: I have just set the agenda. The paper will run the story—*my* story. It will show up in breakfast nooks and commuter trains around the country. People will read it, then talk about it. They'll discuss it, debate it, and it'll all happen because of my story.

"Do you understand what happened here today, Roland?" Carroway's question jerks me from my thoughts and I am temporarily flat-footed. He repeats it. "Roland. Do you know what happened here today?"

I raise my eyebrows rather than answer, because I know enough to know that a question like that is invariably a cuddly toy with a pound of TNT inside.

"What happened here today was the real business of journalism, Roly. Stories and bylines are byproducts of the machine. The news is the story, not the anchors, not the writers, not the editors, not any of us. We're just the paperboys. We just deliver the news on behalf of the machine. And we do what the machine needs, and today the machine needed your story with your pictures. Do you take my meaning, Roly? Today it needed your story. Just watch out for tomorrow."

19

The story runs days later and takes on a life of its own. By the end of the first day Carroway and I are summoned to legal twice—both times to be informed of a pending lawsuit, and to reassure counsel that everything we have presented is based on fact—verifiable fact.

On the day after the names are played out in print, we field interview requests from dozens of radio shows, television stations, and magazines. There are calls from the FBI and Holt's office at USCIS—even someone from the White House. All of these calls are routed to the people in legal and PR, and Carroway and I are updated like tycoons watching the stock market. More trips to legal, more reassurances.

Just as Carroway predicted, Barret has managed to commandeer an element of the story, having provided a briefing to anyone who would listen—and his reputation provided him with plenty of willing ears—on the team environment at the paper. He never actually says it, but through a masterful selection of words and phrases, he's managed to convey that the story was one he handed on down to a promising new up-and-comer. He comes off fatherly, protective of the careful development of paper and industry, and I can't help but be impressed.

The second part of the story runs with the picture of Alex Joiner in a car on University with convicted felon Mike Peelman. It's the picture I took when the dome light in Peelman's car went on, capturing the two men in a suspicious meeting late at night. Essentially, the article ties together a series of seemingly independent threads, weaving them into a loose arrowhead that points directly at Joiner as the key man in the selling of US immigration documents. The tempest that ensues stains Holt by association, although I haven't been able to connect him in any tangible way to Alex Joiner and Mike Peelman. By the third day, Peelman is rumored to be on the run and a week later Joiner is arrested. The story resonates through the capitol like a cracked bull whip.

The day after, Peelman is splashed on TV being led into a police station in upstate New York. I am called into Carroway's office. He shuts the door and offers me a seat with an outstretched hand and an upturned palm. "Quite a week," says Carroway, settling his ever-aging frame into the chair behind his desk. He sits forward and smiles. I smile back; it's a funny moment, but I don't want to go for the laugh. There's too much about to happen. He continues. "So, have you given any thought to what you'd like to tackle next?"

And there it is. I have just been handed the keys to my own career.

He continues with no fanfare: just another day at the office. "This story touches on politics, crime, society—take your pick. The only way I can't see you going is into sports." He chuckles to himself. "So, what's it going to be?"

"The international scene," I say flatly. "I think that's where I want to be."

Carroway ponders it for a moment, then nods. "I can see that. There could be some nice tie-ins from the immigration angle. Have you thought about following up on the impact on the people who bought their citizenship? Could be some great human interest stuff in that."

"That's exactly where I wanted to start," I say, and I'm not ass kissing. Carroway is just that perceptive. "And if it works, I was thinking of following the thread backward, back to their home countries—a perspective on the climate that existed, exists, to set all this in motion." Carroway leans forward, pins his slender elbows on the desk, and rests his chin on folded hands. He thinks for a moment, gazing right at me, perhaps waiting to see if I flinch. I don't.

Carroway nods once. "Personally, I think this—the international scene—is an important area for us, for the *Star-Telegraph* and other large dailies. It's part of what defines us as more than a regional player. But I will tell you that you're investing yourself in one of the areas of our profession that's waning."

In my head, I hear Professor Bowman in the midst of one of his over-the-top and animated pleas to the first-year journo students. *You must be guardians of the Fourth Estate! Emphatically define what it means to report real news—not the frivolous social meanderings of celebrities, their conspicuous net worth, and this week's definition of high fashion. No. Defend the Fourth Estate or lose it to the gathering scourge of infotainment.* I push the Professor roughly aside and nod in understanding. "You think it's the wrong path, you know, for someone starting out?"

"On the contrary," he says. "Myopia is the death of this business. I think we need more than just the society page if we are to call ourselves real newsmen."

I relish the implied inclusion of his use of the word *we*. It is a subtle confirmation that I am indeed part of the tribe.

"All right, then," he says quietly. "I'll speak to Sheila and ask her to keep an eye out for an opening on the international desk. For now you'll stay under me, but I'm sure we can work something out."

And with that, I am a real reporter with a real beat.

. . .

I leave Carroway's office feeling light. There's no way I can work now—I'm too excited, too keyed up, and too much of a rookie to contain it. I slip out quietly and relish the two tasks before me—two tasks that I know will put that final stamp on my new life: quit work at Dory's (although the shifts and hours I've put in over the last year have been lean to say the least), and leave my squalid little apartment—hotplate and all.

In the street, the people walking about seem different. They are less intimidating in some way—hell, I think they might actually be smaller. These people are now at least my equals—or should I say, I am now theirs—at the very least. I felt great when the story broke, and I've been cheering secretly inside when people at the paper—people I haven't even met—slap me on the back and say things like "Nice job," and "Great piece of writing," but now, here on the street surrounded by real people, I know that...

That the man standing twenty paces ahead of me, the man wearing a murderous smile, is Trots.

20

My heart gives a single, massive thump, and it's all I need to start running. I spin and cut immediately out into the street, right in front of a taxi whose fender clips my knee and sends me sprawling on all fours. My palms take the brunt of it, but the pain only serves to get me up and running once again. Tires bark and horns blare, but I make it to the west side of the street, hurdling the railing to the subway entrance. In midair, I flick a glance back; Trots has taken up the chase. I drop over the other side, landing partway down the steps, and realize immediately it's a mistake.

Already committed, I push on, jostling past others on the stairs with a flurry of *Excuse mes* and *Coming throughs*. I vault the turnstile and notice that there is no one manning the booth. There is no train at the platform, so I duck left and low, behind the booth and stop. I hear people objecting as another body forces through the pedestrian traffic. I watch frantically for Trots to pass, and he does, and I immediately sprint back the way I came, over the turnstile and back up to the street. Trots has continued through to the platform and has missed my departure. I have my opening. In moments, I am off the street, into a building and up the elevator. I have made good my escape again.

I wait for an hour, loitering on various floors, trying not to draw too much attention to myself. Eventually I leave the building and after much paranoia, a few false starts, and a good deal of sweating, I realize Trots has moved on. It takes me another twenty minutes to get to Dory's by streetcar—time enough to calm myself down—but as I enter, I realize that despite my near miss, I must still be wearing my news on my face.

Rhona raises her eyebrows—just a shade—as I walk through the front door. The store is empty for the moment, and Rhona is seated at her desk, stabbing her long, painted nails at the unfortunate keys of her laptop. She drops her eyes back to the screen and lightly, almost imperceptibly, shakes her head. "You know what burns my toast?" she says, pushing herself up from the desk. "The people who make the software for accounting." In her overly dramatic way, Rhona waves her hand dismissively at the screen. "There's a group of people who should join the lawyers at the bottom of the sea."

"There's always accountants, you know."

"The sea's getting more crowded by the minute," she says smiling, one hand running expertly along her bra strap and gently heaving her generous right breast. She knows exactly what she's doing—I'm convinced of it—and it's extremely effective. She smiles at me and it's genuine. "I read your story in the paper. Got your name at the top and everything."

"A byline," I reply, with as much self-importance as I can muster. Rhona laughs as she gives her left breast a similar adjustment.

"I haven't seen you for a while, so you're either here to ask me for more hours or to dump me altogether." The smile stays on her face, but I can tell she's disappointed. She already knows.

I spread my legs, put clenched fists on my hip, and cock one eyebrow sharply, ramping up the ham factor as far as it will go. "I'm afraid we have to stop seeing each other, dearest Rhona."

Rhona laughs again, this time reaching out and burying me in a hug. She smells of freshly cut flowers, and the soft press of her body gets an immediate reaction from mine. I pull away and she lets me go.

"I'll be sad to see you go, Roly, because I like you. I always have. You're probably the worst employee I ever had. You know that, right?" she says, smiling. "I'm sad to see you go, but I'm sure glad you don't work here anymore." She's saying it in good humor, but she's dead right. We both know it. We laugh and I see her eyes are nearing the well-up point, but she pulls it back and turns a corner. "So, what's the plan?" she says, flattening out her skirt.

"Well, I've been given a beat now and I finally have some decent management."

Rhona flips me the bird.

The door opens and customers enter. Rhona smiles and walks over to them, speaking to me over her shoulder as she goes. I know it's a sound and sight I will miss. "Your last pay's in the top drawer. And now that you're a celebrity, don't forget us little people!"

As I leave Dory's and Rhona behind me, I am torn between forgetting it entirely and cherishing it as a fond memory. Leaving Dory's is, I imagine, like leaving home. I can't wait to go, but I'll miss the surety of it all.

• • •

Right now, the city is a renter's market. Condos are going up like erections on prom night, and it takes little more than a deposit, a pay stub, and a handshake before I have the keys to a comfortable one-bedroom unit on the East Side at Eighth and Oak. All that's left now is to pick up a few things from the old place and abandon it to my past.

At my old apartment, I pause at the door before opening it. This is a moment I will never repeat. I will never open this particular door again, and never walk into a room that has a hotplate in it. Inside, I quickly realize there is little of value here. A few clothes, toiletries, a stack of bills, and my collection of pawn shop camera gear. The rest, including the hotplate and the black-and-white TV, can all stay.

I take two small cardboard boxes—the kind photocopier paper comes in—and fill one with my camera gear and a few clothes, and the other with a raft of official documents—the kind that follow us around and prove we're alive: birth certificates, driver's licenses, school transcripts, tax returns—and of course, my notebooks. Not much else is coming with me. I roughly grab a few other things and stuff them in, but the boxes have had their fill and underpants and paper spill back out and onto the floor. I snatch at the detritus of my life and stuff it in again. I stack the two boxes and heave them, anxious to make my way to the door, but the load shifts, spilling things once again. I mutter obscenities and take what I have and leave. The rest can all go to hell.

I retreat from the room with my boxes, turn off the light and shut the door.

On the ground floor, I push my key through the super's mail slot and hope he doesn't appear while I'm hailing a cab. I don't want to get into the debate about who is going to clean out the crap upstairs. I know I'm wrong, but it has to be this way.

Outside, where I'm waiting for a cab, I realize just how bad a neighborhood this is. No one does anything about the man who is standing over me. No one seems concerned about the straight razor in his hand or the blood streaming from my ear and puddling in my palm as I cradle my head. I catch a glimpse of an old man watching, but he quickly turns away and pretends not to see.

21

Trots drives his full 250 pounds into me through his knee, and puts the point of the blade to the soft underside of my chin. "You na runnin' now, man" he says, with an almost childlike glee in his voice.

I cannot speak, I am so afraid. The blade is cold on my skin, and feels as if even the slightest addition of pressure will send it sliding up through my tongue from below. "You wan' die now? Right now ou'side you house?" Trots leans in close and I can smell the chewing gum clenched in his bright white teeth.

Everything in me is now fully tightened: my jaw, my arms wrapped about my head, even my eyes are locked open, gazing widely up at him. "Trots, please." I hear my voice high, close to begging. "I can get your money."

"Me already dun write off dat cyash, man." He says, as if speaking to a simpleton, "I jus 'ere to make sure me business reputation nah damaged."

I hear the words but miss the meaning. All I can respond with is, "What?"

He closes his eyes momentarily and shakes his head in mock frustration with the silly child before him. "I got to let folks know whappen when dem default on payment, man."

And then I understand. Trots is not here for money. He is here simply to kill me. Somehow, the realization of it forces me toward a response based in logic—a reaction that both impresses and horrifies me at once. "But the girl…the money…" I am amazed, again, that despite everything, my mind has somehow managed to cling to the big lie.

Trots' response is flat, emotionless, but his eastern Caribbean drawl comes through strong. "Girl dead." He pauses. Then, "No cyash."

I wait for strike three—that I was the one who got in Bosco's way—but it never comes. Somehow Trots has missed my little trip to the headlines. In a flash I recall the old picture of me they used: long hair, ratty goatee and captioned as Roland Keene. Trots only knows me as Joey—a faint sliver of hope rises within me.

I take the chance and speak up, fear clawing at my voice and forcing it up an octave or two. "Please don't cut me. I don't know what happened with that girl. She had the money, I swear."

"Nevah mind she money, man. What 'bout *my* money? De cyash you dun owe me?"

The straight razor slips upward along my jawline, skillfully maintaining enough pressure to immobilize me, but not enough to draw blood. It finds its way to my ear. My voice climbs to new heights. "Listen, Trots—I have a job now. I can pay you."

And suddenly Trots is walking away. He is speaking to me over his shoulder without looking, sauntering down my street like he's got nowhere special to be. "I be back tomorrow. Have it all ready. All of it. Or I gon' kill you." It is a plain, matter-of-fact statement.

Only then do I notice the wetness at the side of my neck, soaking my right shoulder, trickling through my shirt, under my arm, down the line of my elbow before spattering the pavement below. I reach for the side of my head, then stop, scared of the void I will feel, the carved stump where my ear used to be. I am relieved to find it is still there, split in two near the top, but still there. The slice was so quick and precise that I felt no pain, not even a tug as the blade swept through the tough cartilage of that upper curve of skin.

A sound beside me makes me flinch—Trots is back for the killing slice, a downward sweep of that shiny, quick blade. But it's just the old man I saw earlier, this time kneeling and holding out a white handkerchief. He speaks but I don't hear, and beyond him, paused halfway through the building's front door, I see the super, his face a pinched mix of concern and frustration; it seems this particular miserable moment isn't over yet after all. But a policeman and an ambulance arrive in that same moment, and soon I am riding once again to the hospital—again courtesy of Trots—and spared the confrontation with my super.

Hours later, I emerge from the hospital with three new stitches and a gauze dressing about my head that makes me look like a wounded frontline soldier. An orderly places a single cardboard box beside me—someone must've taken the time to put it in the ambulance with me, although where the other one is is anyone's guess. He also hands me a small white business card. It's from the policeman who interviewed me about the mugging, the *random* mugging, and I am urged to call him if I should remember anything else about the attack. The orderly leaves and I'm once again alone at the side of the road, my life's possessions in a box beside me and a world of possibilities ahead.

There is no way I can repay Trots tomorrow. I have a half-decent paycheck coming, but even if I gave it all to Trots, it would just be the proverbial drop. And there's next to nothing in the bank. The good news is that I won't be going back to the old neighborhood—ever—and it'll at least be a while before Trots can find out my new address. He can catch me at work, sure, but at least that'll be in the city with lots of people about, and not on some curb in the low-rent, high-crime dump I've lived in until now.

• • •

Once again, I am the story. It's not front-page news this time, just a few column inches buried on page five. The small headline reads, *Would-Be Dysart Hero Mugged.* It spends a few lines explaining the attack, then dedicates the bulk of the copy to history—a retelling of the shooting and the death of Chloe Dysart.

And so I start to answer the questions of another interview, over the phone this time to a radio reporter, speaking about how amazingly quick the attack was, violent and sudden, and then

I dutifully link it back to memories of the time I was shot. The reporter eventually asks about the Dysarts, about how they reacted toward me at the death of their daughter; it is a mutually understood and unspoken truth between us that the only real reason for this conversation is my oblique linkage to the Dysarts. I gently parry the question in a natural but prepared way. I tell them that the Dysarts have suffered enough and that they don't need such a deep wound laid open once again. He asks me why I'm at work the day after such a traumatic event and I reply that there's really not that much to it—just a cut on the ear. He thanks me for my time and I put the phone down, which rings again almost instantly. I know it will be another reporter, with the same questions.

"Hello," I say, wincing slightly as the receiver touches my ear.

"Roly? It's me, Donna."

It turns out hearts really do skip beats. "Donna?"

"Yes, you might remember me: five six, brunette, from the *Star-Telegraph*?" She laughs and I feel a warmth rise up through my chest and into my cheeks.

"Oh, hi." My inexperience shows through and I am struck speechless. There is nothing. But Donna, true to form, saves me. "I heard about what happened. Are you okay?"

"Oh, yeah, it's nothing really, just a little cut on my ear." I'm forced to stand and walk around; there is suddenly altogether too much energy inside me.

"Is there anything I can do? Do you need anything?"

"Uh, no, no. I'm good." Swing and a miss.

"Are you sure, Roly? You sound different."

"No, really—I'm absolutely fine. Honest."

"Well, then. I was thinking maybe you'd like to meet up later tonight, get a drink? If you're feeling up to it."

"Tonight? Um, sure." I'm still shaky but recovering—and not from Trots's attack. "Where, uh, where?"

"How about Ballaro's, say six o'clock?"

"Okay, six." Silently I pray my conversation skills will improve by quitting time.

"Roly, are you sure you're okay?"

"I'm fine. Don't worry—I'll see you at six."

I hang up the phone and sit in quiet disbelief. For the first time in my romantic life, I may have gotten it right.

. . .

The following morning I am struggling to refocus on the story hanging in electronic purgatory before me. There are words there, on the screen, but all my mind can process is the evening before. Drinks at Ballaro's led to more drinks, and by the end of the night, giggling and able to laugh at almost anything the other said, we stole into the Ambassador Hotel and found ourselves in a quiet function room down behind a series of stacked folding tables. Donna pressed herself into me, and her kiss was so assertive, so demanding that I knew it went well past the alcohol that was certainly fueling us.

It was quick, exhilarating, and when it was over there was no awkward rush, no backs turned and clutching at a tangle of strewn clothes. There was just a comical series of shushes and giggles, and a walk home with my hand comfortably in the small of her back. And this morning, when we met in the hall, we smiled, stopped and talked. The world was still normal, only better.

But the story before me, on my screen, needs my full attention. I push thoughts of Donna aside but she cuts back in again and again. I see the pure alabaster of her breasts, her nipples taut and trembling, and the tiny, almost invisible hairs at the back of her neck. The images are difficult to shake, but slowly I deny them, and dip my head closer to the screen. The story. I must focus on the story.

Okay—calling it a story may be a bit of an exaggeration; it's really a mundane series of questions and a block of background copy on Lesotho, a tiny, desperately poor nation surrounded by South Africa. It's more like a set of loose notes, to be honest, but it represents a story—a real story. Nevertheless, I hammer away, and in a matter of hours I have a draft.

According to the great Professor Bowman, putting time into almost anything invariably makes it better. The same is true for writing, and so I decide to sit on my story for a couple of days. The idea is to put some mental distance between it and me, so I can review it with fresh, and perhaps objective eyes. After all, it'll need to be at its best before I take it to Carroway. I need a distraction, something else to focus on, and the answer comes almost immediately. Maybe I'll ask her out for dinner, perhaps a walk down by the water; whatever it is I know it'll consume my attention fully and the thought makes me smile.

I pick up the phone and begin dialing her extension, then quickly set the receiver back down. Donna works on the same floor on the far side of the newsroom; I'll just go over there, ask her out. I walk through the labyrinth of cubicles, past desks with paper and file folders stacked a foot high, nodding to coworkers whom I recognize but never speak to. I pass Carroway's glass fishbowl, and smile briefly to Janet, his assistant, who smiles back warmly. A quick left and I'm in the main thoroughfare that cuts through the field of cubicles; Donna's is at the back against the wall.

As I get closer I can see there are other people there, some with chairs pulled up and leaning in, others draped over the cubicle wall and craning for a view. Among them, at the center, is Donna, pointing at the screen and explaining something. In the face of the group, my courage suddenly collapses.

I mean to keep walking, beyond her cubicle and the group, but I've passed the last intersection and find myself faced with a white wall and nowhere to go. A light ripple of panic sets in. I'm forced to stop and turn, and I try to pull off some expression that says, *Dang it, I forgot that piece of paper I meant to be walking over here with*, and I even snap my fingers as I turn, to emphasize, of course, the sudden dawning of it all.

Perhaps I might have gotten away with it, been able to sneak back undetected by anyone in the group of five or six hunched around Donna's desk, but my little ad lib finger snap has turned a few heads—Donna's included.

But if I'm anything I'm committed, and so I retreat as fast as I can without running, even putting a little bounce in my step.

"Roly?" It's Donna, but I'm at that point where I'm just far enough away that I could keep going, and people would think I simply didn't hear. Maybe.

"Roland!"

The jig is up. I turn and smile. Everyone in the group is now looking my way, plus a few other random folks nearby who happened to hear Donna call out. I'm supposed to say something here. Something like *Oh, I was just checking if you had that thing, that article, that something.* But I've got nothing. Everyone is looking, including Donna, and finally I open my mouth, because that's what you do when you're going to say something—but I have nothing lined up and exactly what will come out is a complete and terrifying mystery.

Donna reads the situation precisely. "Oh, gimme one sec," she says, her tone implying she's running late for some prearranged meeting with me. "I'm just finishing up." She swivels back to her keyboard and speaks to the group, her attention still on the monitor before her: "That's all of it, guys, I'll email you the pictures. Oh, and by the way," she says, bobbing her head once in my direction without looking up, "that's Roly Keene—he wrote the USCIS Immigration piece."

I'm saved from certain embarrassment, subtly shifted from awkward suitor to professional colleague by Donna's deft touch. Instead of ridicule I get hellos and nods that carry a measure of what looks suspiciously like regard. The others file past, and finally Donna stands and smiles. I am entirely aware of the dramatic social rescue she has just performed, and something in that wide, warm smile tells me she is, too.

"What are you doing way over this side?" she asks, still smiling.

"Slumming, really."

She steps toward me, and stands close enough for me to smell her; it is lavender, I think. "Well," she says, "it's a good thing I know how to deal with the local rabble, then."

I was hoping for a clean escape from that mess with the attempted (and highly unsuccessful) getaway, but no such luck. "I'm sorry, I just...all the people, and the..."

Donna laughs out loud, then quickly tries to stifle it with both hands, but it's too late. "You are *sooo* cute!"

I cringe. "Cute?" Donna laughs again, and this time physically doubles over.

I look around and people are starting to pay attention again. I reach out and take her by the arm. "Can we just go get a coffee or something?"

"Sure, but what will we do if there's people there?" The giggling resumes.

"That's not funny," I say. "Not even a little." But it is, and her laughter is contagious. And so we head for the elevators, Donna still giggling that adorable giggle.

• • •

I knock on Carroway's door and he waves me in, a phone wedged between his ear and his shoulder, scribbling notes on a pad before him. His computer is dark, the monitor little more than a destination for little yellow sticky notes crammed with Carroway's doctor-like scrawl.

"So, what's up?" he asks, setting down the phone.

"I want to know how I go about getting the okay to travel. Well, for a story, that is."

He leans back in his chair, throws his arms behind his head and looks at me with a this-oughta-be-good sort of smile. "That depends where you wanna go."

It's my cue to begin the sale, the pitch for the story I've been working on over the last few days. I set out the rationale, the expenses I expect to incur—flight, accommodation, food— and I explain the story's function. It's to be the follow-up to the immigration piece, and it'll look at the human toll the business of selling citizenship has claimed. I focus on three families, two in Lesotho, and one six hundred kilometers away in Swaziland, all of whom had sons caught up in the federal net and deported back to their homelands.

No, I haven't spoken with the families—none of them have phones—but I have made contact with people locally—two churches and an aid organization—who have confirmed that the families are there.

No, I don't have any experience with this kind of thing, but that's part of why I want to go.

And yes, I think it's a responsible direction to take the piece. It's the evolution of an important story; it moves past the sheer shock value that made the original story so compelling and holds up a bright light to the real cost of selling nationality. It grounds the story and morally legitimizes the newspapers' breaking of it.

When I'm done talking, Carroway nods in thought, then breathes in sharply through a pair of well-haired nostrils. "I'll sign off on it, but I suggest you go pitch it to Sheila first—this is her bailiwick. If she gives you a hard time, I'll see what I can do, but I'm pretty sure she'll go for it."

I nod in appreciation, but Carroway's not done. "There's a spot coming open in her group, but I have to warn you you're not the only one after it."

I raise my eyebrows.

"There's a girl in the society section being considered, Donna Sabourin. D'you know her?"

Inside something lurches hard to the left. "Yeah—she did that thing on hats and horses—'Ladies at the Races' or something, right?"

"You'd be surprised; there's a market for that."

"I guess."

The old editor misses nothing. "Some disdain there?"

"Well, just for the topic, not the person."

"And what do you think of the person in this case?"

"That's kind of an unfair question, don't you think? I'm competing for the same spot with her."

"But it's a question, nonetheless."

I think hard before I answer. "I think she's very capable. She's doing all her work on the society page because—to quote a certain editor—that's what the machine needs right now. She's definitely doing a good job there, and like you said, there's a market, and markets pay the bills."

"So you see value in the society pages, then? In the context of the culture we live in?"

He's baiting me now, and this water feels suddenly shark infested. "Yeah, I see value—commercial value. I'm not sure how much journalistic value I see. I mean real social commentary. The society stuff we get now is all who's wearing what—but that has little to do with the capabilities of the reporter coving it, I think. She's feeding a demand."

The old editor leans back and taps his lips with the arm of his glasses. "There's an interesting debate in that for another day—the whole question of who defines the news, who determines the content...is it the providers or the consumers?"

"Ah, the great chicken and egg conundrum."

Carroway smiles. "Deep waters, my Padawan."

And while Carroway disappears into thought for a moment I wonder over the conversation. Carroway does nothing by chance. He lives and breathes the paper—hell, he's one of its organs, and these questions are not being asked just for the sake of it. Somewhere in all this, Carroway's opinion will carry weight. He's probing my resolve, my determination to say *I'm the guy. I'm the one who should be in that job.*

But as much as I want to blurt it out, and as much as I would if it were anyone else, I find myself holding back. Why? Because it's Donna, and so many of her own hopes and dreams are being weighed in the balance of this very conversation.

Carroway tugs me back to the moment. "So, you see the two

of you on an even footing, then, in terms of qualifications for the job with Sheila's group?"

My teeth clench and I think hard. Finally I answer in as measured a tone as I can muster. "I think her experience is writing about the natty downtown set, and mine's about human impact in an international context."

"Hmm. Light and fluffy versus serious and weighty?"

"Something like that, I guess." And while I mostly believe it, I know part of me is quietly lining my own future. "But like I said, what she's writing—it has nothing to do with her capabilities."

But Carroway just nods; his mind has moved on.

I've tried to be evenhanded, but I know that despite everything I've been tipping the scale in my favor; it's impossible not to. Would anyone put in this position react differently? *You're going to piss the world off, and you're going to be alone.* I shush the voice; there's little I can do now. Instead I resolve to worry about that part later, and for the moment feel positive about the travel approval that appears to be in the offing.

But it's not that easy. I recognize that Donna is something important in my life—or at least, she might become something important—and I wonder if I've somehow put a great tear in any future I might have had with her. Oddly, this tiny betrayal seems somehow more awful than the whole business with Chloe.

Standing up and walking out of Carroway's office is a major accomplishment for me. As I stop in front of Janet's desk and stare blankly, I wonder at the cost of so many good breaks in one streak. Surely, somewhere out there in front of me, out there in the world of botched robberies, grieving families, dead girls, and small betrayals of lovers, the big scale in the sky has to bring things back into balance.

My words to Carroway haunt me lightly, enough that I feel compelled to call Donna. I'll take her out, make her feel good. I also suspect, uncomfortably, that perhaps the person I'm really trying to soothe is not Donna at all.

Donna's arm is linked through my own, and as we walk slowly along the cobblestone streets where the tourists like to wander, she suddenly freezes, and a broad smile envelops her face.

"Oh my God. Look at these!" she says, dragging me toward a glass storefront.

I look up at the hanging sign: *Fox Chocolates*, and through the window there are rows of delicately handcrafted brown-and-white confections of every description. Beside me Donna is now an awe-struck ten-year-old ready to hop up and down and flap her arms in excitement. I can't help but smile at her unbridled enthusiasm.

She catches me watching her and cups her hands over her mouth and nose and laughs. "I know, I know!" she says through snatches of laughter. "I can't help myself—it's *chocolate*!"

I shake my head at her in mock disapproval, then pull her by the arm toward the store entrance. She resists momentarily. "Oh, come on," I say. "If I don't get you something here you're gonna wet yourself." She swats me, then pushes past and into the store, elbowing me lightly and sticking her tongue out for good measure.

Outside we sit on the lip of a low wall, and above us the sun is perched high in a perfect, cloudless blue sky. Donna is trying to eat the chocolate without getting any on her, but the caramel inside has other plans and sags in little golden arcs between her mouth and the chocolate in her fingers. "You sure you don't want some?" she says, offering me the small white paper bag from the store. "You have no idea how good this is."

"No, I'm scared if I reach in there I'll lose an arm."

She smiles again. "Hmm. Wise beyond your years." She finishes the chocolate and sits for a moment, her eyes closed in exaggerated bliss.

"That good, huh?"

She laughs freely this time, and falls toward me naturally, pressing her hands into my chest. I feel her instantly settle, her muscles relaxing and her shape melding with mine. Her head settles against my neck and her hair is pressed to my nose. I breathe the clean smell of her hair, and just as I think it can't get any better, she exhales a gentle sigh that is so satisfied, so tranquil that I realize it is a sense and sound I didn't even know existed.

While I drench myself with the purity of the moment, somewhere nearby the conversation with Carroway is casting a dark shadow. It's something I know I'll never tell her, along with the news of my upcoming trip, but it's something I know she will inevitably find out on her own.

And so I cling to the moment for as long as it will last.

22

A handful of days later I find myself sitting in the departure lounge in O. R. Tambo International Airport in South Africa, staring through the plate glass window and seeing almost nothing. It took twenty-two hours of travel to get here, including eight hours to Heathrow in London, another eleven down the length of Africa to O. R. Tambo, and a final two-hour hop to the tiny mountain kingdom of Lesotho.

The story I've cobbled together over the last few days follows one of three men deported back to Lesotho from the US, three of many caught up in the aftermath of the USCIS immigration scandal I helped break.

The man is Lebo Magagula and he is now dead. His mother tells me the story during my stay in Lesotho, over the course of three visits to her small house in Thaba-Tseka. "House" is a rather grand word for the structure, which is really little more than a few sheets of corrugated steel nailed together and pitched lopsidedly over a hard dirt floor. Six people sleep in the single room, on the dirt floor, including Lebo's mother. It used to be seven, but as I mentioned, Lebo is now dead.

Thaba-Tseka is a tiny village in the heart of Lesotho, surrounded by steep brown mountains that are perennially covered in short-cropped grasses and dotted with deep-set stones. Crystal clear rivers zigzag through the spurs, carving, as they have done for millennia, deep channels that swell with rainbow trout and barbell as long as a man's arm. Rich fishing is perhaps the only advantage these hills still hold, save a few kimberlitic pipes—ancient volcanic plugs—that yield diamonds to the distant mine owners in South

Africa and the Netherlands. Of course, the diamonds are quickly exported, leaving only crushed rocks and tailing to the indigenous people. But Thaba-Tseka has no diamond mines—the nearest is a day's journey in a four-by-four—and none of the jobs, menial as they are, that go with them.

The summers are a perfect mix of hot African sun tempered by cool, high-altitude air, and the winters are bitterly cold with a sun that shines brilliantly but warms nothing. It is a hard place to live for any creature; there are no trees—all long ago burned for fuel—and there is little for livestock to eat. And like all the marginal places where industry and agriculture can find no profitable foothold, the poor set up home. "Poor," like "house," is an overstatement because the family in Thaba-Tseka, Lebo's mother and her five children, have absolutely nothing.

The mother, Mathato, sits on an upturned plastic bucket, wiping at her face with bare hands, pulling at the neck of her threadbare dress, as it seems, to her at least, to be slowly choking her. She is probably fifty, but looks seventy. I sit in front of her on a short, three-legged stool, and record everything on the small voice recorder given to me by Tech Services at the *Star-Telegraph*. Later, when I write the story, I will do it all from memory. Not because I have some prized journalistic gift of total recall, but because her story is so heartfelt, so raw and unfettered with concerns of how it all might sound, that every bit of it stays with me.

She speaks Southern Sotho, a complex, ancient language that evolved hundreds of years ago, when the warring Zulus drove the people that would become the inhabitants of Lesotho into these barren mountains. They embraced the protection its remoteness offered and thrived on its harsh, unapologetic hillsides. One of her daughters translates her words into halting but passable English, and pausing—head bent and hands clasped—patiently and respectfully, whenever the old woman begins to cry.

Her oldest son, Lebo, learned basic reading, taught by a long-departed Irishman who had taken to living in the deep mountains and who had run a makeshift school. Lebo stood out with a clear bent for academia. He learned to speak English, mastered the basics of math, and eventually took the long journey to Maseru, the nation's capital, in search of something better than a single corrugated tin room.

Mathato says he found it, too. His ability to speak English landed him a job as an interpreter at BEDCO—the Basotho Enterprises Development Corporation—where he played the middleman role of translator between expatriate aid workers and locals. BEDCO is a business development project, set up with money from a number of foreign governments. The Americans, Swiss, Germans, Canadians, Brits, and Danish all have nationals working at BEDCO, trying to help get small, local businesses off to a healthy start. Lebo worked there for two years, all the while honing his English and learning everything he could from the white men from far away.

He returned home twice, bringing money and food for his family, along with wonderful stories of the world he had joined in Maseru. On his second trip home, he told his mother that he had been offered a chance to go to America and start a new life, but his mother did not understand. She had never heard of any of the towns he spoke of, and could not fathom the kind of distances he said he would have to travel to get there. He told her everything he had heard about this fascinating new world: about the trees, the forests, the houses, and the cars that everyone drove. He told her about winter and snow, which Mathato was glad about, as it was one thing she could nod to, and say, *Yes, snow. I know it.* Lebo had smiled with her, at this small common ground between them in this expansive idea called America. Indeed, it does snow from time to time in the mountains of Lesotho, but by all accounts it's just a dusting. It was a small handle on a big idea, but one that fit the palm of his mother's hand nicely.

He left her after that visit, promising to return again and that she should expect letters from far away. Nearly another year passed without word from her son, until the letters began, hand delivered in bundles of five or six, passed from hand to hand, family to family through the mountains, until they arrived at the corrugated shed in Thaba-Tseka.

She beams at this point in her story, pitches forward on her bucket and speaks with real pride about her boy in America, about how he left this tiny village, how he made something of himself. Her daughter translates as best she can, but the idea, flowing so easily through smile and tone, is undeniable in any language.

Then she says something that catches me like a fish on a fully swallowed hook. She speaks it first in Sotho, and it's clear by her daughter's reaction and the quick sidebar they have in Sotho that the daughter is having a hard time translating it. Finally, she says to me, in clipped, halting English, that her mother believes her son was not a fortunate man—which I find odd, as he seemed to have done so well for himself. My facial reaction must convey my thoughts, because the daughter immediately raises her hand and says, "No, I mean…mother say…Lebo make his own luck."

Lebo, however, is currently dead, buried a mere three feet down on a rocky hillside in Maseru—five hours from his home, and his mother, in Thaba-Tseka. He died in Maseru—although "he died" implies some passive departure where he perhaps rolled over in bed and exhaled quietly for the last time. This was in fact far from the case; it's more accurate to say that he was torn violently from this life, and what was left behind was done as much for the statement it would make as it was for the result. And without the benefit of refrigeration, modern morgues and barrels of embalming fluid, getting his corpse into the ground was a priority. As a result, his mother has never been to his grave and only learned of his fate about a month ago.

At the end of my last interview with her, I ask if she would like to go to Maseru and visit his grave, but she declines, saying only that he is not there. And so, after accepting her offer of a simple meal of pap (a kind of cornmeal prepared in a *piokikos*—a black three-legged cast-iron pot straddling an open flame), she holds both my hands and smiles goodbye with a nod. I leave her with nothing more than she had before I got there, and I spend the five-hour trip back wishing I had given her all the cash I had in my pockets—which would have been a small fortune to her. I didn't do that because I thought it would somehow cheapen the moment, reduce it to a simple business transaction. But who was I really protecting that moment for? I know the answer, and, distasteful as it may be, I make it right with myself. After all, in my list of sins, this is but a tiny indiscretion.

23

There have been wonderful dinners, walks after work, a romantic harbor cruise and a few movies, but right now there's just the awkward way that Donna is fidgeting with the Starbucks coffee cup in her hand. She's looking everywhere except at me. Our conversation is stilted, wooden, and now that we've gone over my trip to Lesotho (which ended a mere twelve hours ago), there seems to be nothing else to say, which is odd, given that what Donna *really* wants to talk about is *how* the trip came about.

The international desk is what Donna wants, it's what she's always wanted, and here I am just back off my first trip, internationally, for the paper. She's aching to ask how that is, and I am aching to avoid the subject altogether. I don't have the job at the International Desk yet, not officially anyway, but it's starting to look awfully good. And I know it's killing Donna. I can see it in that tight muscle in the corner of her jaw. I can also see that she's torn; part of her wants to be happy for me, and the other part is jealous, perhaps even a tad resentful. But at this moment everything about it—the International Desk appointment and my recent trip—is still ephemeral, vaporous, unclear in its genesis and with nothing set in stone. Somehow we both know that whoever brings it up first actually loses something. Asking the *how* of it, now, before anything actually exists for certain, will somehow sully the asker. No, that question will have to wait, but it hovers around us like a foul odor. And so the coffee break drags on and the conversation pleads for its life. Finally the awkwardness ends with Donna smiling meekly and saying, "I'm glad the trip went well." And then she's gone.

. . .

Carroway looks up from the page and nods. "I like it."

At first, I can't tell if he's serious or sarcastic. He flicks the page with a finger and it floats onto his desk and the bumper crop of paper being raised there. "What about the kid? Her son. You don't go into how he died." He looks at me as if he already knows: "Related?"

And it is. I tell him Lebo's story—a story only hinted at in the draft on his desk. I spent a fourth day in Maseru after the interviews with his mother, digging around in the details of his death. It was remarkably easy to uncover, starting with a cousin who buried him, and corroboration of sorts from almost everyone I spoke to. Admittedly, it was all based on hearsay, but fact committed to paper in some official capacity is simply unheard of. The least helpful people were the expatriates at BEDCO, all of whom regarded me with suspicion. The local US embassy refused to comment and the American BEDCO expat, with whom Lebo had worked to set up his immigration, had long since been rotated out of the country. Only a subsequent application to USAID (the United States Agency for International Development) under the Freedom of Information Act garnered me a name, a Mr. Bob Carling.

"The story at his end—Lebo's end—is that he was offered a chance to emigrate for a set dollar amount. His cousin told me that one of the Americans at BEDCO—Bob Carling, a USAID employee—said he could arrange it, but that Lebo had nothing even close to the kind of money he wanted. Apparently either Lebo or Carling suggested a fee in diamonds, and a month later Lebo produced a bagful of raw stones.

"Most of the mines in Lesotho yield industrial-grade diamonds, although some are of gem quality. What was in the bag is unknown, but his cousin says he made a payment arrangement with someone in the unofficial diamond trade, agreeing to send foreign exchange back to cover the debt. Once the story broke and the illegal immigrants were repatriated, Lebo had no hope of making his payments. His cousin claims he was beaten in the street, had a tire placed around his neck. It was filled with gas and set on fire—what they call a 'necklace' in that neck of the woods."

Carroway looks at me the way a man looks at his recently constructed house of cards as a breeze picks up—with a mix of horror and fascination. "And how's that make you feel, Roly?"

I snap back, surprised at the venom his comment so quickly summons up in me. "Makes me feel like a grade-A asshole, thank you very much. My breaking the story ultimately led to his murder."

"Easy, tiger," he says. "Remember, you're the storyteller, not the story."

"It's a kind of blurry line on this one," I say, thinking more of Chloe than Lebo. Somewhere in my conscience, I am stacking corpses like cordwood.

Carroway continues. "And the USAID guy, this Bob Carlton?"

"Carling."

"Right."

"There's nothing on paper. Nothing that can be traced back to him, and the expat community is a pretty tight bunch. No one was talking, at least not to me. All I can confirm is that he was there and that he was posted to Asia shortly after the story broke."

"Like rats from a sinking ship…"

I nod in agreement and the required reverent silence lasts for mere seconds before Carroway packages it all neatly for business. "Prep it, have Deane edit it, and we'll run it tomorrow."

It's the closest I'll come to a *well done*, and I wonder if Lebo and Chloe understand the real value of the sacrifices they made. No sooner is the thought through my head than I am repulsed by it. I mentally spit and scrape the tongue of my internal narrative, then realize that the very act of thinking it, of spinning these events in such a self-centered act of rationalization, means that I *can* think that way. What that says about me, about who I really am, is the real source of my disgust. Surely only real bastards can bend logic so perversely? This seems an apparent truth to me, and so I begin the process of accepting—just a little bit—that I may just be one of those bastards.

Let's face it, at some level Lebo knew—he must have—that a bag of diamonds passed surreptitiously across a table in a roadside café in Lesotho is not the way citizenship comes about. Once he made that deal, once he crossed that particular bridge, he was complicit. He lost his status as the innocent guy, and became a player in a game that either pays dividends or consumes all—money, people, entire lives, heck, even entire families.

Already I can see that Lebo is lingering too long in my head. He needs to be slotted, carefully classified and filed away. Maligning him doesn't seem to be working, so I take a new tack. At some level, Lebo and I are very much alike, or at least enrolled in the same exclusive club: folks who have decided to go out and get what's not being handed to them. For some, the result is favorable, for others, not so much. And so I settle on seeing him with respect—a man after my own heart, willing to do what was needed to get ahead. Too bad for Lebo things just didn't work out. Tough break, bad luck, unfortunate timing. The clichés all fit and gradually, without too much objection, Lebo's corpse fits comfortably into its slot.

24

The week after my article on Lebo runs, I look up from my desk and find Dave Barret staring at me from across the room. I don't know what it means, but I'll be damned if I'll give him the satisfaction of asking. I'm sure it's a threat of some sort. I ignore him, focus on my work, and he soon disappears.

The light on my voicemail is on. I stab at the keys—a little harder than is really necessary—and retrieve yet another message from Warren. He's left three in all: the first two calling to catch up and go for a beer. This latest one is a little more direct, saying he has some of my shit and I need to come get it or he's going to pitch it. I know he has nothing of mine, but my mind flits back to the Barton cottage: late night, cold beer, loose thinking. And so I disregard the message and move on.

Warren is a genuinely good guy, but he is too closely connected to the whole Chloe affair and speaking to him—thinking of him—just brings it all up again. And of course I have this ridiculous thought that he'll somehow put two and two together and connect my inquiries about Chloe with the subsequent tragic events. Even now I can feel the tension building—ever so slightly—at the thought of him connecting the dots. And in all fairness, he'd have to at least consider it, wouldn't he? After all, I asked about her, then a few weeks later she's dead and I'm bang smack in the middle of it? It had to look suspicious. But before I spiral out of control and start dishing out gangland-style gag orders, I remember the central journalistic tenet of Context. And for Warren, context says I'm the good guy, the would-be hero. I try to leave it at that.

In the last year and half, since the unfortunate business with

Chloe, Warren and I have crossed paths less and less. Of course, there was the trip to his cottage, and we've met up a few times for beer and wings, and a couple more for coffee. While I do regret it, I recognize that Warren and the history he drags along need to be held at arm's length. Besides, he's so close to being an actual friend that it makes him a liability; I can't afford to be around someone so compassionate that I might actually think of confiding in them. It's just another sad reality of my path, and I grit my teeth and accept it for what it is.

The Lebo story is well received—not groundbreaking, not here's-your-trophy-can-you-start-with-your-syndicated-column-tomorrow? stuff—but noted by a few who count on the upper floors as a competently written piece. A week later, it's further confirmed by a call from Sheila Copperhead, who tells me that a position has opened up at the international desk and would I be interested in hearing about it? I don't really know Sheila well, save the one brief pitch I did on seeking approval for the Lebo story, and I make a pathetic preinterview impression by gushing my enthusiasm over the phone unchecked. "Fuck yes, I'm interested!"

Sheila ignores my apparent lack of couth. "Come to my office tomorrow at ten and we'll talk." I switch gears and head for the thank-yous, but I can tell from the deadened sound that she has already hung up. My watch says 4:22, and I take Sheila's call to be a sure sign that I should go home and spend some time feeling good about myself.

It is short-lived.

• • •

I once tried out for the men's soccer team at college and spent some time going up for headers against a six-foot-two, two-hundred-dred-and-twenty-pound keeper. I did okay for a while, just kind of jumping with him without too much hope of ever reaching the ball with my head. After all, he had three inches on me and the use of his twelve-foot arms. Still, I let him know I was there. It all looked good until he decided he'd had enough of this Johnny-come-lately who was trying to impress the coaching staff. We went up for the ball and the keeper went to punch it away, but instead cracked me a perfect right cross to the temple. I went backward and hit the turf, and spent a few minutes confused about why the clouds, the people, and the net were all waving as if painted on a flag in a stiff breeze.

The sensation I feel now is the very same one. From my position on the ground, I can see the sidewalk stretching away from me, and wavy as it is, I can see that someone's blood has been spattered and is pooling very close to my head. It takes a few moments but, as someone rather roughly helps me to the sitting position, I understand that the pooling blood and the spatter are in fact mine.

I look up and see a woman, about forty, dressed in her downtown office get-ahead gear, looking at me and speaking. She is leaning forward and despite my bloody nose (which I discover is the source of the blood), I can't help myself from looking straight down her top at her rather impressive breasts. She sees me do it and I catch her face twist for a moment in indecision—is this guy concussed and deserving of some understanding for his momentary lack of social grace, or is he just a prick? The answer materializes as she stands and backs away, briefly bumping into a large man behind her.

It's Trots and he is angry. Not screaming-bloody-murder angry, but the more vicious, silent, simmering, ever so slightly just-this-side-of-a-complete-loss-of-control angry. I understand that he will kill me, and would have already if the woman with the heaving cleavage had not appeared. Others gather round, mostly ashen-colored smokers who gather to puff at the back of the building. This puffers' haven has been my preferred escape route of late, which, it would now appear, was a rather thinly devised plot to avoid Trots and his violent intentions.

As someone helps me to my feet, Trots edges away, still eyeing me intensely. He disappears, and I retreat back into the building. My rescuers say they didn't see what happened, that they saw a black man bent over me, and then a crowd began to gather. Apparently I let out quite a yelp, which was what drew people over, and the best I can guess is that Trots hit me square in the face, laying me out on the sidewalk. I politely refuse offers of calls for ambulances or rides to the hospital, and instead I head for the front doors. I figure going out the front and flagging a taxi is the best idea; Trots will be long gone and won't like the crowds milling outside the very front of the building.

As I cross the foyer, the pudgy guy at the security desk calls me over. "What happened to you?" he asks, wiping the remnants of a powdered doughnut from his moustache.

"Accident," I mutter and try to push on.

"Hey, whoa. I got a box here for you."

I glance over and think about going to get it, then realize how ridiculous I would look going back upstairs with blood oozing from my nose, both hands clasped around a cardboard box, and nary a tissue in sight. "I'll grab it tomorrow. Thanks."

With that, I am away, through the glass façade, out onto the street, and into the safety of a cab. Trots's attack today has shaken me for sure, but it has done so much more. And while I don't know it yet, meeting him at the back of the building on the eve of my move to the international desk, having my nose bloodied and my tail jammed decidedly between my legs, has set in motion what is arguably everything I deserve.

If only I had collected that fucking box.

25

As with cattle, there is security in numbers. The only thing I'm not doing this morning is mooing. I blend with the herd, the commuter livestock around me, stick to the center, and scout for trouble. I get to work with no extraordinary encounters the next morning, save a few curious glances from those wondering about the two shiners that are so very clearly peeking out from behind my sunglasses. I long for a nice set of wide-swept Wayfarers.

At the security desk there is a replacement pudgy guy who knows nothing about the box, and cares even less.

"They musta sent it up," he declares, never moving his eyes from the newspaper. In the elevator, I catch a few more glances and even a question from an intern named Mark. He is a budding journalist with a tight line of questioning: "Dude, what the fuck happened to you?"

I explain that I was knocked over the day before and hit the pavement face first. Never got my hands out in time. Not sure how it happened.

I'll repeat the story another twenty or so times today, with the only important instance being the time I recount it all to my new boss, Sheila Copperhead. Sheila is nothing at all like Ed; she's a woman of the modern world. She's tuned in precisely to the corporate sociopolitical vibe, and her suits are no-nonsense with clean lines and a cut that says, *Take me seriously or I'll put a stiletto through your eye.* She has impeccable academic and professional qualifications, and is universally recognized as a highly effective, on-the-money editor. Because of all these positive qualities, she is generally referred to as a "bitch."

But the label just doesn't fit. She's a genuinely warm person—just one who doesn't mince her words, which is a good thing given her career choice. Our conversation is almost exclusively about me: a kind of after-the-fact interview. She asks about my motivation to get into journalism, which I have to hastily manufacture as I suspect the reality—that writing was the only thing that I seemed to be any good at—didn't seem to be the kind of answer she was looking for. I speak about Professor Bowman and about being inspired right from the first lecture, and she nods in approval. She mentions that she knows some of his work and that he has a solid reputation in journalistic circles.

She asks about my motivation to join the international desk, especially given the fact that selling papers means pandering to social trends and that, in turn, means less and less focus on what's happening thousands of miles from here. I mention the immigration stories and the subsequent trip to Lesotho. I tell her that despite the shrinking column inches dedicated to the international scene, my own interests in journalism run at the scale of nations—the human condition as described by the meeting of cultural forces, global forces that are compelled to intersect more and more as the planet shrinks and the wealth gulf expands.

I am mildly surprised at my argument and about the clarity that I see in it—regardless of whether I've captured it verbally or not. I can tell by the way I've described it—by the sense of ownership that I feel myself wrapping it in—that these are ideas I actually give a rat's ass about. I sit back for a moment and realize, while staring blankly at a spot just past Sheila, that I have just come pretty damn close to ringing my own bell. Those first-year lectures with Professor Bowman have stayed with me, and his heartfelt convictions of how important this business really is, have been backed up with my own early experiences in the trade. Journalism is becoming everything I have believed it would be, sullied only slightly by the path I took to be part of it.

And the universe, through Sheila, confirms it. "You know you're not very popular with a number of people out there," she says, stabbing a finger at the newsfloor outside her office. "A lot of them think you haven't paid your dues."

I'm still caught up in a little of the wonder of the self-bell-ring, so my answer comes out ultracasual, almost drugged, the kind of response you give when someone catches you staring and you don't want to stop the moment.

"Well," I say, "fuck 'em."

And then I snap back and realize I am still in that after-the-fact interview phase with my brand-new boss, and that potty mouth probably isn't the way to her heart. I think I gravitated to writing because you get to hone your responses, bake them fully and then deliver them with all the odds in your favor. Real life doesn't provide you the luxury of time to create those perfect one-liners.

Despite my shortcomings in the quick wit department, I manage to do the only thing remotely sane given the situation: I say nothing. Instead, I look directly into her eyes and lock every muscle in my face. It's not a carefully thought-out strategy, not some mechanism designed to come off as a hardened, I-don't-give-a-shit news vet, but rather simply a total lack of data input. I am a deer trussed up, with eyelids peeled back and restrained with little metal fasteners. All I can do is stare.

It can go one of two ways here, neither of which I can control. Sheila looks at me with a face that I am having trouble reading. She seems to be at once horrified and amused. Somehow, a bitter lemon has been secretly slipped into her mouth and fully squeezed to boot. And somehow, I still hold her gaze.

Then it happens.

Sheila smiles and then chuckles. "I know what you mean," she says. "I know what you mean."

I have no idea what she means.

"See what else you can develop in the same vein as the immigration story. There seems to be an appetite there. Let's talk in a week and see what you've come up with."

As I leave her office, the conversation begins to gel and I do start to see what she means. She said I wasn't popular with a lot of people out there, and she's right. Live people, dead people, it doesn't matter. I am an equal opportunity offender.

Fuck 'em, I say. *Fuck 'em.*

26

Lebo's mother—the one whose tin lean-to I sat in while she cried and told me about her beautiful, dead son—left an impression that has stayed with me. The idea of making luck, the way her son had, at least in the beginning of his adventure, is fast becoming a beacon for me. She isn't the first to mention the idea, but the concept has been sticky ever since.

Four days after the attack behind the building, I'm sitting at my desk and trying to commit an idea for a story to paper, but I keep being pulled away to the notion of *manufactured opportunity*. Nothing "just happens." Look at Colin Dysart. Did he wake up one day and find a media empire at the foot of his bed? And at the other end of the scale, look at Rhona: late forties and running an independent copy shop and still holding out against the big chains. How? By design. She's doing what needs to be done to survive. For her it might mean a tighter top and a little extracurricular credit, but it works.

In my mind's eye, I equate it to a process of maturation—letting go of the idea that the cream rises, that justice prevails, and that hard work is the key to success. The true brass ring is accepting the ugliness that propels people, careers, and corporations forward.

I look up and Donna is standing there.

Her eyes are puffy and it's clear she's been crying. But she's in control now. I see something stony in her, something resolute and impenetrable, and I know right away she has heard about my new job. "Is it true?" It's more accusation than question.

My reply is pathetic and even I feel it—but I need time. "Is what true?"

"That you're working for Sheila now. Officially."

"Oh, right. Um. Yes, I just got…"

She doesn't speak but simply looks at me the way people look at a schoolyard bully who has just won a fight with a dirty kick to the balls. She doesn't ask the question I know she's burning to ask, and even now I can't help but admire her. That high road is one I've rarely chosen, and she takes it now as she simply turns away from me and leaves, taking everything we had away with her. In my head I can almost hear an audible crack, like a sheet of ice calving from a glacier, and I know this thing has just broken in a way that is unfixable. *You're going to piss the world off…*

My phone warbles and I snatch at it. "Keene."

"Roly!" says a voice that is clearly smiling. "It's Warren."

"Warren Barton. How the hell are you?" I am pleased to hear from him; it feels like a sudden reprieve, a welcome distraction from the strange pain I'm experiencing over Donna and the way she just left. I don't like the feeling; it's all too real, too present, and too reminiscent of Dr. Coyle's predictions…*and you're going to be alone.* I suddenly have the urge to come clean on my coffee debt. "Where are you?"

"I'm at my dad's offices just over the way." Warren's a pro at trying to play things down while almost always achieving the opposite. He doesn't mean it; he just royally sucks at coming off as the common man. What he's really saying is that he's at his dad's penthouse suite of offices in the Barton Building on First and that there's a pretty damn fine chance that the building I'm sitting in—just over the way—is owned by Daddy, too.

"Listen, you want to grab a coffee? I'm sure I owe you a few."

"Sure. When?"

. . .

Leaving work midmorning is simple; research, interviews, dumpster dives—all manner of distractions are available as excuses—and the walk to Starbucks is measured in minutes. I pause at the front door, darting glances toward likely hiding spots for Trots, but I know it's unlikely he's here. Trots will be playing the odds, looking for me at the obvious places and times—on the way in, on the way out, that kind of thing—and waiting for me to make unscheduled and unusual midmorning departures would be a significant waste of his time. It's not long until I move off with a sense of relative safety and I begin to think about the possibility of actually settling up with him.

In terms of a real debt, I owe him something in the order of a few grand. But in Trots's reckoning, including the daily, penalties, surcharges, and all manner of lender's fees, I am into him for upward of ten. I don't have it, and every day his number climbs. Paying him is a pipe dream. I rationalize it all away with the thought that he's probably well past wanting the cash now, anyway. Killing me is the real objective, and his windfall is the effect it'll have on any other loan defaulters in his little evil empire.

Warren is already inside when I show up, staked out at a table and being eyed by little groups of coffee drinkers, two and three strong, all trying to lever him out of the spot with their implied group rights. Warren is oblivious and I immediately warm to him for it. He has two coffees on the table, which I suspect is the only thing that stopped the loitering table-seekers from tearing him limb from limb. I sit down and realize there will be no debt settling today; I can only hope to maintain the coffee debt status quo at best.

"Roly," he says, as if I've been a naughty boy, "you've been giving me the cold shoulder, buddy."

"I know, I know. Sorry, man, it's just hairy at the paper. You wouldn't believe how competitive it is. I kept meaning to call you back." I'm only half convincing, but then again, I'm only telling half the truth.

"Did you get the stuff—your box of shit from the apartment?"

For a moment my brain stalls. "What box?" And as I say it I find the answer—the box left at reception. "Oh…at the security desk."

"Yeah."

"No, no," I say, raising my hands in mock despair. "I completely gapped on that. It's still there. What the fuck's in it? And how did you end up with it?" My tone has somehow become accusatory, I think, so I reach for levity and come up empty-handed. There is a stretched moment there and all that emerges is a ridiculous facial contortion that apparently implies I am having a seizure rather than trying to be funny.

Warren does the classy thing and pretends it never happened. "Your landlord is a freaking stalker. The guy called me a thousand times until I came and got the box of crap you left behind. I was your emergency contact on your lease, remember?"

I nod and vaguely do remember. My mind flits back to that lightless little hovel, the lumpy mattress, and the hotplate. I make a silent promise to hurl it into the lake if it's in the box Warren left me.

"So are you practicing, or vetting, or whatever the right term is for fixing doggies?"

"And you're supposed to be a writer?" he says, eyebrows pinned up high. "Never mind me—I'm following your shit in the paper. If you're not writing the stories, you're starring in them!"

I turn my palms upward and give him my best hapless fool.

We chat aimlessly, frivolously, but eventually the conversation picks up on an old and well-worn thread. "So is there anything happening with the investigation? Around Chloe's shooting?" he asks, and then hurriedly adds, "And yours, of course."

Of course. "Not that they're telling me. The police haven't been in touch in quite a while, so I'm guessing it's shelved."

Warren scratches his head and screws his face up in doubt. "I kinda doubt it. The Dysarts have a lot of pull with the city and a lot of cash to spread around. And Chloe's dad is a one-cause man these days. He was over at my dad's place and I hear he's letting everything else slide. He's focused on catching the fucker and nothing else. That family's stretched thin, man. That's what I hear."

Something large and solid is fighting gravity, forcing its way up from my chest and into my throat. "Is he getting anywhere?"

"Fucked if I know," he says. "But you gotta know he has the resources to take a damn good stab at it." He sips his coffee and shakes his head. "I still can't believe you were right there, man."

"Yeah. Me either."

"I'm still talking to people about it, you know. Or at least they're talking to me. I get calls every now and then asking about you. It's pretty freaky."

"Like who? Who calls?"

"Well, the cops did, but not for, man, over a year now I guess. I've also had some calls from guys in your line of work—shit, had one just yesterday."

"Really? Who?"

"Can't remember his name. Said he was researching a story on Chloe Dysart's death and wanted some background stuff on you—what kind of guy you were, where you went to school. Stuff like that."

"What'd you tell them?"

"Don't worry, pal, you came off smelling like a rose." He sips his coffee again and then realizes I am waiting for a real answer. "Aw, I just said you were a good guy, a talented guy."

"What else?"

"Shit, I don't know…um, that you didn't really know her well. And that you crashed and burned once hitting on her." He smiles but it is short-lived.

"Fuck, Warren. Don't tell these people stuff."

"Hey, take it easy—it was just a joke, a throwaway line."

"You don't know what these people are like, Warren."

"These people?" he asks, dripping with sarcasm. "These people are you, Roly. Journalists."

I back down. "Yeah, yeah. Look, just do me a favor and don't make any more comments." Inside, I am a fully drawn bow; I don't know whom Warren has spoken to, what it was for or anything, but the string is humming with latent energy and the arrow is eager to let fly. It apparently does not go unnoticed.

"Buddy, you need to bring it down a notch." His tone is part sarcastic, part concern.

I shrug and try to guide the conversation away. "Yeah, I know. It's all been pretty weird. So what's up with you, anyways?"

Half an hour later I'm back in my cubicle at the *Star-Telegraph*, clicking away at the keyboard and wondering why anyone is still picking at the Chloe Dysart scab. Christ, it's almost two years old. Why are they looking at it? *Who* is looking at it? I find no answers, but plenty of dread.

● ● ●

My knee bounces incessantly and I know it, but if I don't bounce it I have to pace, and Dr. Coyle's little office is too small for pacing. That and the fact that it would make me look like some kind of manic fool on the very edge of control.

The woman in the blue fog looks like a shadow, half there, half not. "So at some point are we going to get to why you're here? I mean why you're *really* here?" she asks, her hands folded calmly in her lap, a smoldering near-death cigarette pinched between her fingers.

My voice is tight, just like the rest of me. "Like I said—it's been a long time—too long—and I thought I should just check in. You know, stay in touch. Just in case."

"Just in case," she says, parroting me.

I nod and my knee bounces.

"Okay, so let's say right now is that *just in case* time. Tell me what's going on for you. It doesn't take any special insight to see you're on edge, Roly. Something's got you revved up, and your being here tells me *you* know it, too. Now, that in itself is a good thing—we talked about self-awareness, about reaching out. About being your own first line of defense."

Well, you see, someone's asking around about me in regards to how Chloe died, and it's freaking me out. "I broke up with my girlfriend," I say glibly. "Well, she broke up with me."

"Hmm. Girlfriends."

"I deserved it."

Dr. Coyle leans over to a small side table, crushes out the cigarette, and fishes another from her pack. She pauses while she sets a flame to it, then: "Okay, Roly, the therapist in me would pick up on this and say, 'Tell me about the relationship, about your feelings. Tell me about why you think you deserve what happened.' But the real-life person in me, Cathy Coyle, she would say Leo Bowman covered as many visits as you wanted for a year, but that's over now. And this hour's on your tab. So why don't we stop with the bullshit about girlfriends and breakups, and talk about what's got you sitting there sweating like a whore on nickel night?"

I stare at her for a long time. She just sits and smokes. There's a neutral expression on her face—open, but neutral—and she waits with an infinite patience for me to speak. The silence is almost unbearable, but Dr. Coyle is content to sit and smoke and wait.

"Have you ever..." I begin, then falter and scratch at my head. "Have you ever done something that you knew wasn't right, but you did it anyway? And then you justified it for yourself, and did other things, said things—maybe little things—to kind of shore it all up? And before long you'd created something that was impossible to back out of."

"Roly, do you see the pattern in there—in what you're describing?"

I nod and stare at the floor.

"We all tell lies. All of us. Sometimes for good reasons, sometimes not. But all rationale aside, the conviction we place in the lie is what's actually dangerous."

I look up at her, unsure.

"You ever heard of a little Russian named Dostoyevsky?"

"The *War and Peace* guy?"

"Jesus. What are they teaching in school these days? No. Different Russian. I'm talking about Fyodor Dostoyevsky—he wrote *Crime and Punishment, The Brothers Karamazov...*" She expels a blue cloud above her, then waves a bony hand through it to no effect at all. "Anyway, he once wrote: 'Above all, don't lie to yourself. The man who lies to himself and listens to his own lie comes to a point that he cannot distinguish the truth within him, or around him, and so loses all respect for himself and for others.'"

And so I sit with that and stare into the distance for a very, very long time.

27

"Naw, there's nothing here. Musta been sent up already." The guy on the security desk is a regular, but not one I know by name. I don't trust his answer; perhaps it's the fact that he never even lifts his eyes from the copy of *Sports Illustrated* he's reading.

As I turn away, I say thanks and immediately wish I hadn't. Back on my floor, I check with the receptionist, the mail guy, and all my cubicle neighbors but no one has seen any box for me.

I forget about the stupid box and spend another half hour staring at the keyboard for effect, while trying to decipher the mystery of who is looking into Chloe Dysart and me. My enemy list turns up only one candidate—Barret—and I quickly review every sighting I've had of him in the last six months. My mind instantly interprets everything I have seen in Barret as suspicious. Yes, he would love to see me collapse in on myself and be revealed as nothing more than a one-shot wonder—let alone an honest-to-goodness murder-setter-upper. With that thought, I see I am close to coming unglued. I take a deep breath and talk myself back from the ledge. Barret knows nothing. He can't. It's just paranoia.

In front of me is Lebo's mother's story. I reread it again and try to cut away some of the overly expressive references—ones I have injected, rather than the very real moments I have tried to describe honestly, where Lebo's mother had her emotions stripped bare and left, bright and bleeding, in the cool mountain air. The story I wrote about Lebo, the one published on my return from Lesotho, originally contained a good deal about his mother. But, as so often happens to the first draft in this business, it was cut and cut and cut. Ultimately, her part in the story has been reduced to a single rather insignificant line. Not terribly unlike her life. Still there is more here, more I can bring from the story if I can do the job of telling it through her eyes.

I sit with fingers poised, but aside from minor edits, nothing more is coming. I switch tasks and open a document that I am preparing to justify another trip—this time to Zimbabwe, where a delusional Robert Mugabe is leading his country into a new and heretofore uncharted state of want and misery.

There are a number of valid reasons to go, and chief among them is the fact that the rest of the pack, that lens-toting group of fellow self-described Fourth Estate professionals, are all shipping out as well. If approved, I will set out in two days. A hop to London, a four-hour layover, and then on to Johannesburg. From there, it's a short run up to Harare, where I'll join the rest of the traveling journo road show and perform my duties as professional witness.

By four o'clock the details are set and there's little else but to pass it through to Sheila; she has the authority to make the trip happen, and given the general exodus, and the success of the story from the first trip she green-lighted, I think I have a pretty good shot. She says good luck, nods sharply, and slaps me on the shoulder. That's it. The only trouble I'm really having is now that I've left Sheila's office: as I wait for the elevator I find myself wholly unprepared for the awkwardness of Donna standing two feet to my right.

I spend the entire ride wondering exactly where my eyes should fall. She's behind me and to my right, and I know her stare is boring a hole into the back of my head. I feel the heat of her cutting glances, and by the time the doors open I am convinced everyone in the elevator car knows what's going on, and has been infected by her loathing.

But she walks off in the other direction with no acknowledgment of me whatsoever. The others dissolve into various rooms and corridors, and I am left alone save a vague sense of melancholic embarrassment.

Three days later I'm on the ground in Zimbabwe, shoulder to shoulder with Steve D'Angelo, the *Star-Telegraph's* number one man with a camera.

We follow the herd for the most part, catch a few dictatorial sound bites from Mugabe at a rally, interview a white farmer whose land seems likely to be liberated and returned to the people of Zimbabwe (at gunpoint), and speak to a handful of locals about their feelings toward their government.

In total, we are on the ground for four days, and on day three I meet a four-man TV crew from the BBC shooting B-roll for a piece on Mugabe's policy of farmland repatriation. They ask us if we would comment on camera about our perspective, the journalist's perspective, and I immediately turn to Steve, as he's the senior guy. He's in his fifties, has seen and shot everything, and doesn't feel the need for niceties. By the time my eyes have flicked to him, he has already dropped his head and begun walking away. "Fuck that shit," he says, in the same tone most people would say, "No, thank you."

I, on the other hand, am a rookie. I know the odds are pretty slim that whatever they shoot of me will ever end up in the piece, but the thought of showing up on camera has a certain amount of damn-cool to it, so I immediately agree.

They ask about how we've been treated. Have we felt any sense of threat? Are the authorities cooperative and are we generally feeling any unease as foreign press poking our noses around in Mugabe's affairs? At the end, the producer tells me I have a "real comfortable" way on camera and asks if I have any formal training for this side of the trade. We look at the replay and I'm quietly thrilled with the small comments from the Englishman. "Not bad," he says, almost imperceptibly. "Not bad."

On the plane home I spend time thinking about the BBC interview, and while the segment will probably never make it to air, I admit to myself that I really enjoyed sitting on the lens side of the camera. There is a certain immediacy to it, a short burst of focused time into which you can cram so much more than just the words. It's exciting, perhaps a little egotistical, too. I hear Leo Bowman, dusty and aged in a stuffy office filled with books and yellowing newspapers. *I'm a newspaper man, and for me that's the purest form of the art—the written word. But I will admit to one advantage the TV people have—and that's access. You want to hit the masses fast, that's your medium. But be warned: it's fast food. Deep thinkers want to sit down with something they can sink their teeth into. They want a steak. TV can't offer that. Nope, it's quick bites and on to the sports.*

• • •

The stories from the Zimbabwe trip are not earth shattering, but they keep things moving forward for me. I file them remotely, prior to getting on the plane in Johannesburg, and by the time we reach London there is word—and tickets—to get Steve and me to Israel, where tensions are once again rising. I know little about the situation there, and Steve spends the flight educating me so I don't end up looking like an ass when I meet the Middle East bureau chief. After Israel, it's back home—briefly—before heading out again. My tour of duty spins me through a dozen countries in the next three months, all the while with Steve D'Angelo and all the while fully aware of the fact this exhausting series of rather simple assignments is little more than Sheila running an aptitude test. The stories we're sent to cover are mainstream, almost pedestrian, the kind you fully expect to see in the world roundup section—quick snippets about besieged dictators, disillusioned youths trashing Main Street, and citizens without nations lobbing bricks and stones at heavily armed soldiers.

But in truth, the grueling schedule works for me. I have no one waiting at home, no dog to starve or goldfish to float, and the constant state of movement means I spend little time reviewing myself—a factor that has quietly become the cornerstone of my little surge in career building. I go happily from story to story, country to country, taking with me everything I need in a single green backpack small enough to get me on and off planes with no checked baggage.

But, as the winter settles in and Sheila's travel-test schedule lightens, I find myself back in the city, back at my desk, and, after pushing the workday as long as I can, back in my apartment.

Which wouldn't be so bad, were it not for the letter I find slipped under my door.

28

The number in the envelope is ridiculous.

It's preposterous. But then I suppose that's the point. What really bothers me is how the note found its way under my door. I haven't been in my apartment for the last six days thanks to Sheila's Whirlwind Tours Inc., but the building is supposedly secure—there's no doorman, but there is a door for which only tenants are supposed to have a key.

The letter is handwritten and the writing is so bad it would be laughable if it weren't so damn menacing. It's signed by Trots—a single capital *T*—but the body of the letter and the signature are clearly from a different hand. I suspect one of his evil henchmen wrote it, probably Bosco, with Trots doing the dictating. It says:

> *You had all the chance you gonna get. On Saturday the 19th, be at the station at 9:00 (at night) and have 40 BIG. Cash. We aint playin. Be there, or I gonna spend some muny and have some peeps come for you.*
>
> *T.*

It's that last line—*have some peeps come for you*—that creeps me out. It's been three months since the last time he found me, and I guess I've managed to convince myself, largely through omission, that he has no idea where I live now and that any threat I might face is always going to be a downtown, in-and-out-of-work kind of deal. Add that to the fact that my life seems set to have a large on-the-road component, and it's been looking, well, sort of self-managing.

But this note, this note that's in my building—shit, in my

apartment (slipped under the door, sure, but it still fucking counts), is causing something inside me to unravel ever so slightly. I have a burning and sudden desire to withdraw, to shut the windows, pull the blinds, and put out the lights. I need a corner, a dark, defensible corner, where I can stare forward and see the shit coming straight at me when it inevitably does.

Soon everything about my life is awash with uncertainty. There is nothing about which I am confident, nothing upon which I can rely, and no one I can turn to to make it all better. Dr. Coyle's voice sweeps though my head for an instant: *Be aware that these events may yet come home to roost.* And the horror of it wrings me completely.

In my bedroom there is a closet, a disorganized clutter of clothes and shoes and boots and sweatshirts, but it's dark, away from the windows, and I can fit tightly into its corner. I reach up and pull fistfuls of clothes from their hangers and pile them around me, shoring up a barrier that will offer nothing but still insists on being built. I draw my knees up tightly and hide among the clothes and shoes, and finally reach out a tentative foot to swing the closet door closed. Finally, I am overcome with the exhaustion of worry, of fear, and I succumb to a sleep as thick and black as fresh tar.

On the afternoon of the second day I sense the first trace of a turning tide. I finally eat—a slice of well-buttered bread with honey—and look at the calendar pinned on the wall of my kitchenette. Today is Sunday the sixth, and Trot's deadline is the nineteenth…thirteen days. I know there's no way I can come up with forty grand, and even if I could, there's no way I would hand it over to Trots. And as I think it, I feel the worm turn in my stomach.

By Monday I'm like some medium channeling pure frenetic energy from a clawing mass of long-dead scribes, each desperate for one last chance at the pen. It's an exciting, almost sexual experience, and I know I'm smiling wildly as I write, flipping pages, rushing words and leaving them half finished as the next come tumbling through. I stop only long enough to call the office and leave a message that I'm sick, and then it's back to the plans, the ideas, and the giddy euphoria that comes with this unbridled sense of clarity and creativity.

The surge runs its course by early afternoon and I walk away from the desk spent, eat more bread with butter and honey, and then sleep. In the morning it's back to work. My energy is low, my mood somber, and I can tell from the looks I get that I'm broadcasting my disposition with no signal loss. It works for me, as no one bothers me, and it seems to support the story that I was sick the day before.

I stare at the monitor, at the story I've been working on, but in my mind I'm going over the scribbled pages back at my apartment.

"Donna's got a gig with *Foreign Correspondent*." The voice is behind me, to my right, or seven hundred miles away and speaking through a tube. For a moment I can't tell which. "And she starts next week."

I blink and then realize that it's D'Angelo. He's nursing a coffee and looks like a screwed-up piece of paper retrieved from the wastebasket and flattened out by a grimy mechanic. "Really? On-air?" I ask, warming to the idea that this may be a conversation I'm interested in having.

"I dunno, probably eventually. I'd bet it's production for now, but on-air's what she's after."

I nod slowly and dig deep for an intelligent response that will mask the vague sense of jealousy that I feel about her move to a credible television show with a truly national audience. "Wow," is the gem I come up with. In my head the Donna-and-Roly high-light reel starts clattering away, but thankfully D'Angelo shuts it down quickly. "You good for tomorrow?" he asks, rubbing his eyes and settling onto the corner of my desk. With him this close, I can smell the day-old booze. While D'Angelo is no alcoholic, he has a reputation for doing nothing in half measures.

"What's tomorrow?" I ask.

"You should read your email. We're headed back to see Robby M."

"Land grabs?"

"Yup. Two white farmers and their families pulled out of their homes and butchered. Then justified by the man himself."

I shake my head in wonder. Mugabe is reacting to a one-hundred-year-old situation that saw 1 percent of the population (the whites), ending up with 70 percent of the choice farmland. His solution: throw out the whites, kill them where necessary, and hand the land over to his cronies. Two years ago this would have horrified me. Now it's just something we need to get to and cover.

"What time do we fly out?"

• • •

Harare is comfortable, climate-wise, and is a lot less like what people imagine it might be. It has a busy commercial center, shiny high-rise buildings, and all the trappings of your average North American city—until you look to the streets. It's there that you get the reminder that you're indeed in Africa and that the gleaming skyline way above is far removed from life down at ground level. Harare is a concrete-and-glass warning for the rest of the world, a living example of what happens when you have it all and screw it up. Here extreme wealth and acute poverty live side by side, with nothing in between. As a result, the gleaming towers are besieged by a slow but inexorable deterioration, where dirt, refuse—human and otherwise—and every manner of detritus gradually finds a foothold and digs in.

As we thread our way through town toward the south, heading for the vast farms that once made the country—then Rhodesia— one of the richest in Africa, we see the wealth fall away, and, apart from the odd black Mercedes speeding by, almost everything and everyone is afflicted by poverty. The people, the relics of old cars, the skeletal animals hanging motionlessly in huge, dusty brown tracts of land—all of it reeks of decay. An hour later we turn in to a dirt road that leads directly to a farmhouse about a kilometer away across another enormous stretch of land. It is the Cullinan farm, where a white farmer and his family were butchered in the name of land redistribution. There seem to be many people at the building, poor locals judging by their tattered clothing. They linger around the structure as if bereft of purpose: outside, inside, all loitering. It looks like a huge house party that has ended; no one wants to go home, but the music has stopped and there's nothing to keep things going.

As we approach, the driver slows and speaks in hushed tones to the man beside him, a guide we have hired, and the two exchange what I interpret as concerned glances. Up ahead, the group has noticed our vehicle and some begin to stand and look our way. The driver speaks to the guide again, only this time he is more animated. They are speaking Shona, which is lost on D'Angelo and me.

"What's going on?" D'Angelo asks, with the first real hint of concern in his voice. "Why are you slowing?"

The driver stops the vehicle altogether and half turns toward us, one well-muscled arm hitched over the seat back. "Is not so good here, *bhasa*."

D'Angelo is suddenly my own private Geiger counter and I am picking up his clicks with rapidly increasing intensity. "What does that mean?" he asks sharply. "What does *not so good here* mean?"

"Dis people. Dis guys here," the driver says, gesturing at the group of thirty-odd black people at the farmhouse, "Dey are…" he struggles for the word, then, "…*vengano*."

I am suddenly exasperated. "Veng…what the fuck is that?"

D'Angelo lifts one of his meaty hands. "Take it easy, Roly. Take it easy," he says, which has exactly the opposite effect on me. I am about to go off when our guide jumps into the conversation.

"*Vengano*—hot. Ah, angry, you know? Dey not happy jus now."

The driver looks nervously at the group ahead and then back to us. "Maybe we go. I think maybe dey see you and…bad, bad."

Ahead of us, our fully stopped car has elicited even more interest and some of the members are moving closer, craning their necks, trying to see who we are. I can plainly see they're carrying long blades, like pirate cutlasses, swinging them loosely as they point at the car and gesture to one another. I look at D'Angelo and I see the words on his face before he speaks them. "Yeah, let's go. Let's get outta here," he mutters, his eyes fixed on the group now moving cautiously down the track toward us.

The driver wastes no time. He grinds the gears as he searches frantically for reverse, finally seats it, then pops the clutch. The car lurches once, then immediately stalls. He says something in Shona, which is almost certainly *fuck*, then attacks the keys in an effort to crank the vehicle back to life. Ahead of us on the track to the farm, the group has become aware of our attempted withdrawal, and some ancient predatory instinct has kicked in. They cry shrilly, raise their cutlasses, and charge the path. Behind them, those who were only observers have now joined in. A mob has just been born and is headed our way.

The guide shouts at the driver in Shona, and the engine turns over and over without firing. The mob is now a mere fifty yards away. As the driver releases the key for another try, the guide decides he's had enough and abandons ship. He is past us and sprinting for the road before any of us can react. A moment later the car sputters to life with a belch of black smoke and the driver dumps the clutch again, but this time with enough grunt to keep the momentum, and we're suddenly retreating, one door flung wide from our guide's departure, and with a screaming mob redoubling their efforts to catch us. The driver is facing us as he drives in reverse, looking through the back window. I can see terror on his freely sweating face. The car lurches left and right through the overaccentuations of high-speed backward driving, and by the third overcorrection, physics steps in and orders the car off the road.

We spin into the shallow gully only meters from the fence line, kicking up an instant maelstrom of dust and cusses. D'Angelo and I clutch at our bags and gear, the driver is shouting in Shona, and all I can really hear is a high-pitched whining in my ears as adrenaline courses through me and threatens to tear my heart from my chest.

The dust obscures any view through the windows, and before we can tug on the door handles, they clatter upon us.

• • •

Professor Bowman, during one of his well-trodden first-year lectures, spoke about passion. "Whatever you do," he said, "do it with some degree of passion. Go after something, anything, with gusto. And I don't care what it is or what your lot in life is. If you're a mainstream journalist, do it thoroughly, write with spirit and do the work to the best of your ability. Honor the trade and its purpose. If you're a garbage man, do that with the same intensity. Embrace the thing before you and do it with a consideration to beauty. Be passionate!"

I now remember that lecture with the intense clarity afforded by adrenaline sparking my every neuron, and I wonder, for an instant, if the Professor would applaud these people. I wonder this because of their passion. As I sit in the back seat of the car, hands thrown around my head and eyes peeled wide, I understand that the people pulling at the now locked doors, banging on the sheet metal and screaming wildly, are in the grips of the kind of passion Professor Bowman would surely approve of. I know now that I will not just die here. I will be torn to small fleshy pieces.

29

The window behind me stars briefly and, with one more crack of a well-hefted blade, shatters. Then the driver's-side window. I can now hear the driver screaming in Shona, and even though I know nothing of the language, his plea is universal. D'Angelo is putting up a fight, swatting the hands that are clutching and grabbing at him through the door they have now pried open, and in an instant he is dragged out of the car feet first.

Someone has grabbed my hair and I am being drawn up and out through the rear window on my back. Because of the angle, my chin is being forced up, exposing my throat, and I fully expect a blade to hack into me and stop only after it finds my spine. But as I hang suspended and exposed, my throat laid bare on this makeshift sacrificial altar courtesy of Ford, something else happens.

In an instant there is a turn in the way the mob surges. The hands in my hair are still there, but I can feel hesitation, uncertainty, and perhaps just a shade less passion. Through the high-pitched whine, I can hear a man shouting, bellowing. Faces are turning toward him, voices are muttering, and suddenly I am released. Half in and half out of the back window, I am suspended on the trunk, hands and palms skyward, eyes wildly trying to comprehend this sudden turn of events.

The mob somehow changes, morphs. It is abruptly a group of people, panting, out of breath, and still clearly hopped up on adrenaline themselves, but no longer a mob. Moments later another set of hands seize me, but the touch is supportive, and I am pulled out, off the trunk and onto my feet. There is an argument happening to my left, two men heatedly going back and forth, until one, the one with a heavy blade, throws up his free hand in disgust, and dismissively walks away from the other and out of the group.

Now the group, too, is evaporating, and I am seeing individual people for the first time. I realize the man who was arguing is our guide—the one who had fled from the car. I don't understand any of it, and suddenly I remember D'Angelo and whip my head about frantically to find him. I see only his legs sticking out from beneath the car, and as I walk around I realize he had somehow managed to get into the space between the ditch and the bottom of the car. He is completely covered in dust as he slowly comes out, eyes as wild as mine feel, and hands clenched into meaty fists. There is a smear of blood on his cheek, but otherwise he seems whole.

"It is okay," says the guide, breathing heavily and clearly still a tad edgy. "Dis people jus famas."

"Farmers?! Fucking farmers?!"

The D'Angelo I am used to has apparently returned. "Roland, shut the fuck up." And I do.

Some of the "farmers" are wandering back toward the farmhouse, but most are looking at us curiously, the way people look at lobsters in tanks at seafood restaurants. D'Angelo and I are asked to move aside, and the group puts its collective muscle into the car and pushes it back onto the track. It's a bizarre scene: a battered car with its windows cracked and shattered is being carefully restored to the road by the very people who just attacked it. Some even wipe at the dust and brush shattered glass off the trunk, and one man carefully closes the passenger door, sees it does not sit properly, and then closes it again—coming away with a nod of self-satisfaction to his work.

The guide points at the car. "You wan go now? Or you still wan talk-talk with dis people?"

D'Angelo looks at me and I at him, and something in it all strikes us both as hilarious at the same moment. We laugh the laugh of the narrowly reprieved, and eventually I say yes, we still want the interview—only we'll do it here at the car if that's okay.

No need to go over to the house to where all the other *farmers* have now retreated.

As it turns out, we owe our escape to the guide—the one who got out and ran—and it's a good thing he did, too. The mob focused on us, and ignored him, and he was able to shout back at them—from a safe distance—that we were foreigners here to tell their story. I gather from the animated way the conversation is going that the *farmers* are now under the impression that we are sympathetic reporters here to tell the world about their struggle. We are content to be perceived that way, still fresh from the reality that we could have easily been butchered without timely intervention.

Occasionally, and very gently, we nudge the conversation, with the aid of our guide and interpreter, toward details of the killing of the family that once called this place home. At the end we thank them, perhaps a little more enthusiastically than they really deserve, more for what they didn't do rather than what they did.

An hour later we are once again cruising through the open fields of Zimbabwe, the cool air streaming over us (thanks to the broken windows that needed to be kicked out entirely to make the car drivable), headed back to the hotel and relative safety. This "scrape," as D'Angelo calls it, has left me feeling at once terrified and supremely alive. The brown, dusty country we moved through earlier is now awash with vibrant tones and hues, each popping from the land and screaming to be noticed, while somehow managing to still be a perfectly balanced part of the picture. Near death has left me in a state of near euphoria, buzzed, hypersensitive, and acutely aware of the fact that whether we lived or died in the back of that car was a decision neither of us could impact. We were simply passengers in every sense of the word.

Here, thousands of miles from home, on another continent, in another hemisphere, I am reminded that while almost everything is entirely different, so much is the same. People make decisions, react in both contrived and natural ways, and at the end of it all, people die—or they don't—and the reality is, no matter what your faith, your politics, or your personal code of ethics tell you, that conclusion is fucking random. Dead in a car in Zimbabwe and butchered by a mob of panga-wielding wannabe farmers, or shot dead on a city street thanks to the lies of a wannabe journalist, it's all the same. It has almost nothing to do with us.

After showering and changing into new clothes that are free from fear-induced urine stains, D'Angelo and I close out the evening in the bar downstairs. There is the usual assortment of reporters, little cliques and groups that form and fracture as people flow into and out of the room. Our story—what happened to us out at the Cullinan farm—is the major topic of discussion at the bar, and D'Angelo and I never tire at the retelling of it. We are past the beer and into the scotch, and I soon realize I have no taste for it and even less tolerance, but that won't stop me. I soldier on bravely.

And then, draped in the shining glow lent to all women viewed by those well lubricated, in walks Donna Sabourin.

She sits down with her *Foreign Correspondent* crew, four of them in all, and sees me. Her eyes meet mine for a splintered second, and then fall back to her colleagues. That's all the time it takes to dismiss me. But, thanks to the power of some rather cheap and decidedly evil local scotch, I am undeterred.

I arrive at the table just as one of her group is departing, temporarily, judging by the half-finished drink. I slide into the seat and smile at Donna, and in all honesty I'm glad to see her. I miss a lot about my relationship with Donna—brief as it was—and the booze makes the longing all the more intense. But, ever the perceptive one, I can tell that something in the frown she is wearing means the feeling is likely not mutual. Still, I press on. "Donna, I heard about your move to *Foreign Correspondent*, and I wanted to come over and say congratulations. I didn't get a chance to see you before you left, so I saw you here and so I think it's great. Really great."

Donna forces a joyless smile and nods, but offers nothing more.

I realize I am in trouble here on two or three scores: first, my hands are waving around altogether too much and without any real sense of refined motor control, and well beyond what the occasion calls for. Second, because it has suddenly become clear that she is not going to be an active part of the conversation. And third, the other two at the table are looking on with an air of condescending amusement. This has all the earmarks of quickly becoming an embarrassing, possibly offensive encounter.

Donna, to her credit, reads the situation superbly and asks her friends to give us a minute. One asks if she's sure in a quiet, understated tone and then they leave, casting just the correct degree of aspersion in my direction.

Donna's tone is cold, aloof. "What do you want, Roland?"

"Wow, that's a heck of a greeting. You're a familiar face a thousand miles from home. What's the harm?"

"What's the harm?" Donna shakes her head in exasperation. I ignore it by waving over a waitress and ordering two more scotches. Donna says she doesn't want it, but I make some flaky hand gesture that means go ahead and bring them anyway.

The silence starts to sag in the middle so I fill it quickly and with no skill whatsoever. "How are you?"

"Roland, how did you get into this business?"

"What business? The news business?"

"Yeah, Roly, the news," she replies sarcastically.

"Same as everyone else, I guess. I went to school, got a job, and hustled." I shrug.

"I got into this through nothing but hard work. I got in with *Foreign Correspondent* through hard work, and with no support from the people I would expect to get support from."

"You're pissed about something you *think* I said to Carroway."

She crosses her arms in a single twitch. "You deliberately badmouthed me. You—of all people."

"I did not, Donna! Look, I admit I had a conversation, with Ed, but I have—had—I mean, well I've never, you know... In fact, you know what? I told him you were a gifted writer. That's what I said. A great reporter. That's exactly what I told him. There's no reason I'd say anything else, I have no interest in badmouthing you. And I never did!" At this point I am embarrassed by my lack of command over the English language, despite the effects of the whisky.

Donna is growing more prickly by the second. "No reason, huh? So it's just a coincidence that you trash me to Ed and then all of a sudden you get the plum job at the international desk—the job I'd been in line for." For a moment she seems about to boil over, but then reins it in. "I put in my time with the society pages, I paid my dues, Roly. You undermined me intentionally so that you could set yourself up for the job."

"Donna, that's not it at all. All I did was answer a question I was asked, and gave my opinion. And, like I said, I told him you were a damn good society reporter." I see the pit I'm headed for and swerve hard to dodge it. "Not that society was all you could do. No. I never said that. I just said that's what you were *doing*. Back then. You know, for the machine." I know it's starting to look ugly so I change gears. "Carroway didn't understand. Jeez, I even knew it back then. I shoulda said something. Donna, he misinterpreted. He got it wrong—what I was trying to say. And I was not looking for a job with Sheila's group. I'm not that devious."

Donna leans in, both hands pressed into the table. "I think you're plenty devious, Roly, and one of these days you are going to trip yourself up and fall on your ass."

"Come on."

"And just what did you tell Carroway, anyway? Specifically."

"I told him what I thought, you know, my opinion—which counts for nothing!"

Her lips are peeled back tight and she speaks through a clenched jaw. "What did you tell him?"

I know I should just stop now, stand up and run from the room, burst into song, anything but answer the question. But true to form, I babble away. "He asked what I thought about your work, and I said it was good, great—just that I didn't see a lot of value in the society section. But that's the *section*—not you."

Her face is pleated, her mouth hanging open and her color rapidly changing to crimson. "Fuck you, Roland. Fuck you! You waltz into the paper on the good graces of the owner, steal—*steal*—a major story and then suck-ass your way uphill, and you think you have the credentials to criticize my writing? Even if that was your opinion, would it have killed you to say something nice? You knew goddamn well I wanted that post. You fucking knew, you..." She can no longer keep control, and preempts her own public outburst by getting up and storming out of the bar.

I knock back my drink and follow. As I leave I note that no one, save D'Angelo, has noticed the quietly heated debate.

I catch up with Donna outside the bar and follow, imploring her to understand my perspective. She ignores me and keeps walking and eventually we are at the door to her room. She turns sharply, blocking the door, and roughly shoves me out of her bubble. "Roland, you are a despicable person." She simmers, and then, "Stay away from me."

With little else to work with, I try history. "Donna, we were pretty good together for a while there, don't you think? I mean, Christ, I can't be all that bad? Why don't we just go inside and have another drink and..." My words peter out as the look on her face changes from anger to pure revulsion.

My mind briefly escapes the bleak moment swirling around us, and settles on a memory so perfect it seems almost cruel—given the look on the face of the woman before me. In it we are sitting in a small restaurant in the city. Donna is laughing, at what I don't know, but it's warm, inclusive laughter. And as she laughs she brushes the hair from her face, then reaches across the table and takes my hand. It's just a momentary touch. A simple gesture of affection that is so sincere that it takes me entirely by surprise. It is truly a perfect moment for me.

But it only exists in my memory. The woman before me can't see it, can't remember it.

She has something to say, yet can't or won't find the words. I watch as she physically swallows whatever it was, deciding that not telling me was more venomous, more hurtful to me; the act of withholding is a mighty exercise in self-control indeed. Finally, she just walks through the door and closes it sharply.

30

Days later, back at my desk at the *Star-Telegraph*, I set to work on two stories. The first is in the true human interest vein, and draws dotted-line connections between Zimbabwe's current economic decline, the erratic political gesticulations of a cornered dictator, and the desperate lunges of a people caught in between. The second story is less important but infinitely more sellable. It's got that proverbial sizzle.

D'Angelo and I collaborate on the story; I write it, and D'Angelo contributes three photos—which completely amaze me. I now understand why D'Angelo has the reputation he does as a photographer, because it's truly what he is, and not simply what he does. As it turns out, as hands locked onto him in the car in Zimbabwe, as they clawed and tugged at him, and even as he kicked at them and put up a fight, D'Angelo kept snapping away. Two of the three are taken from inside the car, toward the people who are pulling him out. The first picture is angled, rotated about fifteen degrees, taken from inside the car in the back seat and framed by the open doorway. In that opening are three men and one woman in a flowered top, and their faces, their eyes in particular, are mesmerizing. In the moment captured by the photograph, these were not people at all, but rather fevered zombies, carrying out actions demanded and dictated by impulses a million years old. The next picture is the same group, but with D'Angelo's legs captured in the bottom of the frame, and slightly closer to the door as he was being dragged through. In the photograph, you can see something akin to glee in their eyes now, as their quarry is drawn inexorably into their clawing hands. The photographs both carry a real sense of movement and built-in dread, and looking at them invokes that dream where you're running away from some threat, but your damn legs just won't move fast enough.

The last picture is remarkable only in the context of the first two, and shows a group of people milling around, among them a woman who is laughing. According to D'Angelo's fancy digital camera, that photograph was taken a mere nine minutes after the one with D'Angelo's legs in it, and the laughing woman is the same one, the one in the flowered top, from the picture taken only nine minutes before.

I am amazed at her transformation from frenzied attacker to carefree, giggling girl in such a short span. I am also amazed at D'Angelo's presence of mind to pick up his camera again and start shooting, literally minutes after coming out from under the car where (I'm sure) he thought his life was going to end.

The story frames the event as a day-in-the-life piece, with the underlying message of "Shit changes fast, so watch out." Sheila loses control of it in an editorial meeting and it finds a home in the Saturday edition on the front page of the Living section. By the time it sees print, it carries the headline NOT YOUR AVERAGE NINE TO FIVE and by the following Tuesday D'Angelo and I are booked as guests on the nationally syndicated TV show *USA This Morning*.

Steve D'Angelo, I notice during our four-minute live interview, lives up to the other part of his apparent ethos: my work is all in the picture, so what the fuck are you talking to me for? As a result, I take up most of the conversation, even when Carolyn Thomas, *USA This Morning*'s anchor, turns and pitches a question directly to Steve. His answers are generally restricted to "Yeah," and "Sure," and once, in an absolute outburst of wordiness, he says, "Uh-huh, it can be like that." And so I leap in when I can, trying not to dominate and making sure I tell the story in terms of *we* and not *I*, and in what seems a blink, our four minutes are over.

We're stripped of the microphones and power packs by a pretty blonde girl who flits about and doesn't look a day over fourteen, and then shown to a table with bagels and fruit juice, conveniently located near a rear door with a glowing exit sign above it. The show has moved on, the lights are now focused on a woman explaining the art and science of upholstery, and D'Angelo and I are pretty much abandoned.

It's a cool morning and we debate for a moment: cab it or walk? Before we reach a conclusion, the perky blonde appears and pecks at my arm. "There you are, Mr. Keene," she says, dancing lightly from one foot to the other. "Mr. Stewart asked if he could have a moment."

I wrinkle my face trying to place the name.

"Gordon Stewart," she says, jabbing a thumb over her shoulder toward the studio. "The news director."

"Oh, sure," I say, suddenly convinced that we've screwed something up and are about to be reprimanded. D'Angelo and I both turn to head back to the studio and the little blonde chirps to life once again. "Actually," she says awkwardly, "he really only needs Mr. Keene."

D'Angelo doesn't miss a beat and pivots, raising one arm for a cab, toward the street. I feel the need to close the conversation—unlike D'Angelo, who is already stepping into the street for a slowing taxi.

Inside, the blonde girl leads me past the studio and into a more corporate-looking area filled with cubicles and a cluster of private offices. She waves to a man seated behind a desk chatting on the phone and leaves. The sign on the door says GORDON STEWART and I find myself awkwardly loitering just outside. I catch movement and see that Gordon is waving me in, still on the phone, and pointing to the chair. He gives me the universal signal for *I'll be with you in just one quick minute*, and then shakes his head in frustration at the person on the other line. "No, no, Carol. That's not going to work."

As I sit there, I browse his walls and I see picture after picture of Gordon with his arm around people's shoulders, shaking hands, sharing a drink, and even administering the occasional peck on the cheek. A closer look shows the people he is captured with are not just pals but world leaders, A-list celebs, and even a few international villains thrown in for good measure. It appears that Mr. Stewart has been there and done that, several times over.

"Roland—may I call you Roland? Thanks for coming in. And great segment this morning, I really liked it, it really worked. What'd you think?"

Wow. Gordon is velvet smooth, speaks in fully automatic, and while I know intrinsically that I should distrust fast talkers, I can't help but warm to him.

"Yeah," I say rather unconvincingly, "I thought it was good."

Gordon is wearing jeans and a tan corduroy jacket over a faded blue T-shirt that says *I do all my own stunts*; it's a wardrobe I would have expected on a trendy twenty-five-year-old, not on this fifty-something news director. Still, he somehow pulls it off. "That's why I wanted to talk to you," he says, "Because I believe you've got something that's much harder to find than you might think."

I think I know where he's going, but I see this as a chance to practice the art of shutting myself up, so I let the moment stretch and he fills it.

"Have you done any work in front of the camera?" he asks.

"A little. Not much, really."

He leans in. "Tell me."

"I did a little interview once for the BBC on being a journalist. That's about it."

"And how did that feel—to be on camera? I imagine you were okay with it, comfortable. The reason I say that is because in the segment you just did, Roly, you were totally at home. Completely natural and unaffected. That's perhaps the single most difficult commodity to find in this business. Most times you point a camera at someone, their personality packs its bags and heads for the hills. Very few people can disregard its effects, and you have that."

I'm not sure what to say here, so I just nod.

But he does. "Now, you have a bunch of things going for you: you're in the business already, you have some credibility thanks to some of your work in print, you come across well under the lights, which is our way of saying you're a handsome devil," he says, filling his own laugh track, "and you're unaffected by the lens, which is of course the big one."

I'm flattered, but feel somehow uncomfortable with the praise. My response is wooden. "That's great. Thanks."

Gordon chuckles and leans back in his chair. "Look, let me get to the point. I'd like to test you on camera, and if that all holds up, and I'm sure it will—I'm pretty good at this stuff—then I'd like to talk to you about a job. Here at USBN. Well, not here exactly, but in the field. You'd be a US Broadcast Network correspondent."

• • •

The whole process, the testing—which is really just a bunch of lighting guys and makeup people fussing around while you say random things into the camera—the obligatory chats with various management types, all happens in the space of two days. At the end of it, on the Friday after the on-air interview, I'm sitting in front of a job offer that makes a mockery of what I'm being paid at the *Star-Telegraph*. It's been just shy of two short years since I started at the paper and only nine months since I broke the immigration story; how quickly the world can change.

I sit in Gordon's office and stare at the contract. The urge to ask them if the number is right, if it's not a cruel typo that will be caught and changed with some sarcastic remark—*whoops, yeah, I bet you'd like* that *as a salary!*—is overwhelming. So instead I just read, all three pages, and then I fold it and do what you're supposed to. "When do you need my answer?" I ask, waiting for a bunch of USBN staffers to burst into the room, laughing and slapping each other on the back while Gordon snatches the paperwork back saying, "Gotcha!" But they don't and he doesn't.

"Is Monday too soon? This is a key role we've been looking to fill and as you may have guessed by the last couple of days, we move fast when we know what we want."

31

Just because you're paranoid, so the saying goes, doesn't mean people aren't out to get you.

In my case I'm admittedly riding a wave of paranoia, but I have a pretty solid case to support it. With Trots's deadline only hours away, thoughts of shivs are dancing through my head as I move down Eighth Street. The sun is shining and the street is alive with bobbing heads, each of which must be diligently checked and double-checked to see if it's Trots or one of his lackeys. There's an argument going on inside my head as to whether I need to worry or not, seeing as the deadline is tomorrow and technically I'm still this side of that line. The counter is, of course, that Trots is a fucking lunatic and there's no reason to expect that he feels in any way bound by the constraints of his hand-crafted contract.

As a result, my walk down Eighth is a nervous one, characterized by much pivoting of the head and twitching of the eyes. Once home, I head straight for the desk, where I toss the USBN contract aside and pore over my notebooks, searching for the one I scrawled in last. As I sift through the pile, I'm thankful for small mercies; the Chloe notebook is not sitting on the top of the pile and I don't have to pick it up and move it, then deal with its attending phantoms. I rationalize that it's probably buried under paper in the growing stacks around my desk, and having an untidy room is for once an advantage. But the little self-delusion is short-lived; something is quietly gnawing away at me, leaving me unsettled—and worse—unconvinced that I know exactly where that Chloe notebook is. I shake it off with the promise to find it—or at least to look for it—later.

I soon find the one I'm looking for, snatch a Coke from the fridge, flop on the sofa, and begin to read.

• • •

An hour later and it's just after noon, officially half a day before Trots's deadline. I've blown work off for the rest of the day because my morning meeting with USBN means the *Star-Telegraph* is soon to be relegated to an entry on my resume, and because Trots's deadline needs to be met in one way or another. I can't do it with cash—won't do it (even if I could afford it), so I must go with something else.

I can take a respectable photograph—I'm no Steve D'Angelo, but I can get things in focus and I understand the principal of volume: shoot a shitload and your chances of getting something usable are greatly increased. My problem is that I am still in the world of film. My old Pentax was a great camera in its day, but the digital age has made it all but obsolete. Still, it takes a decent picture, and when I was at school I was able to get all the accessories I needed—a decent zoom, a wide-angle, and a motorized film feeder—at the pawn shop for next to nothing. The only hitch is that film and developing are unavoidable costs, and as I sit perched on the highest part of the wall at Union Station, at the far opposite end from Trots's corner, I remind myself that now that I can actually afford it, I'm going to have to think about upgrading.

Through my zoom I can watch the activity from a relatively safe distance and for good measure, I've positioned myself so that my body, at least, is blocked by the umbrella of the hot dog vendor that sits about midway between us. Only my head and camera peek up above. It would take some serious attention to detail for anyone at Trots's end to pick me out.

Through the viewfinder I locate Trots easily. Beside him are two younger guys, both with their backs to me, but clearly part of his entourage. A moment later they turn, scanning the crowd for customers. One of them is Bosco. The other is one I've seen before, but I don't know his name. I let the shutter fall and keep the lens trained on the group as the ebb and flow of activity brings them a steady tide of customers. It's remarkable how many there are and just how out in the open business is being conducted. I guess it's a case of hiding in plain sight.

I let the camera snicker away at every visitor and in the space of an hour I've gone through three rolls of film. For the most part, customers appear to be surreptitiously passing money over—which is the business of laying bets—and occasionally they'll take a walk to the west end of the station with Bosco or the other one, and then disappear southbound around the corner and down toward the poorly lit underpass. These are the drug buys; I know because I've been there—nothing hard for me, though, just the occasional bag of stems that pass for weed in these parts. But I know the full menu is available.

I'm also surprised at the range of his clientele. There are hunched-over, greasy, denim-clad junkies, then pinstriped businessmen, and even one woman pushing a stroller with a sleeping toddler. He's tapping into almost every demographic, and part of me can't help but stand in awe at his enterprise. In fact, the only group he's entirely missing is the tourist set, and that's only because he can't hang a sign.

By two o'clock, I'm done. Done with the pictures, done with the hiding and, as I hop down off the wall, it occurs to me that I am done with the *Star-Telegraph*. Once home, I check the answering machine and find the call I expected—Sheila asking where I am and if everything is okay. I pick up the USBN contract and read through it once more, marveling at my good fortune.

The Roland Keene streak of luck has got to be getting close to its end, but the breaks just keep on coming. From obscurity to the *Star-Telegraph*, and now to USBN—and all in the space of two short years—surely the universe will demand its balance be restored. Not today, though.

I take a plain oversized manila envelope from my desk and

head north to the one-hour photo place on Third, then catch a cab up to The Meadows.

. . .

Like everything born from the scribbles in my notebooks, there is a certain degree of madness built in. I'm keenly aware of this as I stand outside the gates, staring through the ornate wrought iron-work toward the palatial residence of the Dysart clan. I steel myself by trying to remember a quote—one that says something about madness and genius being separated by only the thinnest of lines. But the more I think of it, the more I realize that one implies the other, so either way I'm probably screwed. I abandon the thought. Instead I refer mentally to the pages, to the steps, the method laid out in spiral-bound glory.

I put my hand inside my windbreaker and feel the manila envelope there. In the cab, I had opened the individual photo wallets from Fotoshak and poured the contents into the manila envelope—taking care not to touch the prints themselves. Then I screwed the Fotoshak wallets up into a single paper ball and dropped it on the floor of the cab with the other garbage.

The knowledge that I am following a plan has a calming effect that is good, but I remind myself that too much calm here is my enemy. I will myself to reach out and press the button on the inter-com box fastened to one of the huge stone gate stanchions, and it buzzes in a low and somewhat foreboding tone.

"Yes," says the voice in the box, "How may I help you." There is no real question being asked here.

"Oh, um, I need to speak with David Mahoney."

Silence. Just the static hum of the intercom.

I press on. "It's very important. Really. Very important."

"I'm sorry. Who is this?" asks the voice, the tone either mildly curious or shocked at my audacity—I can't quite tell which.

"This is Roland Keene. Mr. Mahoney knows me."

Again, silence.

"Please—it's very important."

Another long silence, then, "Please wait."

The static hum disappears with a click and I can tell the person on the other end has gone. I stand there, waiting, not sure if I should press the button again or if I should rethink my approach, when through the gate I see the front door open and a man steps out. It's David Mahoney, Colin Dysart's executive assistant.

I smile as he approaches, walking with his hands clasped behind his back, but he doesn't return the smile and nods instead. "Mr. Keene," he says.

"I have new information about the shooting."

Mahoney stops dead, blinks a very large blink, then exhales sharply. "Then you'll want to speak with Mr. Dysart directly." He reaches momentarily into his jacket pocket and the gate rattles to life, then swings inward. Mahoney stands still as the two halves of the wrought iron gateway elegantly sweep by him on either side, and he extends his hand to me. "It's very good of you to come, sir. Please follow me."

32

Mahoney shows me into the small library, the same one I sat in almost two years ago, and little has changed. The wingback chairs still frame the window, the walls still hold a floor-to-ceiling collection of first edition masterworks, and the hollow sense of loss somehow still lingers.

The room itself is almost void of sound, save the *tick-tock* of an old grandfather clock marking time in the corner. I don't remember it being there on my last visit, but it must have been, evenly counting the days and hours of my life between then and now.

As I look at the events that have brought me to this comfortable, opulent room, I wake to the fact that my progress through the ranks has been nothing short of amazing. There has been no end of luck involved, although most of it—hell, *all* of it—has been manufactured by me.

I cannot—will not—let Trots take it all away from me. With a slow and deeply drawn breath, I settle in to wait for Colin Dysart.

This time, I avoid the books and sit in one of the chairs to wait. As the leather creaks its disapproval, the door swings open and Colin Dysart marches in. I pop up reflexively, but Dysart waves me down with one hand. "Please, sit, sit," he says.

He settles into the other chair and laces his fingers in front of his chin. "So, David tells me you've new information about Chloe's case?"

"Yeah, I wanted to come and speak to you directly, because it's sensitive."

Dysart is trying to remain calm and receptive, but behind his eyes there is an eagerness that has very sharp claws. "Please, go on."

"Well, the night that it happened, when she was, well, shot, I saw the guy, but I really didn't want to get mixed up with the police and the investigation, so I just told them what I knew and that was it. I was scared; I didn't know what to do, so I just clammed up. I hardly even trusted myself. And I'm really sorry for that now—but please, hear me out.

"A couple of weeks ago, I came across this guy, completely by fluke. He was just sitting there on the wall with a bunch of other guys, and I walked past him. As I'm passing, I look him in the eye and as soon as I do I realize it: bang, it's him. The guy from the alleyway. Anyway, I see the same reaction in him, so I put my head down and keep moving. A couple of minutes later, I look back and this guy is following me. He's a big guy, so I can see his head above the crowd, and I get the hell outta there."

"Where was this? Where did you see him?"

"Downtown." I hurry on. "So the next day, I head down there again, to the place where I saw him—only I was looking from a safe distance—to see if he was there again, to see if that was his spot, his hangout. And sure enough, he's there again. I didn't know what to do, and I was scared. This guy knows I can identify him, so if he sees me…"

In one swift motion, Dysart snatches up the phone from its base on the table.

"Hey," I say, alarm instantly in my voice. "What are you doing?"

"I'm calling Jim Garland; he's the lead detective on the case."

I reach for the phone in Dysart's hand and hold it. There is a strange standoff, both of us holding the phone, and for a moment I think he will physically shove me across the room for my inso-lence. The moment passes when he registers the fear on my face. "No, Mr. Dysart—please, you can't. You can't call the police," I plead with all finality I can muster.

"Why not?"

I let all of my fears flow through now. "I can't get in the middle of this. This guy has already killed one person, and I'm sorry, but I'm not putting myself in the position to be the next one."

"Nonsense," he says, tugging the phone from my grip. "This is a police matter and we need—"

"No!" I bark. As I do so I stand bolt upright, again purely on reflex, and turn almost imperceptibly toward the door.

Dysart falters: "Wait. Sit down. Let's talk about this." He sets the phone back in its cradle and shows me his empty hand, like a croupier after the deal.

"Mr. Dysart, you don't understand. I looked into this guy. He's a bad guy, a criminal, and part of some kind of network…an organization. Look, there are others that he's always with and even if the police pick him up, his guys are still out there, and I'm the one who put him in jail!"

Dysart takes a steadying breath and waves me back into the chair. Adrenaline is coursing through me and I make a conscious decision to ride it. "And I work at your paper—I'm bylined. I'm easy to find. Do you understand what I'm saying? If you go to the police, it's a death sentence for me." I am shaking now, and the fear is real—although not born of the source Dysart thinks.

He stands and walks slowly to the bookshelf and pinches the bridge of his nose.

I go on. "I want to help you, I do. I know you need to know who did this to your daughter, but please understand that things are different on the street. It's not tidy, it's not all buttoned down. After the police do their thing, people like me get left behind. I'm sorry, Mr. Dysart, but I don't want to die trying to help you."

Dysart lets out a long breath. "What are you asking?"

"I'm asking that you not take this to the police. If you do, I'll end up like Chloe."

"But the police…"

Adrenaline lets me slice through his objections. "Mr. Dysart, do you really think the police will give any credence to my testimony two years later? Not to mention that you gave me a job at the *Star-Telegraph*, and that I'm basically your employee. Christ, the lawyers would shred me."

I see a small rent in his armor, so I push on with everything I have. "And let's say you do go to the police and he is convicted—and remember that would be on the back of a memory that miraculously reappeared two years later. He gets sentenced to life, and with the system the way it is right now, he'll likely have his first parole hearing in a decade, be denied a couple of times, and be back on the street in fifteen. And in the meantime, I'm dead, Chloe's dead, and he can come up here and press the buzzer on your gate to say hi."

It is a pitiless finish and I know it. But right now I can't afford to be gentle.

Dysart closes his eyes briefly.

I reach into the pocket of my windbreaker and remove the envelope of photographs. "There are two facts I know for sure here, Mr. Dysart. One is that the man in these photographs is the one who killed your daughter, and the other is that if you take him through the courts there's a damn good chance he'll walk. At best he does fifteen years. Then he's out. Scot-free."

I wait for a moment and let the pause stretch out. "Mr. Dysart," I say finally, calming my voice to as steady a tone as I can make it. "You can't address this inside the courts."

He looks at me and I see something steely there, something hard and unrelenting. Something I wanted and needed to see. It's there for just a moment, then gone.

"Look at these," I say, placing the manila envelope on the table with four rolls' worth of prints inside. "I took these just yesterday. He has a spot at Union Station. I think he's a drug dealer and maybe a bookie, but he's regular. He's there two, three days a week. Always around the same place."

Dysart picks up the envelope and pauses. For a brief moment he's the man I met two years ago, freshly grieving for his little girl. He's no media magnate, no one-man economic lightning rod; just a helpless, heartbroken father.

As quickly as it came, the moment is crushed and Dysart upends the envelope and removes the pictures. He moves through them quickly, flipping the front one to the back, until he settles on one that catches Trots clearly among the sea of heads milling around Union Station.

"This is the man?" he asks almost in a whisper.

I nod and watch as the muscles in the corner of his jaw clench and put his teeth under all the collective pressure of two years' worth of unanswered questions. There's a shift in his eyes, like a cloud moving in to block the sunlight, and I can see a flood of crimson push up past his collar and into his face.

Dysart never lifts his eyes from the photo. "How sure are you?"

"Mr. Dysart, there is absolutely no doubt. I watched this man kill your daughter."

I remind myself that there is some degree of atonement to be had here, and providing this information to Colin Dysart is in part doing the right thing.

"His name is Trots," I add. "I don't know if it's his real name or a nickname, but that's what they call him."

Dysart looks through the rest of the pictures, shaking his head gently as he does, until the last one is filed back into the wallet. "May I keep these?" he asks.

"Sure, but no police. Or I'll be dead a week after they pick him up. I'm bringing this to you because I remember how much you needed answers the last time I was here, and I had nothing to give you. At least now you can put a face to the person responsible."

Dysart is still looking at the picture, and I'm not even sure if he has heard what I've said. He's far away, his mind already five steps into something else. I stand and move toward the door.

"And what about you, Roland? What will you do with this guy out there, this guy who knows your face?" Finally he looks up at me.

"Me?" I say, looking into eyes that now seem hollow, yet fixed with a frightening determination, "I'm just going to go home, and hope that this problem just…goes away, somehow."

. . .

On the cab ride back home I understand, for the first time, the concept of delayed gravity. It's that sensation that Wile E. Coyote is so familiar with: a wild run at full tilt taken with absolute commitment to the cause that takes you unknowingly over a precipice and for a moment—about four heartbeats—you hover. Nothing but yawning canyon below. A moment later you intellectually grasp the peril, and then—and only then—delayed gravity kicks in. Down you go.

In the back of the cab, something in my gut is plummeting south to the canyon floor. I catch myself muttering a mantra of "Holy fuck, holy fuck," and only after the cabbie says, "Pardon, I didn't catch what you said" do I realize what I'm saying and zip it. The handhold I go for helps calm me: if it's in the notebook, don't question it.

The day is still in its prime—a little after two in the afternoon—and what a day it has been. Ahead of me is the weekend, and, after I hand in my notice at the *Star-Telegraph* on Monday, two weeks of pure throwaway. I'll get no real assignments, I won't be asked to cover anything. For the most part it'll be two weeks of marking time.

And time, I note, is all that needs adding to the mix. For now, the most important thing is staying alive. I remember that what I'm doing is simply forcing a favorable shape on an unfavorable situation. I'm designing an outcome, taking charge of my future, making my own breaks. I'm joining the ranks of the Makers, not the Takers.

33

If ever there was a time to have a weekend out of town, this would
be it. My main concern is Trots, of course, and the fact that the
deadline he's given me is here. I flip through the spiral-bound
notebook, past pages of hieroglyphs and something akin to spirit
writing, and on to the blank page at the end where the plan ceases
and all eyes turn to me. What next, boss?

The security of autopilot is simply not there. For a moment
I think of Dr. Coyle, of the surety of those conversations, of the
strange and temporary sense of refuge that her office provided—
that crappy, smoky little dive above the laundromat. But I can't go
back there—not in any sense.

I place the notebook on the table carefully and then, in an act
of singular bravery, I pick it up and pitch it into the trash. It has
served its purpose and there's no more to be squeezed from it. Over
the course of the next two hours, I decide that whatever I do to
stay clear of Trots need not be grand and dramatic to be effective.
The city is large and filled with nooks and crannies ideal for the
business of hiding. In the end, I decide on simply switching to the
West Side, and with a small backpack stuffed with a few clothes
and toiletries, I slip out of the building and into the safety of a cab.

I check into the trendy Metropolitan Hotel and order a bottle
of wine and a burger, enjoying the fact that my career is on the
upswing. I gulp at the overpriced wine; I insist in reveling in my
good fortune, celebrating the way anybody would who was just
offered a high-profile gig with USBN.

It's only a matter of minutes—about twelve of them—before
I'm sitting in front of the TV twitching my thumb through channel

after channel of mindless drivel. I'll spend Saturday and Sunday here, check out Monday morning, drop off my acceptance letter at USBN, and head to the *Star-Telegraph* to tender my resignation.

In the middle of the fifteenth or sixteenth loop through the channels, I come across a scene that holds my attention just long enough to temporarily paralyze my thumb. It's a Bible-thumper station and for some reason that escapes me, I watch and listen just long enough to hear a man's voice speaking. The words he is saying scroll across the screen on a background of what I'm guessing is a desert scene from the holy land. "Do something good," he says. "Not by chance, but on purpose. Even if it's just once. Go on, do something good."

The scene changes and I lose interest. My thumb resumes twitching and the channels flick by in a comforting, predictable way. An hour later, I give up on celebrating and accept my act of hiding for what it is. I climb into a gloriously soft bed and wonder if the service people here at the Met, the ones who selected this bed for this room, can count my sense of wonder at just how goddamn soft this bed is as their "something good."

As I mentally wrestle with yet another small and insignificant debate, I become slowly aware of a creeping sense of dread tied directly, but somehow indefinably, to doing my own "something good." The voice/writing said it had to be on purpose, so I rifle my thoughts and try to come up with something that qualifies. I strike out almost immediately. Nothing. So I move on to the unconscious—things that I've done that may have inadvertently been something good, but a quick rummage reveals another big fat nothing. Dr. Coyle's voice echoes hollowly in the back of my head: *...and I don't even want to know what it is, to be honest, but it doesn't sound like something good.*

34

Things happen quickly for the rich.

It's Sunday, my second day at the Met, and I cross the street—still cautious, but fairly confident that an encounter with Trots on the West Side is unlikely—to have breakfast at Sunshine's, one of the city's best breakfast spots. I get a booth in the corner and help myself to a copy of the *Sun* as I wait for my eggs.

The front page cries out DOUBLE MURDER, and, sadly, it's the kind of headline that's become less and less surprising over the last few years. The *Sun* tells me that murders numbers eighty-one and eighty-two of the year were discovered floating in an inner lagoon in Waterview Park, a small, lonely spit of land jutting out into the harbor.

After toast, eggs, and coffee, I return to my room and hover about while housekeeping straightens things up. Once she's gone, I sit down and craft my letter for the *Star-Telegraph*, and wonder if it should be short and sweet or appreciative and slightly forlorn about my leaving. It takes me an hour to finish, all of it longhand, and after a quick visit to the business office downstairs I have in my hands my first ever resignation letter.

Satisfied, I flop in front of the television once more, and turn it on just in time to learn that the dead men in Waterview Park, one black and one white, were apparently beaten to death, and then tossed into the lagoon where they were discovered by a jogger sometime late on Saturday. Both, the pretty woman at the anchor desk says, were known to police and their names were Matt Cassidy—a local hood—and Terrance Richard Ottley, a native of the Caribbean island of Saint Lucia.

At first it doesn't register; the name Matt Cassidy means nothing to me. But then the penny drops and it all comes into crisp, clear focus. Terrance Richard Ottley. T. R. Ottley. Trots.

I hold my breath involuntarily. He did it. He really did it.

• • •

After stuffing my belongings into my bag, I check out one night early from the Met, and smile acidly as I get screwed on the late cancellation fee. I don't care, not really, because as of late Saturday night, I've shed one very large monkey from my back. The cab ride home takes me along First Street, right past Union Station, and I see that Trots's spot is conspicuously empty.

Once home, I sit down and continue mechanical tasks—tasks that occupy my mind and provide evidence that the world is rolling along just as it always has. I unpack, toss in a load of laundry, tidy my apartment, and stack the magazines that litter the coffee table—two of them with Colin Dysart peering up at me. Finally, I reread my resignation letter and immediately throw it away. There is absolutely nothing wrong with it, but the act of sitting and pounding away on my laptop is therapeutic.

Once I have it written, rewritten, and then rewritten again, I'm satisfied and I save it for printing at the office tomorrow. The phone rings and I'm saved from dark pondering. For now. I reach out and snatch it up. "Hello?"

"Roland? Roland Keene?" The voice is vaguely familiar: strong, authoritarian, but strangely soft at the edges. I can't place it.

"Yes, this is Roland."

"Good, good. Roland. Thasgood."

I can sense what it is now, that soft edge, as if the voice is being spoken through numb lips: he's drunk, or at least drinking. "Mr. Dysart?" I ask cautiously. "Is that you?"

"Of course, yes." His tone changes now and becomes quiet, but I can feel the tension at his end, humming like a taut wire in the few words he has spoken.

He says nothing, and predictably I fill the void. "Is everything okay?"

"Roland," he says quietly, almost reverently. "I wanted to call and speak to you."

"Yes?"

"I wanted to ask you again—about that night. About Chloe."

"Sure, sure," I say, as if talking to a child. "What do you want to know?"

"Look, I apologize for calling, but—"

"No, no—"

"She was so young and, so..." He takes a steadying breath or perhaps a drink, and then, "In the street, that night. Was she frightened?"

It's a question I remember him asking before, and one I've answered. But something inside me immediately understands his need to hear it answered again and again. "Mr. Dysart, she was—"

He suddenly cuts me off, and his voice comes through the phone as if the receiver is mashed tightly against his lips. It comes across tight, drawn and quivering, like a cable stretched to the point where the braided strands are beginning to part. "How sure are you about the man you said did this?"

I am jarred, off balance. "You mean Trots?"

"Yes, Trots."

"It was him. Without a doubt." I steady myself. "Are you okay, Mr. Dysart?" I hear a long breath drawn and exhaled, and then the sound of ice against crystal. "Mr. Dysart?" I ask again.

And then the tension is suddenly gone. He is quiet, contrite. "Look, Roland, I'm sorry. I shouldn't have called."

"No, it's fine, Mr. Dysart. I understand."

"I'm sorry, Roland," he says. "Forgive me."

And the line, much like Trots, goes dead.

● ● ●

"Well, I'm not entirely surprised, Roland," Sheila says, putting her reading glasses down on the desk. "What was it, two years here at the *Star-Telegraph*?"

"Yeah. Nine months with you."

"Nine months. Well, that's some kind of record for sure." She smiles, and then, "Of course, you know I'll have to spin this and take at least partial credit for your speedy rise."

I am glad, now, that I opted for appreciative and ever-so-slightly forlorn. Sheila asks a few harmless questions about the new role, not in any line-of-inquiry kind of way, but more collegial, and with perhaps a hint of maternal pride. At the end, she stands and shakes my hand, crushing it, then assumes the Superman stance with hands placed firmly on hips. If she'd had a pair of balls, she would have reached down and scratched them.

It's decided that my last two weeks will be filled with the work of editing fellow scribes, proofreading, and generally tooling around with no real direction. There will be no more story development for me. No assignments. No travel. Just a series of pointless days punctuated by editorial meetings from which I'm carefully excluded.

I head down to Carroway's floor, past his guard dog, Janet, without so much as a growl from her. Two years ago I wouldn't have made it to the door, but today she just gives me a crisp smile and then drops her head back to the monitor. I knock once and Carroway peers over the top of his glasses and then waves me in. "Ah, Mr. Keene. Come to say your goodbyes?"

I am mildly annoyed that Sheila broke the news before I had a chance to do it myself. But then again, that is kind of her job.

"You already know."

"Of course," he says, smiling a rare warm smile. "This is a small town, Roly, and an even smaller business."

"Well, I had wanted to tell you myself, seeing as you gave me, you know, my first break."

Carroway crosses his arms and leans back in his chair. "Hmm. It's a nice-sounding sentiment, but I don't think even you believe that, do you, Roland?"

I say, without pretense, "What do you mean?"

"Well, if you're referring to how you came to the *Star-Telegraph*, I think Colin Dysart is the man you should be thanking. And if you're talking about the immigration story that got you that first byline, then it's really yourself you should be thanking."

I shuffle awkwardly, ever the rookie in Carroway's presence.

"Sit down," he says, and then, louder and over my shoulder, "Janet, would you mind getting the door, please?" Janet obliges, and Carroway gives her the standard nod/smile combo. "She's great but loves the gossip."

"Yeah, she's great."

"So, off to the land of network television."

"Yeah. I'm assuming Sheila gave you the details, so I won't bother repeating it all, but I'm really looking forward to it."

"No, I haven't spoken to Sheila in days."

I dig through the morning and can't come up with anyone else I have told. My first stop was Sheila, and then I came here. "So who told you?" And then it dawns on me. Small town… smaller business.

Carroway sees the realization in my face. "Gordon and I go way back. We worked the police beat at the same time in our first couple of years." He leans back dramatically in his chair, eyebrows raised and cheeks puffed out. "Christ, that was awhile back," he says wistfully. "My start wasn't as dramatic as yours, Roland. Still, it's worked out okay."

"So, Gordon called you today?"

Carroway smiles and shakes his head. "Nope."

"—."

"Sure, we've had a few chats about you, about the possibility of you in front of the camera. But it was Steve D'Angelo who told me it was coming."

"After the thing on *USA This Morning*?"

"No, actually. He called it well before that—after your bit with the BBC in, where was it? Botswana or somewhere in southern Africa, I think."

"Zimbabwe." My mind is reeling and I'm trying to catch up with the activity that has been so clearly happening around me, without my having even the faintest idea. It's a little flattering, for sure, but also kind of creepy. "So you and Gordon were—"

"He sounded me out about you. What kind of guy you were, if I thought you had a pair large enough for the TV game, if I thought you could pull off a report without editors reworking your script for you. Stuff like that."

"So I guess I do need to thank you after all."

"No again. I told him you were still too green. Don't get me wrong, I told him I thought you would be great for it—given a few more years, but I guess he's investing early."

"Well," I say haltingly, "Thanks—ish."

Carroway laughs. "I'm sure you'll be great, Roly. Plus it gets you away from here and out of certain people's crosshairs."

Carroway sees the blood run up from under my collar immediately—and perhaps the full body rigor as well. He smiles. "Do you think this latest move of yours has put the problem behind you?"

I'm stunned. What does Carroway know about me and Trots? How the fuck does he know anything at all? I stare blankly, wide eyed. Thoughts ricochet around in my head as I frantically jam puzzle pieces together and find nothing that fits.

Carroway continues. "You know, you leave enough bodies in your wake, at some point one of 'em's gonna come back to haunt you."

All I can do is go for the clarifier. He can't know. He simply can't know about Trots, about Chloe, about any of it. "What are you talking about?" is all I can muster. It comes out an octave too high and all squeaky with stress.

"Barret. I'm talking about Barret and the big step up you took on his back."

My heart performs a full-gainer in my chest and Carroway interprets the shock on my face—which is really a spasm of relief—as horror: some kind of posttraumatic realization of having grievously wronged a genuine news somebody. "Now take it easy there, Roly," he says. "I'm not saying Barret is going to wait for you in a dark alley and brain you with a baseball bat. Just that at some time in the future you'll likely feel his influence in a negative way. That's all."

The blood roaring in my ears is calming, and I physically will the scarlet from my face with only limited success.

"Right, right," I say, "but I never set out to get him or anything. He was just there, in the way, when I needed to move. It was nothing personal."

Carroway shrugs in that noncommittal, *maybe you have a point, maybe you don't* kind of way. "Look, if you ever get the chance, throw him a peace offering. Put it behind both of you. I'd just hate to see this fester and have it drag something up that didn't need dragging up."

I leap in with both feet. "Something like what?"

"Nothing. I'm just illustrating my point. I'm merely suggesting you try to do something good for the situation—should the opportunity arise. Bring things back into balance. That's all."

Do something good. Christ, it's some kind of cosmic echo.

Again, Carroway leans deep into his chair, arms thrown back behind his head. "Just giving you the headlines, Roly. What you make of them, how you interpret them—well, that's all outside the scope of what we do here at the *Star-Telegraph.*"

I think for a moment, and then ask a question that a real newsman would never have to. It feels crass somehow. Distinctly high school. "Has Barret said something?"

Carroway chews on the inside of his lip. "Mmm, sort of. I'm not sure what he's up to, but my ear to the track tells me he's looking into you at some level. Probably just hoping to find something embarrassing in your past. I like you, Roly. I have from the get-go. That's the only reason I'm telling you this. I'm presuming nothing—we all have our share of skeletons—but if I were you, I'd make sure mine were well buried."

35

I fade quietly from the *Star-Telegraph* and at the end of my two weeks, I pull a no-show on my last day in order to dodge the inevitable embarrassment of the poorly attended farewell party in the lunchroom. I get a few calls from well wishers, from the likes of D'Angelo and Sheila—and one from Carroway himself. I collect them all on the answering machine.

There's one other call, not from a well wisher, and it's the only one I return. I dial the number and listen as the tone warbles at the other end. It never finishes the first full ring. "Dysart," comes the voice at the other end. It is commanding, secure, unflappable.

"Mr. Dysart. It's me. Roland." And then, because I foolishly believe he may not know who Roland is, "Roland Keene."

"Ah, Roland. Appreciate the call back."

I am about to speak but he continues. "I understand you've left the paper."

"Yes."

"Onward and upward. Look, are you available to come down for a lunch, perhaps a drink? I'd like to chat. This afternoon would be good. Let's say two at the club."

"I'm sorry, which club?" I ask, confirming I'm from another world entirely.

"The Empire Club. And you'll need a tie." And then he's gone, the line dead.

The Empire Club—arguably the city's most exclusive—sits at the center of the financial district, shamelessly preening in its tony address, welcoming a select few and casting disdain on all others. I've walked past it, but never dared to venture inside.

Two hours later I'm looking up at the red brickwork, the large, squatting white pillars and the black wrought iron fence that wraps around it all—carefully emblazoned with the club crest.

I brace myself and step inside.

The man at the desk looks up and smiles warmly. There is no spotlight, no henchman sharply raising his eyebrows. "Mr. Keene, I presume?" he says, still smiling. "Mr. Dysart is waiting for you in the Cumberland Room. Right this way, please."

Upstairs, at the end of a long marble corridor lined with busts carved in polished black stone and paintings of pasty-faced dignitaries, I'm shown through double doors into a private members' room.

The walls are paneled in rich woods, and in each corner four pinstriped wingbacks cluster together, creating semiprivate alcoves where groups can sip brandy and smoke fine cigars.

The only man in the room is Colin Dysart, and he waves me over from one of the chairs. The doors close behind me and I feel it in my ears, as if the room is sealed airtight. "Roland. Good of you to come. Drink?" he says, raising the crystal tumbler in his hand.

"Sure," I say, then immediately regret my decision. He'll ask me what I want and I'll look like a fool and ask for something distinctly low rent, like a beer. I don't know anything about wines and fine scotches.

Dysart stands and pours something amber into a glass, and now I notice that each wall has its own polished wooden table, inlaid with marble, upon which sit crystal glasses and decanters. "Here you go. Sit. Please."

He crosses his legs and sips at the drink in his hand, eminently comfortable in these surroundings. I, on the other hand, perch on the edge of my chair, waiting for Dysart to speak. I don't know why I was summoned here, and the not knowing is gnawing cruelly at my insides. But Dysart lets the moment ride. I, however, cannot. "This place is beautiful," I say, looking up at the ceiling.

"Yes, it has its charms." He sets his glass on the small table beside him. "So tell me, Roland, why the change to broadcast? I rather thought print was your preferred medium. And you've done quite well with us. Written some important pieces."

"Well, thank you. I mean, again—I would never have had the chance without your recommendation to Ed Carroway."

"Happy to have helped. But that was just a start—this thing at USBN sounds interesting."

I'm reminded that the man before me wasn't always a business tycoon. He was once a reporter, like me, and I can see that his interest is genuine, not small talk. "Yeah, I think so," I say. "I had no interest in broadcast in school, but I was interviewed by a BBC news crew a little while ago and it kind of stuck. So I thought I'd give it a shot and see if it's for me. Did you do anything on camera? I know you were a reporter early on."

Dysart steeples his hands, touching his fingertips together just below his nose. He doesn't answer right away, but then: "No, I've always been more interested in print. It's in the writing. There's something in a printed word that television and radio can't match. I swear it has as much to do with the look of the letters, the way they sit on that white field, the curl of the font. It's hard to describe, and I've been at this a while, but I really do love print."

"They say you still read every word of every one of your papers."

Dysart snorts, something close to a laugh. "I own fifty-seven newspapers around the world. It's a wonderful sentiment—and God knows I'd love to sit and read them all—but it's simply impossible."

"Do you miss it?"

Dysart looks at me curiously.

"The writing, the reporting. Getting out, asking questions, building a story."

He draws a long wistful breath and I can see him casting back, through the years, to a time when the Empire Club and all its luxuries were just a part of someone else's life. "You know, I don't think so. Doing what I do now seems to be working." He glances at his watch, and I can see a deadline is approaching. He goes on. "But it has come at a cost, as everything does."

I know there is more here, so I let the silence ride—despite a gnawing urge to lunge in.

"Excelling in anything exacts a sharp cost. In my case it's been decisions around time—it's become a commodity and I've had to make trades, some very hard ones. It's paid off in business, but sacrifices had to be made in other parts of my life." He reaches for the glass again and gazes at the light playing in the crystal. "I'm sure you can relate—even at this stage of your career I'd bet you can point to a few sacrifices of your own."

Something large and immovable has appeared in my throat. *What does he want?* Dysart drains the glass and stands to refill it. I look around the room, relieved to see we're still alone. "I hear you studied under Leo Bowman," he says, returning to the seat. "Did you know he worked for me at one point?"

This catches me by surprise. "Professor Bowman? Really?"

"Absolutely. He covered the crime beat, as I recall, for a daily we ran in New York. He's quite a legend in academic circles now, I hear."

My mind flits back to a campus bar and the ridiculous, life-affirming permission slip I received from him. "Yeah, he's the real deal. I really got along with him."

"That makes sense. Did you know he was an orphan? Some common ground there for the two of you."

I'm left momentarily stunned by this simple revelation, and as my jaw slackens the Professor's voice floats through my head as clearly as if the man were sitting across from me now: *Your circumstances, where you start from in life, Roly—that can't be the definition of you. It's what you do next that counts.* I want to linger here, to think about the impact of his being an orphan, but very quickly I am aware of something more pressing, something elbowing its way to the front. Sure, Dysart knows the Professor was an orphan, but what really has my attention is that he knows my story as well. What should have been apparent to me from the start now tumbles in on me like a collapsing mine shaft: Dysart has spent time looking into *me.*

I can't tell if his comments about the Professor (and me) are just conversation fodder or if he's subtly communicating his reach, but suddenly something inside me has finally had enough. The chit-chat has to stop. I need to know why I'm here and I need to know now. I take a steadying breath, and then: "Mr. Dysart, is there some reason in particular you wanted to see me?"

He smiles a contrite smile, and his head bobs up and down lightly. "Yes. Yes, there is."

Whatever it is, it is decidedly difficult for him. This man has the power to sway entire economies, to influence elections and advise heads of state, but what he is trying to say now, to me, seems to wither him.

"Roland, I'm trying to find an easy route to the subject, but there doesn't seem to be one. First of all, I want to apologize—for the call, a couple of weeks back—"

"Mr. Dysart, you don't—"

"No, please let me finish. I've been—we've been—my wife and I…we've been going through a difficult time lately. Dealing with Chloe's death. It was the same this time last year. You see, tomorrow would have been Chloe's twenty-second birthday."

"Oh shit," I say, unintentionally out loud.

"You see, everything becomes magnified on important family dates, and when I called you I'd had a few scotches. Perhaps a few too many. Calling you then was a lapse in judgment, and I apologize."

He sees I want to interrupt, to say it's okay, but he gently half raises an open palm to stop me. He goes on. "Roland, one of the strange quirks of human nature I've been forced to confront is that my daughter's death has become a kind of bottomless pit that I have to somehow fill. And I mean every day." He places his hands on his face and runs them up through his hair, one hand coming to rest on the back of his neck. "I know rationally that I can't do it, that there's no satisfying that hole. But knowing that doesn't matter. I have to do everything I can. I have to *know* everything I can. And I have to touch every part of what's left of Chloe."

He stops and gathers himself. "I'm sorry. I know this is probably very odd, and perhaps a little disturbing for you, but you're part of Chloe's..." He struggles to find the word, then: "Experience." He drains his glass for the second time. "You were there at the end, when I couldn't be. And again, I know this sounds like madness, but you're connected to her in a way that just feels important." He looks up into my eyes and there's pleading there, but for what, I don't think even Dysart knows.

"Mr. Dysart, I don't understand it, but I do *get* it."

And so we talk some more, about Chloe, about what happened. He asks many of the same questions he did two years ago, and he asks them again and again, worded differently each time, hoping to find something new, something to feed the pit. And in the end there's only one thing I say that seems to bring him any comfort at all.

No, I say. *She wasn't frightened*, I say. And Dysart offers a painful smile below eyes lined with tears that are not allowed to fall.

It is truly a reprehensible moment for me, one that I think can drag me no lower—until he places his hand on my shoulder and says, "Thank you."

36

Four days later my life begins anew at USBN.

There are no strained relationships to manage in chance hallway encounters, no awkward smiles and hollow *how are you*s. There's no impending threat of professional violence from the resident hotshot, and no accusing glances from staffers passed over that imply *we all know how you got the job, asshole.*

Gordon Stewart's crew moves quickly, and by the end of my first week I've spent over twenty hours in front of the camera, reporting whatever comes over the wire and then dissecting my performance with my producer, Phil Sudbury. Phil is direct and unapologetic, and critiques me with a bluntness that at first I find offensive, but soon learn to trust. I learn quickly and change, adopting virtually everything Phil suggests. It's the kind of training media students dream of.

I listen as Phil outlines my strengths and weaknesses, on and off camera, and rather than work on improving where I fall short, he adds focus to areas where I excel. Over a coffee between sessions in the studio, he says I have two assets and that playing to those strengths is the way we're going. I don't miss the subtle hint that I'm not a part of this decision, but I find the automatic nature of it somehow comforting.

The first of my so-called assets is what he calls a natural intimacy with the camera. He frames it as "presence" and "gravity," and while I don't fully grasp how this is conveyed through a camera, I do recognize that it exists. It's a curious thing, the power of a camera; intelligent, composed people routinely cave in on themselves and begin to babble uncontrollably once they are fixed in the unblinking eye of a television camera. It seems not to affect me that way—I don't know why—but in this, my new line of work, it is apparently a valued trait.

The second of my two alleged assets is my ability to write copy. Phil likes what he describes as my style. He describes it as compassionate but without bias. Evenhanded but grounded in our Western perspective, our culture. I understand this more than his discourse on camera intimacy, but there's still much I find myself learning from him, particularly in the delivery.

The copy, or script, technically, is one thing, but how you convey it—from the words you choose to emphasize to the placement of something as simple as a pause—is an entire skill unto itself. Phil is a master of subtleties and is clearly fascinated by the art of delivery: the onscreen mechanism that supports the words being spoken, and which, according to Phil, is responsible for almost the entire mood of any given piece. We watch hours of tape together and I quickly understand what he means. It's in the smallest tilt of the reporter's head, the half-hitched breath before describing a tragedy, the way he holds his hands or the sense of tension stiffening his shoulders. It's thin, almost gossamer in its existence, yet its collective layers can couch a story even before the first word is spoken.

"It's the dark stories you want," Phil says to me, staring at archived footage of Christiane Amanpour reporting from somewhere in war-torn Sarajevo in the mid-'90s. "Don't let them put you into anything fluffy. And I mean never."

"Dark stories?"

"If you want credibility, that's where it is. And credibility is your stock in trade. You need to acquire it fast and hang on to it. Lose it, and you might as well go get a job in the mall. 'Cause you're fucked without it."

"And you expect Stewart will start me out with fluff." It is half question, half statement.

"If you let him."

"So when he hands me an assignment to cover the Santa Claus parade I should say, 'Bah Humbug'?"

"Something like that. Just remember this is a team sport. Where you go, so goes your cameraman—and a producer if you're lucky. Understand that everyone is tied to the feed."

"No pressure, then."

"Not for me."

• • •

After three weeks of dry runs, endless copy, and far too much together time in confined editing booths, Phil announces it's time to start earning my pay. My cherry-popper comes in the form of an economy ticket to Saudi Arabia, where an American is being held in prison after having been charged with murder. The diplomatic channels are humming and the world is watching to see what the Saudis will do: a potential death penalty, flimsy evidence, allegations of torture, and the need for the royal family to save face all make for compelling TV.

Chaperoned by Phil and a cameraman named Vince McMillan, I spend three days on the ground and file six stories, only one of which sees airtime back at USBN. At the outset of each shot, Phil and Vince argue about vagaries—light levels, filters, angles, and framing—and I watch and wait until the skirmish dissolves into a series of halting compromises. Phil outranks Vince in the pecking order, but as the routine of their argument settles into a well-worn path, I understand that what I am watching is Phil's deft handling of a budding talent.

I notice how Phil's challenges are often on things Vince is well versed in, and after a while I see that the challenges are designed to see how vigorously Vince will defend himself and his point of view. At first Vince yields to Phil's rank and authority, but as the days progress and the squabbling continues, I begin to see a new Vince emerge, one that is prepared to say no, that's not the right way to do this, and as he emerges I see something akin to satisfaction in Phil.

"You're a fucking bully, Phil," I say, laughing, as we sit at the airport in Riyadh waiting for our flight home. I jab my thumb in the direction of the washroom Vince has disappeared into. "You've been baiting that poor bastard for the last three days, haven't you?"

Phil smiles. "Two things. First, I am not a bully. What you're seeing is someone skilled in the art of social acupuncture. Second, Vince is no poor bastard. That little lens monkey relieving himself in there will one day be the most celebrated man in his profession. You mark my words."

After Saudi Arabia, there are trips to Palestine, China, and South Korea, chasing political flare-ups and military brouhahas. I file stories on human rights abuses, border skirmishes, and tin-pot generals bent on clinging to power no matter the cost. With Vince, I cover small tragedies that frame wholesale calamities: mothers weeping over children blown to bits by land mines, villages leveled by disease and famine and left to quietly expire, babies with bellies swelling mightily with malnutrition and choking in the red dust kicked up by government officials in big black Mercedes-Benzes.

And as I travel and file stories, I begin to see the same faces again and again. I learn the therapeutic value of the local bar in whatever place we might be and the informal debrief it provides. The humor is caustic and dark. The daily horrors are chased away by bouts of loud, if slightly forced, laughter and liberal helpings of local brew. There is an uneasy fraternity in this traveling road show of pseudoprofessionals. In the evening-before, there is back slapping and camaraderie; in the morning after, there are quiet and hasty departures, whispered talk of where the story might be, and where the day's lead will be found. Often, the group miraculously convenes at the same place from a dozen different routes, and some odd conspiracy of silence allows us all to nod straight-faced in recognition but mention nothing of how we each got wind of the story. To discuss it would be an inexcusable breach of decorum.

I learn how to live in threes: three shirts, three pairs of underwear, three pairs of socks, three pairs of pants. As I wear a groove in the road I discover that my anniversary—the start of my life as a foreign correspondent—is marked, year after year, with a call or an email from Colin Dysart. Chloe's birthday is so close to my start date at USBN that the two are now inexorably linked, and as the day approaches I know he will reach out, perhaps with a scotch or two under his belt, perhaps not. Often we don't actually talk, just swap emails or leave short messages on answering machines around the world. For me it has become a macabre tradition; for Colin Dysart, something else.

The routine is the same: Dysart asks after my progress, how I'm doing, where I've been working, and eventually, sometimes elegantly and often not, he begins to talk about Chloe. I understand the calls, the emails, and I do see them as a penance of sort, but I hate them. They keep my own demons alive, despite what I chase around the world for USBN. Still, the calls and emails come year after year, reminding me of how all this was paid for, and by whom.

Of course, the sins committed out here by arrogant military bullies and political jackals make a mockery of my own small transgressions. Their size and scope dwarf anything I've done, and cast large, dark shadows in which I can hide. In fact, I soon understand that muddling through the obscenities of others in faraway places is, for me anyway, a soothing balm. If Dr. Coyle could prescribe *this* shit for all her patients, well, she'd be on to something for sure.

• • •

After three years of being almost constantly in motion with USBN, and with only short hiatuses back home, I have started to develop something of an appreciation for the thrill. The work pattern is much the way it's said to be for soldiers: long hours of boredom and drudgery punctuated suddenly and without warning by fleeting moments of sheer panic. Getting jacked up on adrenaline is a powerful drug and seeing wide grins on animated, giggling crews as they pile into the bar, still caked in concrete dust from some explosive near miss, can't help but make you think the word: *junkie.*

Chase the four horsemen. Get the shot. Land a printable quote. That's the entire job description.

Vince and I cover story after story, tragedy after tragedy, year after year, always paying heed to Phil's doctrine of the Dark Story. It pays off and we slowly eke out a solid reputation in our professional community. Our stories seem to get noticed for their relevance, and somehow Vince and I develop a knack for finding the right face, the right quote, the right shot. As our credibility grows, we discover that the stories and leads come more easily; we're far from attaining any kind of celebrity status, but somehow the locals and their stories always seem to come to us first. We load the feed with famine, genocide, assassination. We cover bloody coups and dictators laden with ribbon and braid. We watch for the world as they step from shiny black cars, the shoeless masses smiling hollowly, waving small paper flags issued by the soldiers moving among them.

On the second to last day of my fifth year at USBN, I cycle back into the city. At the airport, the crowds are thick with tired travelers and as I move through customs I see something in the agent's eye as he recognizes either my name or my face. Once clear, I check my cell phone for messages and find the battery dead. At the luggage carousel I get more bad news as I wait for a bag that isn't coming. I find the lost bag desk and join the slow-moving line with the others. I plug my phone charger into the socket in the wall beside me and pick up my messages.

What I hear on the phone stops me cold.

37

I become aware of the round, middle-aged woman behind me in the lost baggage line. She is huffing and tutting, trying to convey her displeasure at the fact that I have not cinched up the line that has now moved ahead of me a good three or four spots. I stare at her blankly, still processing the last message on my phone, and finally she simply moves past me and back into the line. I offer no resistance, unplug the charger, and fall in behind her.

I haven't spoken to him in almost two years, but his message was all Leo Bowman: congratulatory in a backhanded sort of way. "Hi, Roland, it's Leo. I keep seeing your on-location reports on the news, and one of these days I'm actually going to turn on the sound."

Hearing from the Professor is not what stops me cold, nor is it his (only half) tongue-in-cheek comment about my move to the journalistic equivalent of fast food and away from the purity of print. No, it's his last comment, a quick dig about my being a big shot, so much so that now the media has turned its harsh glare on itself. He'd even been called for some background material on me by an intern journalist at the *Star-Telegraph*.

An intern working for Dave Barret.

· · ·

My heart is racing and my mouth is dry with dread. "Hi, Professor, I just got back," I say, being entirely truthful. I've been back in my condo for only moments, having thrown my bags to the floor and paused just long enough to scatter files and papers frantically as I searched for his number, finally locating it in an old journal that doubles as an address book.

The trip from the airport was too long. Trapped in the cab with a dead cell phone meant I couldn't act, couldn't call and quiz Professor Bowman the way I was burning to. Instead, I had to sit and silently urge the car on, clenching my teeth while my thoughts began coiling, turning slowly in on themselves where they found fuel to grow and take on every horror lurking nearby.

"Roland!" he says back to me and I hear suspicion in his voice immediately. Or do I? "I left that message a week ago. I had assumed you were far too important now to talk to old out-of-touch academics like me."

I know the game, the one where we trade clever jibes, and I've always enjoyed it, but the implications of the call from Barret's intern are moving in my gut like well-brewed morning-after vomit. Still, I try to play along for normality, so I can get to the asking. "Well, like fashion, you'll eventually be relevant again. Someday," I say, trying to sound carefree and chipper. "But considering your age, that day had better be soon!"

"Well said!"

I can't wait any longer. "Leo…" I realize suddenly that it's the first time I've ever called him by his first name. "I'm sorry, but look, what did the intern want to know? Specifically."

"Do I detect a bit of unease at her having called? Well, I guess it is a bit odd having someone look into your life. Perhaps that'll give you some insight into the feelings of those on whom you report. I'm sure you remember Schlesinger's book—"

"Seriously, Leo, um, Professor. What did she want?"

He pauses and I feel a new weightiness on the line even before he speaks. "Is everything all right, Roland?"

"Yes, sure. Just, what did she say?" I'm fighting a rising frustration. I want to shout into the phone, I want to scream at Leo and tell him to hurry the fuck up. But I choke it down and force myself into the appearance of calm. In my hand, the phone creaks as I channel all my frustration into my fist. "Sorry. I've just come off a fifteen-hour flight and I'm feeling it. But I will admit I'm not used to people looking into me. So I'm pretty curious as to what it was all about."

"Fair enough. Well, let me see. She was mostly interested in your habits. The kind of person I remembered you to be. Oh, and she asked if you enjoyed the ponies, that sort of thing."

I sit hard on the chair beside me. Not because I meant to, but because my legs are suddenly incapable of supporting my weight. The daisy chain connects with remarkable speed: The ponies. Gambling. There is only one reason gambling would be on the question list for an interview about me, and that's Trots. I'm clutching wildly for answers in my head, reaching and finding nothing—nothing save the feeling that the air in the room is evaporating, leaving me breathless and near panic.

"Roland, are you there?" The Professor's voice is tinged with concern, and I know he's leaning forward in his chair the way he always would when he saw me in his offices, especially when we spoke about my doubts for the future, my fears of the world I was being prepared for.

"Yeah."

Always direct, he asks, "Are you in some kind of trouble there, Roland?"

"No. No, sorry. I'm just having a hard time with a bunch of stuff right now. Nothing too crazy, just the usual."

"You know I'm always here if you need to bounce ideas off someone. And there's always Dr. Coyle."

"Yeah, I know. But I'm okay. Thanks, though. Look, Professor, I've got to go. I have all kinds of things to tie up—you know what it's like when you've been on an assignment for weeks on end."

"Actually, no. I've been a print man all my life."

Even in my state of near panic, I pick up on the dig. "I hear you. Anyway, thanks for the heads up. I'll let you know how it all works out."

"All right then, Roland."

"All right." I hang up and pace around my condo, energy aplenty but no clear understanding of how to direct it, where to go, or what to do next. I try to recall those years-old conversations I've had with Dr. Coyle—conversations about coping strategies, about mechanisms and tools and skills, but I can't focus on a damn thing.

The phone rings and I know it's the Professor again, his intuition forcing him to call and make sure I'm not stretching my neck or taking a hot bath with a razor blade. I snatch up the receiver and say, with a little more edge in my voice than I mean, "I'm fine, Leo. Really."

"Roly?" comes an unexpected voice. "It's me, Warren."

"Warren? Fuck, sorry, man. I thought you were someone else."

"Hey, no problem. So, how's the life of an international jet-setter?"

"Tiring," I say, and immediately I remember the call Warren had from the *Star-Telegraph* years ago—it was similar to the one the Professor had and my paranoia ramps up one more notch. I have tunnel vision and all I can think of is that the *Star-Telegraph* was—*is* looking into my background. Warren starts to speak, but I cut him off as I did Leo.

"Hey, Warren. Do you remember that time you got called about me from the *Star-Telegraph* way back when?"

"You mean the time you chewed my head off for speaking to them?" he asks sarcastically.

"Yeah, that time. Do you remember who it was that was calling?"

"No, sorry, man. I just remember it was a woman. And I know where you're going with this, Roly, but trust me, I learned my lesson, and I do just like you told me now—I say nothing."

I feel another wave of panic creeping up behind me. I know what's coming next. "So you're telling me there have been other calls since then?"

"Yeah, sure, that was why I was calling. I got calls twice in the last two weeks or so—but don't freak. Like I said, I gave them nothing!"

"Who called? And what were they asking about?" I'm trying to sound cool, aloof, but there is an edge to my voice that even I can hear.

"Jeez, Roly. You okay, bud?"

The question is getting repetitive, and I want to tell him—and the Professor—to just answer the goddamn, motherfucking question.

Deep breath. "Yeah, just tired and pissed off." Another deep breath and I command myself to physically calm down. "Anyway, what'd they want?"

"It was a woman that called, but she never got as far as what she wanted. She told me she was from the *Star-Telegraph*, working on a story about you and that she wanted to ask a few questions. That's when I told her you were a friend and I'd prefer not to comment. She tried to sweet-talk me, but no dice. Then a week or so later—just this past Friday—I got another call, from a guy this time—and fuck me if it wasn't the man himself, Mr. David freaking Barret! The face of the *Star-Telegraph*!"

My breathing hitches. I can feel panic moving in.

"Anyway, I guess they thought I'd spill once he called, but I followed the Tao of Roly and gave him jack shit."

Warren is looking for kudos, but all I have is a quickly evolving urge to hurl. "So he didn't ask any actual questions?"

"No, he asked plenty, but I just kind of laughed it off and said I really can't say."

"What kind of questions?"

"I dunno. How you knew Chloe, where you went to school, what you liked to do in your downtime, where you grew up, where you've lived in the city, stuff like that."

My mind is a blender set to liquefy, and I notice that my hand is clenched into a fist so tight my fingernails are close to drawing blood. I can't stay on the line with Warren any longer. I need to get off. I need to have a full-blown panic attack and run screaming through my apartment. I mutter something about having to go, that I'm sorry, and hang up.

* * *

In the corner of my bedroom, tucked down between the bed and the wall, I clutch my knees to my chest, watching helplessly as darkness gathers around me. But it's as if there are two of me: one weeping uncontrollably and feeling sorry for himself on a world-class scale, and another coolly observing the whole pathetic scene.

The evening comes and hours later I'm still tucked in my corner. By the end of the night I've moved only once: to send an email telling work I won't be in for a day or two—sick with a bug or something I picked up on the road.

Even if I could remember what Dr. Coyle taught me back then, I know in my heart there are no clever strategies to employ here—no breathing techniques, no mantras, no exercise regimen that can get me out of this one. I'm alone, save the restless ghosts with whom I plead. I try to strike bargain after bargain for forgiveness, but they're having none of it.

38

After two days of darkness, I begin to write myself a new chapter. I set it all down in a modest brown notebook. It's new, unspoiled, bound by an unopened cover that means whatever goes into it has no history. It is hope.

As I write, I feel the veil lift. My longhand scrawls about the page, unrestrained by the powder-blue lines or the center spine, sometimes in carefully crafted sentences, sometimes in solitary words, and sometimes in nothing more than a deeply etched scribble that threatens to rip the paper. There are arrows, circles, underlined names, boxes with bulleted points, and lists cribbed into the margin.

The cool observer in me is aware of how it all looks, how unstable the whole idea would seem to an outsider, but still I scribble on. As the words come, so too does a sense of excitement. The pen flicks at the page and the words and letters become flatter, longer, more akin to squiggles: childlike doodles of snakes and worms. My hand begins to cramp.

What I've written here is perhaps not as dramatic as what I first set out where Chloe was concerned, but at least it's not designed to hurt anyone. Well, no one but me, that is. Still, the gist of the thing is there, laid out with a purpose that is for once not just for the good of me. And why? Because like Zimmerman once said, that evening's empire has returned into sand.

There's a price for everything, and like I said once to myself: perhaps my something good is just paying it.

39

Like practically everything else in life, it's the accepting of the facts that causes us the most pain. Once that's complete, the rest is relatively easy. As I ride in the cab over to the USBN offices, I'm surrounded by an almost blissful calm, an afterglow left by that dark mistress I have not seen for so long. It persists and stays with me. The cab is filled with warm, soft light. I'm comfortable, breathing easily, undisturbed by the living or the dead. I suspect I'm as close to being at peace with this world as I'll ever come.

I know that the source of this Zenlike state is the result of my own cowardice—with no room to maneuver, I'm forced into a corner by the actions of others. I wonder: would I have had the courage to get here given sufficient time to reflect on things? Maybe. Maybe not.

Before being cornered, there seemed to be options, wiggle room, a space to squeeze through, and the acceptance that a life might still be grudgingly eked out alongside my demons. But not now. In the end, it makes no difference. I'm here.

I move through the USBN offices and smile and nod to all the right people, and work my way down to Gordon's office. He waves me in and says all kinds of nice things about my last assignment, then sends me on my way. I'm to find Jane Tanner, who apparently has all the details on Rwanda, and on what appears to be poised to happen there again. I smile and nod—unruffled by the thought of a new wave of genocide that needs witnessing in Central Africa—and set off to find her.

Hours later, sitting with one ankle perched on the opposite knee at gate 47, I watch an old man with what must be his granddaughter as they giggle and poke at each other on the seats opposite mine. After a while the little girl, who can't be more than five or six, calms down and pops herself up onto the old man's knee, pressing herself into his thinning cardigan until she almost disappears.

The PA crackles to life as the flight is announced, and the little girl's face is now pleated with concern, eyebrows tented as she lifts her eyes to her grandfather's. She says something I can't make out and the grandfather smiles and says to her in the kindest, clearest voice, "Everything's okay, sweetheart. Everything's just fine."

And I know it will be.

• • •

A day later I step off the plane and into the heat of Rwanda.

At the Intwan Hotel, a familiar voice calls out to me from the entryway of the main bar, where I'm alone nursing a cold beer. "Hey, Roly, I just got in." It's Vince, lugging his backpack and two cases of technical gear. "What do we know?"

I nod to him in welcome. "Rumors mostly," I say. "Memories of '94. People are saying the Hutus are organizing, caching weapons and making lists. Folks are scared."

"You have a game plan? Anywhere you want to go? Anyone you want to interview?"

"I think so. We've got a little cash to spread around. Hopefully we'll get a bite." Vince's disdain is immediate and poorly camouflaged. He hates dropping dollars for callers, but it works, and if we don't do it, someone else will and we'll miss the story. It's just the business.

I continue, ignoring his sour expression. "There's supposed to be a guy here soon—says he can take us to a spot where a bunch of kids were executed just last night. He says they were dumped in a pit, in a whatayacall it—a latrine."

"Fun, fun, fun," says Vince flatly.

"Where'd you come in from?" I ask, redirecting him.

"I was with Jamie in Somalia. He's working on a warlord

thing. I touched base in New York for one night and then turned around to catch up with you here. In the lovely Intwan Hotel," he says in mock approval.

And with that, our conversation runs dry. Vince tolerates me as he's fully one half of our deft little two-step. The relationship works, each doing our part, dutifully filing stories on time and on spec that are routinely hitting the mark for the network.

The pause doesn't last long. "Well, I'm beat," says Vince, half turning away. "I'm going up to my room. Call me when your guy shows."

"Sure thing," I say, and drain the last of my beer.

As Vince is walking away he stops, snaps his fingers, and points back at me. "Almost forgot. I have something for you." He puts his bags back down, rummages briefly through his backpack, and comes up with an envelope. It hasn't traveled well and is creased and dog-eared. Vince hands it to me unapologetically.

"Who's it from?" I mutter.

"An old workmate of yours. Dave Barret over at the *Star-Telegraph*."

As Vince disappears from the empty bar, I run my fingers over the creases in the envelope. What's inside specifically, I don't know, but what I can tell, what is sure beyond the shadow of a doubt, is this: the letter Vince handed me and what I scribbled into a brown notebook only a few dozen hours ago are effectively the same thing. They are my opportunity to atone.

I place the letter on the bar in front of me, then raise my eyes in time to catch the bartender and order another beer. When it comes I take a sip, set it down, and look at the letter and the beer, my hands folded in my lap.

40

The road is lonely and dark in almost every way it can be this far from Kigali—nothing but the glow from my instrument panel, the pool of yellow light cast in front of the Land Cruiser, and the white dots hung high in the African night sky. I'm scared, as scared as I've ever been, but also filled with something that strangely seems like hope, a sense of nervous anticipation as if a long-held goal draws near.

I push on through the darkness, past the dirt road cut off where we found the executed children earlier in the day, and on into the ever-blackening Rwandan night. The police roadblock I was stopped at only twenty minutes ago seems another world away, as do the warnings they gave me through giddy, toothy smiles. I'm alone now in absolutely every sense of the word (*you're going to piss the world off, and you're going to be alone*), and the only handhold I provide myself is that what I'm doing is all I can to atone, to dull their pain, and provide some small respite from the jarring impact I've had on their worlds.

My hand rises to my breast pocket and touches the outline of the folded letter stowed there, the letter Vince handed me yesterday morning when he arrived in Rwanda. Perhaps now is the time to read it, with nothing but blackness on the road ahead of me, save the brightness that I know is coming. I swing the Land Cruiser onto the dusty shoulder, although with no one daring to drive this far from the city at night, I could just as easily stop the car in the middle of the road. I snap on the map light, and under its sallow glow I carefully remove the single sheet, and begin to read.

The letter is on *Star-Telegraph* letterhead, with the words

FROM THE DESK OF DAVID BARRET printed in raised blue ink at the top. Beneath them, written in Barret's almost feminine cursive handwriting, is a letter that outlines the end of me—which in itself is no surprise—but it also contains the answer to the one question I've not been fully able to answer. The letter, in its entirety, reads:

> *Dear Mr. Keene.*
>
> *Over the course of the last year, my team, on behalf of the* Star-Telegraph *and the news magazine show* Foreign Correspondent, *has been conducting a detailed review of the circumstances surrounding the death of Ms. Chloe Dysart, daughter of Mr. Colin Dysart. In the course of our inquiries on this matter, documents have recently come to light that implicate you specifically, and outline a detailed plan that led directly, if not expressly, to her demise.*
>
> *The document I am referring to is a notebook that appears to be yours, filled with details of the alleged plan. This notebook was in a box of personal items delivered to the* Star-Telegraph *by your associate, Mr. Warren Barton.*
>
> *This story will be produced and aired in cooperation with* Foreign Correspondent, *and as a courtesy we would like to conduct an on-camera interview with you to capture your side of the story. A crew from* FC *is currently on the ground in Rwanda and will be in contact with you to arrange the interview.*
>
> *I would strongly advise you to take advantage of this opportunity to speak on your own behalf and comment on the documents and interviews we have collected to date.*
>
> *Yours with all sincerity,*
> *Dave Barret*

My mind slips back to the day I searched for one of my notebooks at the condo; I remember being relieved that Chloe's was not there, not sitting on top, waiting to remind me of all I had done. I remember thinking it was just somewhere nearby, that I'd look for it later. Then my mind flicks back a little further, to the day I moved out of my squalid studio apartment. I'd collected my notebooks, I remember that clearly. But then there was Trots at the sidewalk, the ambulance ride, and an orderly placing a single box beside me after my ear was dressed and wrapped. Where was that second box? The super. He was there. He probably gathered up the contents of the box spilled when Trots knocked me down.

"So that's how they knew," I whisper aloud to myself, shaking my head gently at the revelation. The box that I never collected at the *Star-Telegraph*, the one Warren dropped off after the super hounded him to pick it up. In that box would have been a few old shirts, some underwear—junk, really, just the replaceable clutter of my life. And, of course, the notebook.

If I'd collected that box at the *Star-Telegraph* would it all have been any different? Either way, it changes nothing now. It can all only end in one way.

So I fold the letter into my pocket, swing the Land Cruiser back onto the darkened road, and push on.

Moments later, it happens.

Out of the darkness, I hear the rounds impact the car and the engine block. The Land Cruiser dies, and I emerge from the vehicle with the camera light on, shouting into the blackness of the night that I'm a journalist. Seconds later the camera explodes in my hand in a shower of plastic and shattered lens glass, and I shout out again, "Journalist! Journalist!" I make out the form of a small man in rags, and see by the black swatch pinned to his shoulder that he's a member of the reformed Hutu Interahamwe. There's a small pop and a moment of brightness near him, and I'm knocked backward into a wet heap on the road.

I can't move. I can't speak.

And so this is how it all ends. I had been wondering what it would be, how exactly I would atone for my sins, and this seems at least fitting. An eye for an eye, the Bible says, and as I think it, mine are snuffed out.

41

I am aware of intersecting lines.

Fuzzy at first, then clearing. The image swims in and out of focus briefly, then fixes, and I try to move my head to the left but discover a tightness there. The intersecting lines make sense now: ceiling tiles, white squares neatly arranged in the ceiling of what I slowly come to understand is a hospital room.

As consciousness returns fully, I become aware of pain in my upper chest and in my left shoulder, and a thick pressure on my tongue and throat, like a mouthful of meat frozen in midswallow. My left hand won't rise, but my right hand moves haltingly across my chest and neck, past a hard white collar bracing me from sternum to chin, and on to a heavy tube disappearing into my mouth and down my throat.

There are monitors of some sort beside me, but unable to move my head, I can only catch their outline. The room is small, off-white, and bordered with a heavy wooden rail at hip height. The door to the room, just past the foot of my bed, strikes me as overly wide and as I study it, a woman comes through. She speaks to me but I don't hear her, or maybe I do, but I can't make sense of the sounds. And so I close my eyes.

• • •

Someone is speaking to me, then touching my face. A bright light stabs into my right eye, then my left. I recoil from the shock of it and swear.

"Easy, Mr. Keene. Relax, you're fine." It's a male voice, and as soon as my eyes recover from the blinding flash I see a man with a round face, glasses, and a closely cropped beard. He speaks to a nurse beside him, and then turns back to me. "How are you feeling?"

My right hand comes up to touch the tube disappearing into my mouth, but I find nothing there, and I realize that while my throat is slightly sore, the pressure is gone. But around me something else is struggling to the fore, something tattered and ragged, images that are unfinished but frightening nonetheless: the dark road in the Rwandan night, the letter, the Land Cruiser dying. Then, nothing.

"Where am I?" I ask with a voice that is half whisper, half croak. "What happened?"

The doctor folds his arms and raises his eyebrows. "You've had quite an adventure these past few weeks. You're in Germany now, but you spent a night in Nairobi at the Aga Khan Hospital. They stabilized you and then you were transferred here. And now that you're doing so much better, we'll be sending you back home. In a few days, of course."

And in those few days, I learn all about what happened that night. I learn about being left for dead and about being found by a French television crew in the morning, lying in the middle of the road next to the stripped Land Cruiser. I learn that my heart stopped momentarily on the way to Nairobi in the back of a small Cessna, and how a young male nurse performed CPR on me for the last half hour of the flight to Aga Khan. I learn about being stabilized, about being airlifted by a chance American military flight bound for Germany, where I'm told I underwent surgery to repair my shoulder and a shattered scapula. I hear about the blood loss, the infection, and finally the induced coma. And I remember none of it.

In three days I'm met by a representative of the network, strapped into a medical evacuation plane, flown home, and deposited in yet another hospital room. All the while I manage to keep the questions that are swirling around inside my head at bay. I know that if they land, if they find purchase and are allowed to bloom, I'll be forced to think about the unthinkable: what do I do now that I am alive?

· · ·

My first visitor is a long, gangling fellow I've not set eyes on in almost six years. It's Ed Carroway. He hovers in the doorway until I see him, and my first reaction is a broad smile, but it's not returned and so mine is stolen away too. "Ed," I say hollowly. "How long have you been standing there?"

Ed walks into the room, hands thrust deeply in his pants pockets, and pushes the door closed with his foot.

"Just a little while," he says, and I swear he's wearing the same cardigan he was the day I first met him.

It's awkward, and I realize right away what would have been patently obvious had I bothered to think it through: Ed would know everything Barret did. He'd have to; Carroway would be the editor for the piece.

"If you've come to cry at my bedside, don't worry. The doctors say I'm gonna make it," I say in a sad, failed attempt at humor.

Carroway ignores it and instead reminds me of the direct man he has always been. "Did you get Barret's note when you were down there?" he asks, as coolly as a man inquiring about the weather.

Somehow my eyes can no longer hold his gaze. "Yes, I did."

"But you never made the interview, I'm guessing."

"No. I did see Donna, but we didn't get as far as an interview."

Carroway slides the chair closer to the bed and sits down, and it's only now that I can see the weariness in his face. He rubs at his eyes with his thumb and forefinger. "Roly, I'm going to ask you this once. Not as an editor, not as a newspaper man, hell, not even as a friend. Just two fellas sitting in a room." His hands fall to his knees and sit there, deathly still. "The journal—the book thing that was in the box left for you at the *Star-Telegraph*, all the writing, planning, all of it. Is it legit?"

In the corner of the room there is a dead girl with a hole in her chest. Her arms are crossed, her chin is stuck out, and her eyebrows are raised in anticipation. In another corner there is a dead man standing in a puddle. He's clenching the little muscle in the corner of his jaw and cleaning his fingernails with the edge of a straight razor, one eye flicking in my direction to catch my answer. He seems aloof, but I know he's listening intently for what I will say. And in the third corner there's another man, this one charred and smoldering, stooped over slightly by the weight of the steel-belt radial around his neck. He, too, is watching me, waiting to see if there's any redeemable scrap left to be had.

I had decided some time ago that I would atone as best I could, and in every way that I could. And part of that now needed to include taking responsibility for it, all of it—even if there was a case I might make for myself that it had all just gone terribly wrong in that alley off Harbord Street.

But of course, this is all new ground, as things had also gone terribly wrong in Rwanda, leaving me alive and convalescing here instead of dead and decomposing north of Kigali. And so, in the absence of any plan scribbled frantically in a notebook, I have to stay the course and make my very best efforts at atonement. Nothing can be fixed, but I can be some form of balm for all those whose lives I had crashed through. And so my answer is a simple one, witnessed by all the souls in the room. "Yes," I say to them. "It's the real deal."

Carroway does not flinch. His head bobs slowly up and down in silent agreement with something he's been thinking, and then he draws in a full lungful through his nose and looks at me. "I've read it, the whole dang thing. And if you're telling me it's legit, top to bottom, then that has to include the fact that what you set up, as near as I can tell, never included Chloe dying."

I look in his eyes and say nothing.

And Carroway continues. "Not that it really matters, though.

I just wanted to understand the kind of man you actually are. Here's the thing: your getting shot in Rwanda is big news here, and it's engendered a lot of goodwill from the fine people of this city. You should see the flowers at the USBN studios. And as a result, there're a lot of people pulling for you, which has a nice spin effect for ratings at USBN. So, as you might imagine, there's a lot of pressure on me to make sure the story we want to run on you is ironclad.

"I called in the team that was working on this, which is basically Barret, his staff of two, and Donna Sabourin—who, as you know, left us at the *Star-Telegraph*—and is now working with *Foreign Correspondent*."

"Despite my criticisms."

"Despite your criticisms. Anyway, she was the one who came into possession of the notebook. Long story short: when she brought the notebook to light she was already with FC, but because it was acquired during her time here, we worked out a deal where the *Star-Telegraph* and FC would break the story together. As it turns out, both Barret and Sabourin have axes to grind with you, so they were more than happy to work on it together."

I have nothing intelligent to say, but there is a natural pause, and I feel compelled to fill the void. "Well, I can't say you didn't warn me..."

Carroway ignores me again. "After you were shot in Rwanda, I called the team back and had them comb through the details for me again. Crucifying a news personality who's just been shot in the name of chasing the truth can be a dangerous occupation if your facts aren't straight. And that's when Donna came clean on how she got the notebook. She originally said it was given to her by a source close to you, whose name she withheld. Barret and I assumed that she was referring to Warren Barton."

"It was Warren, sure. He sent that box to me. At the *Star-Telegraph*. Just like Barret said in the note."

"That's right, but if you reread Barret's note, it implies that Warren Barton delivered the box to the *Star-Telegraph*, and not to you. When Donna was pressed on it, she admitted that the box was dropped off for you, sealed and with your name on it, and you never collected it. The reason for that was that Donna had collected it from security downstairs, and told them she would put it on your desk. But she never did. She hid it and forgot all about it. She eventually admitted that she wanted to get back at you for screwing her over, and hiding the box was a petty way of doing just that—juvenile as it seems. She was pretty embarrassed. Anyway, she'd been with FC for four or five years when she came across the box while she was clearing out a storage locker. She opened it and found the notebook."

What Carroway is telling me is interesting at best, but it changes nothing. The deeds are all still mine. "Well, I guess I deserve whatever I get."

"What you do and don't deserve is not a question I'm in the business of answering. All I can tell you is that the story isn't going to run."

I hear the words, but they bounce off me like a stone skipping across the water. Finally they lose momentum and sink in. "What did you just say?"

Again, Carroway ignores me. "The box was sealed and delivered with your name on it, and was ultimately opened without your consent. There is a reasonable expectation of privacy where the box was concerned, and anything resulting from the search of that box must be excluded from the investigation. And without the notebook, there's simply nothing to investigate."

I am stunned, thrown temporarily into a literal state of unresponsiveness. Stunned. Eventually I mutter, "What?"

"There'll be no story."

"Really?"

"Really." Carroway draws in another lungful through his nose. "But that doesn't mean I have to like it. I just thought you should know." Carroway stands, returns the chair to its spot on the wall, and turns to leave.

"Wait, Ed," I say, and ask a question that, while it embarrasses me, I am compelled to ask. "Who else knows about all this?"

He looks at me with disappointment, and my embarrassment is complete. "Four people: me, Barret, Donna Sabourin, and one of the in-house lawyers. Barret's staff ran research at arm's length, and we kept the details to ourselves as we knew this was going to be explosive. But now that we're at this impasse, Donna and Barret have been instructed to keep things to themselves. There's a lot of room for damages against the two companies, and against Donna and Barret, should these *unsubstantiated rumors* leak out. So I guess you're free and clear."

"And the police? Aren't you going to pass over the notebook to them?"

"Nope," he says, staring at a spot on the floor. He seems so tired. "The lawyers see no benefit, only risk. They don't care much for what you did. They just see bad PR, potential lawsuits, and damage to the corporate bottom line. It's cheaper and safer just to let it all go."

Another embarrassing, humiliating question rises to the surface, and again I can't stop myself from asking. "And Dysart? What will you tell him?" In my mind I see the man as he was when his daughter first died, shattered and torn. I hear his voice as he asked me about how she died, over and over again through the years, and the shame comes on like a hot bed of asphalt laid thickly over me.

Carroway is still staring at the floor, but I can see the wrinkles in his face being drawn tight, like a man grimacing as he swallows something vile. Finally he speaks. "Nothing. I'm not going to tell him anything. The paper's made it clear it wants no part of this. I've been part of this institution for a long time, almost forty years, Roly, and so I'll support that position, despite what my personal sentiments might be."

He raises his eyes to meet mine and there's something very final in his expression. It's equal parts sadness, disappointment, and regret, with a dash of frustration thrown in for good measure. He turns, pulls open the door, and ambles through it with his head held just a little lower than when he came in. He turns the corner out of sight, and the door closes gently on its pneumatic dampener, hissing at me in a gentle reproach.

And I know with complete clarity that we will never speak again.

• • •

Hours after Carroway leaves, lying alone in my darkened hospital room, I begin to understand the magnitude of the bullet I've just dodged, and I'm unsure of what to make of it all. Living through Rwanda was the first wrinkle, but penance could still be paid by the forced "outing" I would get at the hands of my own fellow professionals. And now, with the quashing of the story, even that has been stripped away. I'm left somehow unscathed, just Roland Keene, dragging around everything I've done and can't undo.

So what do I do? How can circumstances conspire this perfectly to rob me of my chance to check out with perhaps the tiniest shred of decency? How can it be that I'm now back here, career and reputation still intact, and all avenues that connect me and a series of dead people neatly and nicely tied up? In my mind I tally up the kind of life that has led me to this point, and I try to find the high ground, the places where there was something good, something to build on.

Among them I find Rhona, smiling motherly, almost proudly when I cracked my first byline. I find Donna, perhaps the only woman I ever truly loved, and to whom I never said the word. I find Professor Bowman, who believed in me, or at least made every effort to make me feel that he did, and I find that safety net he so generously cast my way the day I left school—that year of Dr. Coyle. I find Warren, a rich kid to whom I could really offer nothing; yet time and again he reached out to me—often rebuffed—as a friend. And of course there was Ed, that walking allegory for everything it really meant to be a newsman—which, of course, leads me to perhaps the only thing to which I ever really gave myself completely: the idea of calling myself a journalist.

And what have I done to earn any of it? The question takes me back to a hotel room at the Met, and the challenge some random televangelist laid out before me: *do something good.* I don't need to check; I know instinctively the challenge has gone unmet. At least so far.

Here, in this warm hospital bed, my life has come to a pause. I'm filled with the understanding that my legacy to this world is little more than a harrowing debt. I look back over everything, over everyone whose life I have run roughshod over, and I'm overcome with a sense of regret that may simply be too weighty, too expansive to ever crawl out from under. There have been so many reverberations from my actions, so many lives drawn helplessly in, thanks to my determination to be what I set out to be.

I can never bring Chloe back. I can't soothe the suffering I've sown throughout her family. I can't make amends to Lebo, to his mother, or even to Trots. I can't undo the pain. I can't fix any of it.

But perhaps there is something, tiny as it is. Perhaps pathetically so. My life from here on will be lived in a perpetual state of regret and remorse, I know, but I can at least open my eyes, accept what I have done, and spend every last effort trying to wipe out the bad with my own *something good.* There's a chance here, a corner to be turned, and I make a simple and solemn vow to do it. Yes, *something good* will be my mantra, my guiding principle, and while I can never expect to earn forgiveness from any of those I have wronged, I can perhaps make some small contribution in an effort, at least on some grand, universal scale, to restore balance.

Oh, shit.

In the doorway of my room, there is a man. I recognize him instantly, and the recognition fires a daisy chain in my head that connects with frightening speed. It starts with a voice on the phone, then a ride in a limo. Next, a library lined with first editions and a grieving father. Then a leap forward to the library again, only this time the father is holding photographs and looking purposeful, like a sharp blade suspended at the top of a guillotine. The chain flurries on, catching image after image, all happening inside the span of a single breath. Trots facedown in the water, my move to network television, and then a thousand random images of the career it all launched for me, and then, finally, a single crystallizing memory: the letter I left on Vince's bed at the Intwan.

The letter was supposed to be my final act of goodness, of sorts, and was a confession of what happened, all of it—Chloe, Trots, everything—to Colin Dysart. It would not fix things, but it might diminish the pain, lessen something about the whole experience; it would be my final effort to atone.

In the doorway, the man steps forward and while I cannot see his face because of the light in the hall, I know from his size and stature that it's David Mahoney, Colin Dysart's assistant. I can also tell that while I remember him as a kind, caring soul grieving for the loss of someone he considered family, this is not the same man. This one has a hard edge, and now that he has closed the door firmly I can finally make out his face, and I see it is resolute and set firmly with intent.

He steps to the edge of my bed, looks at me solemnly, and says, "Mr. Dysart says goodbye." And with that, he picks up the pillow from the visitor's chair and places it over my face. I know what's coming, and I don't fight it. I hear the metallic snicker of the hammer being drawn back, then feel the pressure of the barrel at the center of the pillow, pushing into my forehead.

And then I am free.

ACKNOWLEDGEMENTS

There are a few people I need to thank here.

To my agent, Carrie Pestritto, whose infectious enthusiasm for this project kept it going when many others—myself included—would have just packed it in: Thanks for believing, Carrie. It's great having you in my corner.

To my editor, Randall Klein: Thank you for your insightful work on *The Journalist*. Quite frankly, the whole damn thing was just better once you were done with it. Thanks, Randall. I'm also fortunate to have had the backing of the talented team at Diversion Books, especially Sarah Masterson Hally and Lia Ottaviano. My sincere thanks to both of you

I want to thank my dad, Peter, for having the balls to make my childhood such an international adventure, and my mum, Lena, now passed, for gamely going along with what surely must have looked like a never-ending series of mad schemes. Thanks also to my son, Ethan, who knows how to give a hell of a hug, and better yet, knows just when to give them.

And above all, I want to thank the most remarkable person I've ever known: my wife, Laura. I'm not sure of many things in this life, but I am sure of this: I love you, Laura, and there's not a person in this world I'd rather spend my days with than you.

Oh, what a lucky bastard I am.

DN

THE
CLEARING

With the eerie thrills of Dean Koontz, Dan Newman's seething suspense brings a young man back to St. Lucia, where he grew up, and where his guilt for the part he played in a murder continues to haunt.

Now, thirty years later, Nate responds to his father's suicide with a trip back to St. Lucia, the land where he was raised as an outsider, tolerated but not accepted. As a boy he ventured out to the plantation of Ti Fenwe with three others—weak-willed Pip, and cousins Richard and Tristan. Surrounded on all sides by dense jungle, the boys explore, their only rule to be back in the house before nightfall. Because at Ti Fenwe, something ancient stalks the jungle, its reputation more horrifying than any of the boys can comprehend.

But it's a very real enemy who changes the boys forever, and snuffs out a life. Decades later, Nate comes back to finally gain a measure of peace over his role in the killing, and to uncover the deadly secrets of St. Lucia once and for all.

CPSIA information can be obtained
at www.ICGtesting.com
Printed in the USA
LVOW07s0203300617
539888LV00001B/104/P